FACE
OF
GREED

FACE OF GREED

A DETECTIVE EMILY HUNTER MYSTERY

JAMES L'ETOILE

OCEANVIEW PUBLISHING

SARASOTA, FLORIDA

ISBN 978-1-60809-587-2

Published in the United States of America by Oceanview Publishing

Sarasota, Florida

www.oceanviewpub.com

10 9 8 7 6 5 4 3 2 1

PRINTED IN THE UNITED STATES OF AMERICA

Greed has poisoned men's souls

—CHARLIE CHAPLIN

FACE
OF
GREED

CHAPTER ONE

EMILY HUNTER LEARNED to be wary of open doorways when she rolled up to a call. In the five years of her assignment to the detective bureau of the Sacramento Police Department, she knew bad things often lurked in the dark behind partially open doors. When it was the front door of your own home, at seven in the evening, the anxiety bit deep.

She crept close, listening for anything or anyone who didn't belong. Her hand tapped the grip of the Glock on her hip as she climbed the stairs. The lights were on, and the television blared an infomercial for a product promising the end of dry skin.

"Mom?"

Emily had moved her mother in with her four months ago after the seventy-year-old retired teacher suffered a series of memory lapses and household accidents. The advancing scourge of dementia meant Connie Hunter was unable to live a safe, independent life in her own home.

"Mom, are you there? Sheila?" Emily called out for the caregiver she'd hired to stay with her mother while Emily worked long hours as a detective.

When no response came from within, Emily's subconscious went to a very dark place. She'd investigated a series of home invasions in the city where gangbangers targeted the homes of elderly people to terrorize and loot money and prescription drugs from the weak and powerless.

The front door hadn't been kicked in, and there was no sign of a forced entry. Emily entered and scanned the living room— except for the missing mother and caregiver, the home appeared normal.

She turned off the television and heard the kitchen faucet running. A quick look into her remodeled kitchen found the water running over a sink full of dishes—but no one there. She shut the water off and spotted Connie's GPS-enabled pendant on the kitchen counter. She held the tracker in her hand.

Then Emily heard the front door slam, followed by the metallic click of the deadbolt. She heard the voices before stepping into the living room. Sheila had draped a comforter from the sofa over Connie's frail shoulders. Her mother was wearing a light housecoat and a pair of fuzzy pink slippers. She shivered as Sheila rubbed her arms, warming her.

"What happened? Where were you?" Emily asked.

"I found her wandering down the street, near the park," Sheila said.

Connie looked small and fragile in the housecoat, one too thin for the cold spring air.

"Mom, what were you thinking?"

"It was time to go," Connie said with a shiver in her voice.

"Go? Go where?"

"Home."

Emily bit her lip. It wasn't the first time her mother mentioned going home, or a need to do something somewhere else. Sundowner's Syndrome, the doctors called it. A little gift that came with dementia—confusion, a sudden surge in anxiety, and a feeling that she was lost. In a way, she was.

"Mom, this is home now," Emily said.

"I swear, I turned my back for a second while I was finishing up the dinner dishes, and she slipped out."

"She hasn't pulled that one before. What happened?"

"She seemed a little more confused than usual but couldn't tell me why. She was watching her shows, then walked out. I can't be responsible for her wandering off. You might want to think about moving her into a facility—"

"I'm not putting my mom in a home." Emily draped the GPS locket around her mother's neck.

"Why weren't you wearing this?"

"That's not mine."

"Yes, it is. Remember? We talked about it."

Connie didn't respond, but the look behind her eyes was one of confusion and uncertainty.

Emily's work cell phone vibrated in her pocket. Calls after seven in the evening weren't telemarketers who should be banished to a leper colony. These nighttime calls invariably meant someone suffered a beating, rape, or another murder in a city with no shortage of victims. In earlier years, she'd wondered if she didn't answer the phone—if she let it ring until it stopped—would the crime still occur? Could she prevent another victim from ending up in some desolate field? A few hundred calls later, her naïve hope evaporated, and she came to terms with the fact that the flow of victims in this city was never-ending.

She stabbed the answer button. "Hunter here."

"Evening, Detective, please hold for the Watch Commander," a woman's voice instructed.

While Emily waited, she plodded to the office in the rear of her home and removed a fresh notebook out of the bottom drawer. On the first line of the first page, she wrote, "*1935 hours, rec'd call from Watch Commander.*"

"Hi, Emily, Lieutenant Ford here. Initial report is a home invasion gone bad. One victim dead and one injured."

"Another one? Where are we talking about?"

"The location is..." Emily heard rustling paper in the background. "Here it is. It's 1357 46th Street. That's a nice neighborhood."

"It used to be anyway. I'll call Medina and get there as soon as I can," Emily responded.

"I called him first. His name was up on the rotation. Javier said he would meet you on scene. Emily, there's something else you need to know."

Emily fell silent.

"The Chief's already there. He's taking a personal interest in this one."

"Oh sweet Jesus! That's never a good sign." Emily tossed the notebook on the desk.

"Gotta mean this is a high profile case. So, watch your back."

"I appreciate the heads-up. I'll be there as soon as I tie up something." She disconnected the call and tried to figure out how she could work the case remotely. Maybe her partner, Javier, could hold up his phone and livestream the crime scene. Who was she kidding?

"Sheila?"

Emily found her mother and Sheila parked in the living room watching a television show that was popular in the sixties. Connie had calmed, and her face was relaxed.

"I can stay," Sheila said. "I overheard the call. I think she's calm now. It won't be long until she's off to bed. I'll keep an eye on her."

"Thank you. Call me if there is any problem and please make her wear that GPS pendant. I'll figure something out . . ."

As Emily changed into a fresh blouse, the thought of Chief Clark wandering through the crime scene kept surfacing. Whatever drew the top cop out to a crime scene after dark wasn't going to bode well for the assigned detectives.

Once in her dark blue Ford Crown Victoria, Emily let the defroster attack the rapidly forming condensation on the windshield. Sections of the window cleared and showcased the obnoxious blue Christmas lights her neighbor clung onto four months after the holiday season. They blinked on and off at once, stabbing a constant strobe into the detective's bedroom window—another flimsy excuse for her insomnia.

As the car warmed up, Emily got out and scraped a thin film of ice from the driver's window with the side of her hand. She stole a glance down the quiet street, gathered her shoulder-length dark hair in a ponytail, and stepped back into the shadows, away from the car. She followed the fence line to the neighbor's glowing stale yuletide shrine. Emily pulled the seventh and tenth small bulbs from their sockets and partially rethreaded the maddening electrical orbs back in the strand. The entire string blacked out, and she basked in the electric silence without the hellish current knifing out into the night. Then she returned to the car, backed out of the driveway, and wondered when her lazy-ass neighbor would recognize he'd become a victim of a drive-by bulbing.

Emily made a right on J Street and sped to 46th, where the glow from the blinking red, blue, and yellow lights of emergency vehicles exacted some sort of revenge for her neighbor's light display. Residents of this upscale enclave didn't typically park their Benz, Jag, or Maserati on the street. Their precious status symbols were locked away in garages, or behind walled court-yards. She recognized the silver Crown Vic in front of her as the Mayor's car and crept forward until her front bumper came within an inch of the Mayor's sedan, effectively boxing the poli-tician's ride against a fire vehicle with a bright red and white sign warning, "Keep Back 100 Feet."

"The Chief and the Mayor at the crime scene. Fricken awesome."

The residence dwarfed the other homes on the block by double. A massive red brick front, coupled with heavy black iron gates to the right side of the residence, gave the place the feel of an embassy compound. Emily approached the front door, where an officer stood post, ensuring only official personnel entered the crime scene. She identified herself to the young officer in his freshly pressed dark blue uniform. After signing in on a clipboard held by the officer, Emily snagged a pair of blue paper booties from a box on the porch and pulled them over her shoes. She stepped through the front door and immediately noticed blood spatters on the marble floor, each marked with yellow plastic numbers. She grabbed a set of nitrile gloves and pulled them on before she acci-dentally contaminated the scene.

Emily followed the sound of voices and the strobes of camera flashes to a room down from the entryway. She paused at a large living room space where a petite blond woman sobbed on a white leather sofa. A paramedic knelt in front of her and tended to a red lump on her forehead. Detective Javier Medina sat in the chair next to her.

Javier and Emily became partners six months ago, and while he had more time in the department, Emily's tenure in-grade as a detective made her the senior investigator. Unlike many of his fellow officers, he didn't resent a woman—particularly one with fewer years behind the badge—holding the lead position.

Emily thought Javier possessed a natural inclination to the job. He could coax a confession from a suspect, or listen to a victim with an honest sense of compassion.

Javier nodded at Emily and pointed toward the kitchen. The Mayor came strolling out with a glass of wine, handing it to the woman.

"Thank you, Johnny."

Mayor Stone perched next to her on the sofa and held her hand—the one not holding a wineglass.

"It's probably not a good idea to drink anything until we make sure you're checked out. You took a pretty solid blow to the head," Javier said.

"Lori needs a little something to calm her nerves, something you certainly aren't doing," Mayor Stone said.

Emily continued down the hallway and located the hub of activity in a well-appointed office. It gave off more of a library vibe, with floor-to-ceiling polished mahogany bookcases on the two sidewalls and subdued lighting through Tiffany glass lampshades. A set of French doors with large windows opened out onto a manicured garden.

Chief of Police Thomas Clark, a tall man with the weathered face of a ranch hand, stood off to one side as an evidence technician framed up a series of photographs of a dead man, facedown in a pool of blood, in the center of the room.

"I'm glad you and Medina caught this one, Detective," the Chief said, somber with a glance toward the Mayor.

"Chief," Emily replied with a quick nod of her head to the living room and the city politician.

Chief Clark shrugged. "Long-time family friend is what I understand. Sure seems there's more to it than that. She called him first thing after 911."

Emily circled behind a medical examiner's assistant who secured paper bags over the victim's hands to preserve any forensic evidence. A uniformed officer stood near the patio door and observed the activity.

"You first on scene?" Emily asked.

"That would be me," the officer said. "My partner and I responded to a 911 call from the residence. We found the wife in here kinda hanging over him. She seemed pretty messed up with what she stumbled into."

Emily scanned the overturned furniture, files strewn on the floor, said, "What were they looking for? Wife give you any indication?"

The officer shook his head.

She noticed a red smear on the officer's gloved hand. "Did you touch the body?"

The officer held up his bloody right latex glove and explained, "Yeah, I checked for a pulse and found his throat slit from ear to ear."

Emily nodded. "You have an ID on this guy yet?"

"Yep, sure do. That's the homeowner, Roger Townsend. He and his wife, Lori, are the only two occupants. She came home and interrupted the suspects."

"She able to give any ID on them?"

"Detective Medina is with her now."

A medical examiner's assistant unfolded a plastic tarp next to the body to contain any fibers or trace evidence. The assistant said to whoever listened, "We're gonna roll him now."

The body stuck on the hardwood flooring where the thickened blood adhered to Roger Townsend's face. A sickening elastic snap sounded as his head released from the floor. When the body rolled faceup, Townsend's dead eyes stared up at the assembled group hovering over him. One eye was puffy, his cheek welted from a blow. The body settled, and Roger's jaw fell slack, exposing the gaping slash wound to his neck. The wound severed the major blood vessels and nearly cut through to his spine. The victim's head remained attached only by the thick muscle bundle at the back of his neck.

Deputy Forensic Pathologist Elizabeth White knelt alongside the body. "Ward, get a shot of this, please." She pointed to the gash in Roger's throat.

One of her staff stepped in and snapped a series of photographs of the victim's body in the new position.

"Our subject suffered a gunshot wound to the back, but I see no evidence of an exit wound," Dr. White said.

"COD?" Emily asked.

"There's no surviving an attack this severe. Exsanguination—he bled out right where he dropped."

"Looks like he took a beating before he died. Any defensive wounds?"

"None evident now. I'll be able to tell you more later, Emily. We've taken liver temps and gotten everything we can from the scene. I'm ready to transport the body. I've tentatively set TOD approximately two hours ago. You need anything else before they cart him off?" Dr. White asked.

"When can I take a look at your crime scene photos?"

"By the time you return to the bureau, they'll be downloaded and emailed to you."

"Thanks, Doc," Emily said. She remembered a few years ago the same photos would take hours. A vestige of the past that labeled her as one of the last dinosaurs to leave the comfort of paper and convert to the digital age. New detectives coming on board now would never know the joys of film developing, paper map books, and carbon paper.

The Chief motioned for Emily, who had paused behind the victim's desk over a stack of papers spread out on the slick bloody surface. She felt the papers were too neat, too tidy, in a room that suffered a tossing. Emily used her phone and snapped a photo.

"Here's what they came for," the Chief said and pointed to the open floor safe.

Emily approached the floor safe, squatted, and shot photos of the high-end safe and the sliding cabinet capable of hiding it from view. She ran her gloved hand around the lip of the safe. Nothing felt rough or out of alignment, telling her the safe wasn't forced or cut open; someone opened it using the combination lock. Emily started to stand when a white smudge in the bottom of the dark safe caught her attention. A small trail of light-colored crystalline powder stood out on the safe's black steel floor.

"Hand me an evidence vial, would you," Emily said to one of the crime scene techs behind her.

She grasped the clear plastic tube in one hand and swept up the powder into the container with a plastic scraper. After she capped the vial, Emily used a pen from her pocket, labeled it with her name, badge number, and sequence number of the sample. "I want to make sure this is tested back at the lab. Not enough to do a field test without destroying the whole sample, but I'd swear it's meth."

"Then it belonged to the killer. He must've dropped it when he stole whatever Roger kept in the safe," the Mayor said. So much for keeping the crime scene secured.

"We don't know yet, Sir," Emily answered.

"What we *do* know is Roger Townsend wasn't involved in the drug trade."

Emily stood and faced the Mayor. "And exactly how do we know that?" The irritation on the detective's face bled over into her voice. At five-six, she needed to look up at the politician.

"Townsend held power and influence in this community. He ran my last reelection campaign and donated a significant amount of money to several prominent legislators. He had no need to be involved in drugs."

Emily shrugged and replied, "Maybe it's how he raised his donated cash. If he was involved in politics, then he's dirty."

The Chief stepped between the two, and Javier caught his partner's eye as he stuck his head in around the corner. He had a knack of sensing when Emily's fuse of self-destruction burned short and knew to extract her before this confrontation with the Mayor exploded.

"Excuse me, Mr. Mayor, I'm done with Mrs. Townsend. I'm sure she would appreciate a moment of your time," Javier said.

Mayor Stone's eyes narrowed, and the muscles on his jaw tightened into thick cords on his square face. He glared hard at Emily, then turned and strode out of the room toward the front of the home.

The Chief turned to Emily. "Don't poke the bear."

"What? Because our victim here ran in some high-powered political circles, I'm supposed to ignore the evidence?"

"No one is saying sweep it under the rug. Make sure you use a little diplomacy and document the hell out of everything."

A metallic rattle interrupted the conversation, and the medical examiner's team rolled a compact folding gurney into the room. One of the two men opened up the gurney and lowered it close to the ground next to the victim's plastic-wrapped body.

"You ready for us to take him?" one of the ME's staff asked.

Emily turned to Javier, who nodded and responded, "Yep. He's ready for you. We've gotten what we need."

While the ME's technicians bundled the body and placed it onto the gurney, Emily asked her partner, "When did the Mayor get here?"

Javier leaned back against a bookshelf. "He was already here when I arrived. And I got here twenty minutes after the first units rolled up. They caught me on my way home from a date." He grimaced and closed his eyes immediately after divulging his abbreviated date.

"Really? A date? Ended kinda early, didn't it? I take it you struck out?"

Javier's cheeks flushed, and he approached the victim's desk and sorted through the documents. "It was fine, thank you very much." Javier changed the topic. "I called the Chief and let him know Mayor Stone happened to be here consoling the widow when I arrived."

"Yeah, good call."

"Turns out Mr. Mayor lives a few blocks away."

"Uh-huh," Emily responded. "What did you get from the wife?"

"Not much. She came home, found her husband on the floor, and someone clocked her from behind. When she came to, she worked herself free from a phone cord, but by then the killer had disappeared."

"She get a look at who hit her?"

"No."

"How long was she out?" Emily asked.

Javier paused from sifting through the paperwork on the victim's desk and said, "She doesn't know, but it took her about ten minutes to work free from the phone cord around her wrists."

"You buy her story?"

"I don't know. If someone clocked me from behind, I wouldn't have a goose egg on my forehead."

"You think she's holding back?"

"I do. Perhaps not intentionally. Could be shock," Javier said.

"Did the wife tell you if anyone else knew the combination, or what he kept in the safe?"

"No, she didn't mention the safe."

"Well," Emily said. "Let's go ask her."

The newly widowed Mrs. Townsend parked on the white leather sofa with Mayor Stone, her hands held tightly in his. "Lori, we'll handle everything. You need to take care of yourself now," he said.

"Mrs. Townsend, I need to ask you a few questions," Emily said in a soft voice. For all of her faults, the detective handled the survivors of murder victims with sensitivity and compassion. She didn't refer to them as the "next of kin," which implied they weren't victims of the crime. Wives, brothers, husbands, and children who experienced a loved one ripped from their lives were victims. The only difference is they remained behind and continued to suffer the loss. They bore the pain of surviving.

Mayor Stone dropped Lori Townsend's hands and said, "Detective, this isn't necessary right now—she's been through quite enough, I would think."

The small-framed blonde turned in her seat and crossed her legs. Blood stained the knees of Mrs. Townsend's spandex tights, and when she noticed the red patches on her legs, she became conscious of them and tried to cover the spots with her hands. The red polish on her right index fingernail was chipped and she seemed self-conscious about it. "I've already told the other detective what happened. I don't know what else I can say," she said.

"I realize you've spoken with Detective Medina, and we know you've been through an ordeal. I'd appreciate a few moments of your time to help us find the person responsible for the death of your husband." Emily sat on the corner of a large white marble coffee table directly across from Mrs. Townsend.

"Detective," the Mayor warned.

"It's all right, Johnny," Lori responded, putting a hand on the Mayor's knee. "Go ahead, Detective. I'm not sure what happened. Maybe it will help me put the pieces together, too."

"Thanks, Mrs. Townsend."

"Please, call me Lori," she responded while she pulled her blond hair together, quickly securing it back in a ponytail, readying for a fight. Her stiff posture told Emily this woman was used to being in control.

"Tell me, how many people knew your husband kept a safe in his office?"

"I really couldn't say. I mean, he didn't do a great deal of business here at the house. Every so often he'd hold a meeting in his office, so someone could've seen him open the safe."

"I'll need a list of those people, Mrs. Townsend."

"Really now, Detective." Lori let out a nervous laugh. "I'm sure Councilman Perkins, Senator Rodriguez, and the Mayor didn't conspire to murder my husband."

"How many people knew the combination to the safe, Mrs. Townsend?" Emily asked.

"That was Roger's safe. I don't think anyone else knew the combination." Her face hardened as she thought about the question. "You don't think I had anything to do with this, do you? Roger never gave me the combination. That was his baby."

The Mayor puffed up and put his hand on Lori's shoulder. "I'm sure that's not what the detective meant. Did you, Detective?" He cut an icy glare at Emily.

"I asked if anyone else other than your husband could've opened the safe?"

"No, Roger was the only one with the combination."

"What did your husband keep in the safe?"

"I know he kept some cash in there, along with business papers."

"How much money would he keep in there?"

"I don't know, not much; maybe ten—twenty thousand or so?"

Emily considered her response and wondered what kind of world it would be where ten grand was pocket change. She decided to throw her a curve and asked, "Did your husband keep any drugs in the safe?"

"Hunter, damn it! I've already told you Townsend was not involved with illicit drugs. You're done here. Lori, I'm taking you to the hospital," the Mayor announced as he stood and extended his hand to Lori.

Lori Townsend drew herself up from the sofa in a slow and calculated way that carried a feline quality. She stood up on her toes and kissed the Mayor's cheek. "Thank you, Johnny, I've had quite enough for one night."

As the Mayor held out a jacket for Lori, she turned her back on Emily. "Roger wasn't into drugs. He wasn't that kind of man." She shrugged into the jacket. The Mayor put his arm around her shoulder and escorted her out of the room.

Javier leaned against the hallway near the living room, said, "Well, that went well." He paused until the front door sounded. "The Mayor's all twisted up with this one. There's more here than some family friend connection. Trying to cover some shady campaign financing?"

Emily stood at an assortment of photographs of Mr. and Mrs. Townsend arranged on a small white enamel table. Javier picked up one of the silver frames and handed it to Emily. A group of smiling people in black tie dress: Roger Townsend and his wife, Lori, with another attractive blond woman and Mayor John Stone.

From behind them, a young uniformed officer called out, "Hey, Hunter, move your car so I can drive the Mayor home with his prom date."

Emily tossed the officer her keys. "I'll follow you out. Give me a minute to finish up."

"Poor kid, I wonder what he did to deserve his assignment?" Javier asked.

The cell phone in Javier's pocket played the first few notes of Pat Benatar's "Hit Me With Your Best Shot" and he pulled it out quickly. "Detective Medina." He listened for a few seconds and hung up. "That was the Medical Examiner's Office. They've scheduled the post for eight in the morning. That's quick."

Emily nodded. "Everything about this case is quick—too quick."

CHAPTER TWO

BEFORE THEY LEFT the Townsend residence, Emily agreed to meet Javier at the Coroner's Office on Broadway at a quarter to eight. She made it home with time to grab a few hours of sleep before they started fresh. Emily tossed her keys on a silver tray in the entryway and kicked off her boots. It was more than a comfort thing. Sure, Emily enjoyed the feel of the hardwood under her feet, but what she enjoyed more was the satisfaction from the hundreds of hours sanding and hand-staining the flooring. Resurfacing the floor turned out to be one of the biggest time-draining projects in the renovation of Emily's 1800s-era Victorian home. All of her blood, sweat, and tears were worth the effort—the place snagged a spot on one of those before and after home remodeling shows. But few in the department other than Javier knew she poured her overtime checks into woodwork, antique light fixtures, and plaster.

Emily bid Sheila goodnight and thanked her for staying to watch her mother. After a calm, uneventful evening, Connie had gone to bed early, unfazed by her escape attempt. Emily hoped her wandering off was a one-off thing as she peeked in at her mother, sound asleep in the upstairs guest room. She worried over how long her mother would be able to make the climb up the stairs. So far, her physical condition was good, but her mental faculties were noticeably deteriorating.

Back downstairs, Emily locked her duty weapon in a safe on her closet shelf and changed into jeans and a t-shirt. She felt the sensation of being watched from the patio door.

"You, again."

The watcher stepped closer to the glass and rubbed up against it.

Emily unlatched the door and cracked it a few inches, which was just the chance the cat needed. The generously proportioned black cat shoved the door open and sauntered inside.

"Yes, please come in. Does Mrs. Rose know you're out again?"

The cat ignored her and trotted to the kitchen.

When Emily got there, the cat settled before an empty bowl and gave her a side-eyed glance.

"Go home if you're hungry. I made a mistake the moment I gave you a snack during the storm last year."

A black paw scratched at the bottom of an empty bowl.

Emily pulled a bag of cat food from the pantry and dumped the last of the dry kibble in the bowl. "That's it, that's all there is. Go find another buffet."

She poured herself a nightcap and held the Irish whiskey under her nose. Emily tried to piece together the few facts she pulled from the Townsend homicide scene while the cat that was not her cat crunched away. The Watch Commander described the scene as another home invasion robbery gone wrong. That's how it appeared: a homeowner killed over a few valuables. The number of violent home invasions in the city trended down in recent years, but when they did occur, the invasions fell into two categories: gang-related robberies, or crimes where the victims knew their attackers. The current spree was gang-centered, but this one, from the initial evidence, did not clearly fall into either category. The victims weren't elderly and infirm, and the invasion crew left behind high-end electronics and pricey baubles they could pawn off in a snap. The widow couldn't identify her assailant, and gang-bangers usually opted for the quick hit, not a lengthy beating and near decapitation. Without a list of the items stolen from the victim's safe, it would be difficult to track down "who-dun-it," as Chief Clark would say.

The Chief's reputation as a good detective in his day made Emily question why a cop's cop would aspire to wear the Chief's badge. It was a job far removed from the front lines of police work, for a man passionate about public safety. He spent most of his time dodging political backstabbing and constant attacks against his cops from political, media, and activist groups. Emily knew Chief Clark tried to keep the line staff out of the political and media wood-chipper, but it had to wear a cop down. The shelf life of a Chief of Police in this town wasn't long.

She'd witnessed a small example of what could happen without a Chief with a spine tonight. God only knew what the Mayor might order the responding officers to do in the name of protecting Lori Townsend. John Stone rose to the mayor's office with a short stint as a minor state assemblyman before he ran against a handful of unknown names. His platform, if you could call it that, centered on making Sacramento a destination city. He avoided specifics on how the transformation of the city into this imaginary cultural attraction would happen, but he laid claim to all things slightly positive in the city. He even claimed West Sacramento's revitalization happened only because of the Stone Plan, something the West Sacramento Mayor rolled his eyes over whenever the claim surfaced.

Stone typified the ego-driven politician, ever eager to burnish his own image at the expense of everyone else. Why would the

Mayor show up at a murder scene? There was more going on here than looking out for Lori Townsend. Stone wouldn't cross the street unless it made him look good. What was in it for him?

Emily woke with a start when the trespassing cat jumped on her chest. She'd fallen asleep on the sofa, never having changed into her nightclothes. "You're still here."

The cat turned a circle on Emily, the feline way of telling her, *you're in my spot.*

Emily quickly showered and downed a cup of instant coffee while wrapped in her towel. She pulled a grey suit off the rack in her closet and poured another cup for the road.

Sheila let herself in and set to preparing Connie's breakfast tea. "You call me if there's any problem," Emily said.

"We'll be fine. I have some errands to run today; we'll make a day of it."

Emily shooed the cat invader out and balanced the coffee cup on the car's roof while she dug the car keys from her pocket. She noticed the Christmas lights on the neighbor's house were dark. With a self-satisfied grin, she backed out of the driveway. Emily knew the blessed darkness contributed to the few hours of deep sleep she'd stolen.

With time to burn before she was due to meet Javier, Emily drove to police headquarters on Freeport Boulevard to take a look at the crime scene photos that would be waiting in her email inbox. The parking lot of the Sacramento Police Department headquarters building teemed with personnel at the early hour. She pulled the sedan into someone's reserved spot near the front of the building, confident there wouldn't be a problem over a few minutes picking up the photos, checking for messages, and then off to the Coroner's Office.

The receptionist recognized Emily before she reached the door and buzzed the lock open. Emily waved and stepped inside, a place unlike any other police department she'd ever seen. A large atrium dominated the center of the building, and offices ran around the edges of the green space. The lights were on in the detective bureau, where the vice guys finished their early morning work booking "Johns" from a prostitution sweep. Other detectives pored over the day's search warrants. Emily was suprised to find Javier at his desk.

"I thought we were gonna meet out at the Coroner's place?" she said.

Javier got up and handed her a photo of the floor safe at the Townsend home. "I needed to do some homework. I printed out the crime scene photos and left copies on your desk. Oh, the safe— it wasn't the kind you'd use to hide grandma's pearl necklace or stash sensitive business documents."

"What'd you find?"

"This is an Olympic Gold, grade 2 floor safe with a stainless-steel door, with an added tempered steel layer to resist cutting equipment," he said.

"Townsend really wanted to protect whatever he stashed in there. How much does a grade whatever cost?" Emily asked.

"Grade 2, and they run close to five grand, plus installation," Javier said.

"Able to find out when Townsend had the thing installed?"

"About three months ago, by a company out of Reno." He read her expression. "I found the invoice for the safe on Townsend's desk."

"Good work, partner. What happened three months ago to cause him to go out and buy a safe?"

"Check out the invoice," he said and handed Emily the yellow document now covered in a plastic evidence sheath. "Look who signed for the safe."

"Lori Townsend," she muttered.

A scuffing sound from down the carpeted hallway announced the Captain's presence before he darkened the doorway. Captain Howard's portly figure tested the tensile strength of the dark blue uniform fabric across his belly, which hid most of the thick black Sam Browne duty belt. Howard's face, slick with sweat, contorted as he spoke. "I understand you two caught the Townsend case last night?"

Emily thought about messing with the Captain, but his perspiration, rapid speech, and ragged breathing signaled an impending stroke. While considered a department-wide sport to cause grief for the incompetent Captain, Emily didn't want to perform CPR and lock lips with an unconscious fat man.

Javier sensed his partner's internal moral struggle and answered for them, "That's right, we did."

The Captain began a lecture. "This is an important case, and we need to bring it to closure quickly and quietly. Townsend's legacy is important in this city, and his dignity will not be dragged through the mud. You understand me, Detectives?"

"I always treat the victims with the dignity they deserve, Captain. Some deserve more than others, that's all," Emily said.

"I'm giving you a direct order, Hunter. You stay away from Mrs. Townsend. I got an earful from the Mayor about the way you treated her."

Emily shrugged and asked, "You want me to hurry and solve this case, but I can't talk to the primary witness?"

"You already got her statement. Move on."

"What's the Mayor's interest in this case, and why would he reach out to you about it?"

"Old family friend is all you need to know. The Mayor wants me to give him a full briefing every day—let's start with today's briefing. What do you have from last night?"

"Captain, I'd love to indulge you, but we're heading to an appointment over at the Coroner's office in less than ten minutes." Emily gathered up the photographs, motioned for Javier to follow her, and they left Howard behind in the detective bureau offices.

"One of these times he's gonna snap if you keep poking him," Javier cautioned as they walked out to her car.

"And I'll feel really bad for a minute." She unlocked the car, and they both got in the Crown Vic.

As the car backed out, Javier shook his head and chuckled. "You realize you parked in Howard's reserved parking spot?"

"Actually no, but it explains the sweat. I think we did him a favor, he needs to exercise more."

Emily pulled the sedan out into the morning sludge of northbound commuter traffic on Freeport, toward downtown. She picked up the pace after they turned on Broadway. Emily jumped in her seat when the cell phone vibrated in her pocket. She fumbled briefly before she answered. "Hunter here."

"Hi, Emily, it's Sharon." Sharon Pixley served as the Chief Forensic Pathologist and was responsible for the forensic operations of the Coroner's Office. She treated each of the deceased with respect and provided the survivors with the answers to the most difficult question—why did they die? "I thought we had a date at eight this morning?"

Emily checked her watch; five minutes after. "We're a few blocks away."

"I'm getting Mr. Townsend ready for our postmortem exam, and there's something here you need to see."

Emily parked the sedan in the front of the modern brick and concrete structure, the home of the county's center for death and its attendant mysteries. The smoked glass doors opened up to a brown marble waiting room for families, made as pleasant as possible, with intricate framed quilts hung on the walls. Even at this early hour, a few seats were taken by family members waiting for news of a loved one. Nothing other than bad news came to those who waited in this space. Emily didn't want to make eye contact with the mourners.

Once through the locked doors, Emily and Javier made their way to an office marked with a small sign, S. PIXLEY, CHIEF FORENSIC PATHOLOGIST. Sharon stood at her bookshelf, one foot propped on the bottom shelf with a pile of death certificates on the top. She carefully reviewed each one and signed off; occasionally, she pulled one from the stack and put it aside for correction. She caught the detectives in the far corner of her vision but kept plowing through the certificates. "I thought I'd take the time and catch up on my paperwork. Glad you could make it, Emily," she said.

"Sorry, Sharon. Howard jammed us up as we were heading over here."

"Did the Captain ever lose his extra weight? I would've thought the heart attack last year would get his attention."

"No, he looks ready to pop any minute." Emily felt a twinge of regret for her contribution to Howard's heart condition, a small twinge, but a twinge, nonetheless.

Sharon turned to the two detectives and in a hushed tone, barely above a whisper, said, "I caught a couple of the attendants putting together a pool to predict the next heart attack."

Javier's eyes grew wide. "You're kidding? That's cold."

Sharon motioned toward the door, and while they made their way down the hall, she said, "What's cold is all the good office pool squares were taken."

Two of the six open bays in the autopsy suite held bodies and their attending staff. Contrary to popular images of dark and dreary morgues glamorized on television, natural light brightly illuminated the Sacramento County Coroner's facility through rows of windows mounted high on the walls. Neutral tones and green plants softened a harsh, sterile, and clinical environment. A paper sign taped on a workspace warned staff against pouring formalin down the sinks, hinting at the room's true purpose.

Beyond the six open autopsy bays, a separate space designated for homicide victims contained Roger Townsend's remains, half covered by a white sheet.

Sharon flipped a switch, and an overhead light illuminated Townsend's exposed upper body. His head lolled to one side, the muscle structure supporting it cut away by the killer. What caught the detectives' attention, however, was a small-diameter clear tube protruding from the mid-chest area under the sternum. A long red scar ran alongside the tube and followed the rib line for about six inches.

"The paramedics didn't put that in, did they? It's healed up around the tube."

"Very perceptive, Detective Medina." Sharon stepped to the table where the clothing and belongings of the deceased were laid out. With a latex gloved hand, Sharon selected a small plastic rectangular box from the table; no more than two inches thick and perhaps double in length. "You know what this is?"

"I had an old cassette tape player about the same size," Emily said.

Sharon grinned. "No doubt you made mix-tapes for your high school crush. What if I take this box and do this," she said as she plugged the chest tube in a socket on the back of the device.

"An insulin pump?" Emily guessed.

"Close. It is a chemotherapy pump. Turns out Mr. Townsend had cancer. By the location of this tube, pancreatic."

"How long had he been sick?" Emily asked.

Sharon disconnected the pump but left it on the dead man's chest. "I won't know until I do the autopsy, but pancreatic cancer has a devastating mortality rate. This approach isn't common, and it's typically a treatment avenue of last resort."

"Terminal?" Emily asked.

"We're all terminal, one way or another. The difference is Mr. Townsend knew it."

"Medical records?"

"None I could find offhand. Did the next of kin mention anything?"

"Not a word. That's understandable from the shock of what she'd witnessed," Emily said.

"I've called the company producing the pump to see if they could tell me where it was distributed. Typically, in cases where medical appliances come with the deceased, a sticker, or engraving on the device provides contact information for the doctor and hospital. But there's nothing on this pump."

Javier examined the purple stains, lividity, caused by the pooling of blood no longer pumping through the body. Townsend's mottled forehead, chest, and stomach confirmed he died facedown. Pointing to a slight depression near his abdomen, Javier asked, "Sharon, this outline here." He traced the faint line on the body with a finger. "Could this have been caused by Townsend falling on top of the pump?"

Sharon moved the tubing down to the spot Javier identified and turned the pump in different directions, working a jigsaw puzzle piece, until it lined up. "Based on the bruising, he wore the pump at the time he fell—and there's a small crack in the plastic frame right here." Sharon pointed out a hairline crack caused by the fall.

"Even though you say he had cancer, he didn't show any cancer patient pallor," Javier said.

"Pancreatic cancer often goes unnoticed until jaundice shows in the eyes, followed by weight loss and upper abdominal pain. By that time, the cancer has advanced and metastasized into nearby healthy tissue and lymph nodes. But we'll know more after we open him up."

Sharon shifted into clinical mode and switched on a tape recorder to begin the postmortem exam. "Deceased is a white male, approximately fifty years of age, six-foot two inches in height, 175 pounds." She gripped his head in both hands and tilted it back, exposing the neck wound. "Evidence of sharp force trauma to the left and right portions of the anterior triangles of the neck. From the depth of the wounds, the attack came from behind, and the laceration worked in a left to right direction. Two small hesitation marks are noted on the far left side of the wound. The wound track shows a start and stop at the midline of the victim's throat. The laceration cleanly severed the left internal and external jugular, carotid sheath, across to the larynx, severing the thyroid gland in two, and continued across, severing the right anterior jugular, terminating at the posterior muscle group on the victim's right." She clicked off the recorder and moved around the body.

"Doc, any idea on the type of weapon we're looking for here?" Emily asked.

Sharon put her hands on the table, closed her eyes for a moment, and then said, "This wound was cut in three separate motions.

Indicates a shorter blade and the killer needed to regrip the weapon to continue the attack. No indication of a serrated edge—the cut is very clean. I'd look for a bladed instrument, beveled with a blade length of four to eight inches."

Sharon rolled the victim on his side and turned on her recorder. "The deceased presents with a GSW in the upper right posterior quadrant." Sharon gathered a small-diameter fiberglass probe and carefully placed it in the jagged open wound. "It appears the path of travel came from the left and above the victim. Entry wound has limited stippling from gunpowder, and no exit wound noted." The recorder clicked off.

Emily pointed at a patch of dried pink blood around the entry wound. "Was he alive after the gunshot wound? And which came first, the shooting or the slashing?"

"Our victim suffered a collapsed lung from the gunshot and aspirated through the entry wound." She allowed the body to roll on his back once again. "Well, it's time to open him up and be certain."

The Chief Forensic Pathologist deftly cut a Y-shaped incision from beneath each shoulder, where they joined at the sternum and continued to the pubis.

No matter how many autopsies Emily witnessed, the next few moments always made her stomach flip; the pathologist pulled back the skin, muscles, and fatty tissue and used what amounted to bolt cutters to snip out the rib carapace in one piece. Worse than the snap of each rib reverberating off the walls was the sickening sucking sound as the rib cage detached from the chest cavity—a sound that always made Emily hold her breath.

"Deceased's right lung is collapsed." Sharon manipulated a pair of long forceps and tugged up on the deflated lung. "There it is."

With some effort, she pulled out a flattened metal slug embedded in the clavicle.

"There's very little blood here, the heart is shrunken, and the aorta is flattened. We're looking at the cause of death here: exsanguination, followed by cardiac failure. The gunshot wound occurred first, but didn't kill him; the killer finished the job by slashing his throat so that he bled out. I'll be able to confirm the COD with samples of lung, brain, and heart tissue, but I'm certain it will bear out."

"Thanks, Sharon. Do you need us here for the rest of the autopsy? We need to go track down a couple of loose ends," Emily asked.

"Go ahead. I'll call with new developments; tox results and the chem panels. If I learn more about the chemo and the pump, I'll pass it on."

Javier retrieved a small evidence bag from Sharon with the slug taken out of Roger Townsend.

Emily met Javier outside of the homicide room in the larger open bays of the autopsy suite. Her forehead creased.

"What's up?" Javier asked.

"What's missing? There are too many pieces that don't fit."

"You mean the cancer thing?"

"It's more than that. Our victim is dying of pancreatic cancer, and the wife doesn't mention it. Kind of ironic the man got murdered when he already carried a death sentence from the disease, don't ya think?"

"No kidding. The killer did our guy a favor by not letting him linger in pain for months. What do you suggest we do?"

Emily thought for a moment, then responded, "We need to talk to Mrs. Townsend again."

"Are you out of your mind? The Mayor and Howard already ordered you away from her."

"I'm going to fully comply with Howard's order. I'm not going to talk to her, you are. The Captain ordered me not to talk to her. He never mentioned you."

After a long, awkward silence, he replied, "You're trying to get me canned, aren't you? Let the brown man do it." Then with a sigh and a grin, "Come on, let's end my career. It was good while it lasted."

CHAPTER THREE

THE NEW WIDOW wasn't at the 46th Street residence; survivors often avoided spending the night in the place where a violent crime left fresh and raw emotions close to the surface. Lori Townsend's neighbors offered few suggestions where she would choose to hide away from the media. Perhaps she took to one of the local hotels as there was no family in the area. Lori apparently turned off her cell phone, avoiding the flood of "thoughts and prayers" calls from casual acquaintances.

Emily unsealed tape along the doorframe. Once inside the Townsend home, the detectives entered the home office, where the murder occurred. Emily stood on one side and made a mental sketch of the room. She typically returned to the crime scene and let it sink in. Often, the alley, riverbank, or in this case, the richly appointed room, would tell her something about the crime she missed the night before. There were no signs of forced entry. Roger Townsend was beaten and forced to open the hidden floor safe. No one else knew the combination according to his wife. It was curious other valuable items were left behind. It didn't scream "smash and grab" to Emily. How did the killer know about his safe? Did Roger Townsend give it up begging for his life? Questions, but not many answers.

Javier searched through a filing cabinet packed with records and documents for an indication of other family properties where Lori Townsend might choose to stay. Based on the state of his desk and work papers, Mr. Townsend bordered on obsessive-compulsive in his attention to the labeling of his files.

"I swear this guy even filed away the dust," Javier observed.

"There's a file marked PENDING LEGAL over here," Emily said. "But it's empty." She put it back down on the desk.

"No medical or medicine files either."

"Here we go." Emily pulled out a binder labeled PROPERTY, from a bottom desk drawer and put it on the surface. She opened the thick brown cover and the first page listed the Townsend property interests in the area. "Seven homes in Sacramento, Elk Grove, Wilton, and Granite Bay." Emily ran a finger down the list and discovered all but the Granite Bay home were managed by a rental company on behalf of the Townsends. She jotted down the addresses in her notebook and said, "She could be at any one of these places."

Emily found a receipt from a local upscale organic grocery store for a two-hundred-and-seventy-dollar delivery of various grocery and liquor items. The receipt was dated two days ago. "Apparently, the missus. didn't demean herself by doing her own shopping. I didn't see a stocked pantry in the kitchen last night." Emily pulled out her cell phone and called the number on the receipt.

"Hello, yes . . . this is Lori Townsend," Emily said into the phone with a slightly condescending tone. "I need to know you have my temporary address for my deliveries for the next few weeks."

A young woman's voice responded, "Let me check. Can I call you back with the information?"

"You most certainly cannot! I have better things to do than talk to grocery clerks. Check your records now and tell me the address on record."

Javier whispered, "Bitch!"

The nervous clerk on the phone responded, "Here it is, Mrs. Townsend. We show 2387 Lakeview Circle in Granite Bay. Is that correct?"

Emily hung up on the woman. "Up for a drive to Granite Bay?"

*   *   *

Perched on the western shore of Folsom Lake, Granite Bay attracted successful businessmen, professional athletes, rock stars, and those who wanted the status of the address. A few of the homes were actually four- to five-acre estates providing the seclusion the residents prized and paid for, handsomely. The Townsend estate featured a wrought-iron gate opening to a brick paver driveway that led to a Mediterranean-style villa perched on the crest of a small hill.

Emily eased up to the gate, and before she pressed the intercom button, a delivery truck barreled down the driveway from the home, tripping a gate sensor. Emily left the car, stopped the oncoming truck in the center of the drive, flashing her badge. "Is the lady of the house in?" she asked the pimply-faced driver.

With a shrug, the driver said, "I don't have a clue. I packed in two hundred and fifty bucks' worth of stuff to the kitchen and the maid, or whoever, signed for it. Oh yeah, no tip."

"Did you see anyone else?"

"I heard some music."

She waved the delivery boy on his way and pulled the Crown Vic up to the front of the grey two-story stacked stone edifice.

Javier got out of the car and pointed out the fountains on both sides of the front entry, each over six feet tall, but appropriate in scale to the sprawling building. "I couldn't even afford the water going through the fountains on my paycheck."

Emily pushed the doorbell, turned to the fountains, and said, "The fountains drown out the noise from unwanted religious peddlers, I guess."

She pushed the doorbell a second time, and within seconds, a middle-aged Hispanic woman opened the door and yelled, "I told you not to use the doorbell—" then shot a hand to her mouth, afraid she'd said too much. "I thought you were the delivery boy again. The missus doesn't wish to be disturbed."

"Detectives Hunter and Medina to see Mrs. Townsend," she replied.

The woman realized her response let the officers know she'd given away Lori's privacy; she couldn't now tell them her employer wasn't in.

The pause gave Javier an opening; he stepped inside and introduced himself. "Don't worry, we're not here to get you in trouble with Mrs. Townsend. And we're not from Immigration."

The housekeeper's shoulders relaxed. "Where are you from?" she asked Javier.

"My family comes from Sinaloa. My parents came over before it got bad with the cartel," Javier said.

"Ah, I thought I recognized your accent. I come from Hermosillo."

"My uncle is from Hermosillo," he replied.

"Did your parents make the crossing with you?"

"Before I was born. We were separated after. They got sent home, and I went into foster care here in the States."

"I still have family there. I worry. I send money home for them."

"It's good you can do it for them. My parents didn't have anyone left down there."

She nodded. Thousands were victims of the cartel violence over the decades. She didn't need to know more.

"Can you point us to Mrs. Townsend?"

The woman gestured to the back of the home.

True to the delivery boy's statement, Emily heard music coming from another part of the home. The entry opened up to a spacious great room, furnished with a grand piano, silk rugs, and a polished dark wood bar. Behind the bar were four Michael Goddard paintings—not prints, she noticed. Emily once owned a print of one of the paintings, an orgy of olives running around a martini glass. She sold the piece to help pay for the home renovations. She hated parting with it, but the modern art didn't fit with the Victorian fixtures in her place.

The music came from a sunroom, a protective bubble of sunlight over a cobblestone patio. Soft music wafted in from the sun-soaked room ahead of them accompanied by a clinking sound. Emily entered the sunroom and noted the temperature soared at least twenty degrees warmer than the rest of the house. At the end of the thirty-foot patio, Lori Townsend lay on a thick padded recliner, sunning herself in a barely-there dark blue bikini.

Javier said, "We've found the grieving widow."

Lori picked up a tall ice-filled glass and drew a deep swallow of a clear liquid before she returned it to the table next to her. She noticed the two detectives, untied her skimpy top, and placed it across her breasts, leaving very little to the imagination.

"I think that was for your benefit," Emily said.

Javier whispered in reply, "Women don't throw their clothes off at the sight of me. I think she connected with you last night."

Emily reached over, backhanded Javier in the shoulder, and prodded him toward Lori Townsend. "Excuse me, Mrs. Townsend? May I have a word with you?"

Without even opening her eyes, Lori said, "I thought we were done with your questions? I've told you what I can remember."

Javier perched on the edge of an adjacent recliner while Emily parked in a rocking chair about ten feet away. Emily pulled out her cell phone to answer an incoming call.

Javier continued, "There are a few loose ends I'd like to go over with you."

"I don't know what I can do. I was attacked, and my husband—"

"Did you put together the list of people you remembered in your husband's office who may have known about the safe?"

"No, not yet. I haven't found time."

Emily noted she'd had time to get a fresh manicure. Lori pulled a bottle of Belvedere vodka from an ice bucket beneath the table and topped off her glass with a trembling hand. As she returned the bottle to the bucket, her top slid down, and Lori made no move to cover up.

"Were you intimate with your husband?" Javier asked.

Lori shot upright in her chair and gave a harsh look at Javier. She fumbled with the fabric of her bikini top, reattached it, and demanded, "What kind of question is that?"

Javier returned the stare and replied, "Please answer the question, Mrs. Townsend. Were you and your husband intimate?"

Lori gathered her glass and took a long pull. "Not that it's any of your concern, but of course we were intimate, we were married."

"I'd like to ask you about your husband's health, Mrs. Townsend."

"Health? How can you sit there and ask me about Roger's health when you saw him last night?" Lori put the glass down heavily on the table next to her. She glared at Emily, across from her, and said, "My husband's dead, and you two come here to ask about our sex life?"

Emily leaned forward in her chair. "So, what about it, Mrs. Townsend? When did you and your husband—"

"Fuck? Is that what you want to know?" Lori angrily cut her off, trying for a reaction with her response.

Lori fidgeted uncomfortably for a moment. "Roger worked long hours. I wouldn't see him sometimes until late at night. He had excuses for being out of town for a day or two here and there. I know he cheated on me. We hadn't been together for a month, maybe two."

Javier waited for a moment and then asked, "Did you know your husband had cancer?"

"What? That's not possible—he wasn't sick." Lori braced herself on the edge of the recliner. The revelation of the hidden cancer diagnosis mixed with the booze made her appear light-headed.

Emily put away her cell and said, "The coroner confirmed Roger suffered from stage four pancreatic cancer. He had less than six months to live. Did you notice he wasn't around about four months ago?"

Lori shook her head. "No, that can't be. Roger told me he attended a trade show in San Francisco. He stayed about a week, I think."

"He underwent surgery. His oncologist attempted what they call a Whipple procedure, and halfway through, they found the cancer had metastasized. They closed him back up and told him about the terminal prognosis. The medical examiner confirmed it just now." Emily held her cell phone.

"Everything I thought I knew, everything he said, from then on, was a lie?" Lori asked. Her eyes watered, in contrast to the tight expressionless forehead. She stood slowly and wrapped a sheer white cover-up around her narrow waist.

"Mrs. Townsend? Mrs. Townsend?" Javier tried to regain her attention.

Lori's blue eyes clouded over, and she opened her mouth to speak, but no words came out.

"Who would want to kill your husband, Mrs. Townsend?" Javier asked.

"No one would want to murder my husband." She tucked her feet into a pair of sandals and then added, "He was a generous man. He invested in community organizations, foundations for the arts, and children's literacy programs." After an unsteady step, Lori turned, reached for the Belvedere bottle, and said, "I'm sorry, you need to show yourselves out." Lori disappeared through a set of French doors behind her.

The detectives retraced their path back to the front door and didn't encounter the woman from Hermosillo. However, as they got into their Crown Victoria, Emily caught movement from an upstairs window. The drapery pulled aside, and Lori Townsend observed them while holding a phone to her ear.

Emily motioned to Javier and said, "Wanna bet lunch she's calling the Mayor?" Lori hid behind the drapes when she realized they both watched her.

"Great. You know how that call will go, don't you? She calls the Mayor, who calls the Chief, who puts us on parking meter duty. We might need to back off on her a bit. She just lost her husband."

Emily pulled the car into gear and made their way to the open front gate. She slammed on the brakes to avoid a landscaper in an older green Chevrolet pickup truck. The detective waved the truck through, and the man in the front seat adjusted his frayed maroon baseball hat and returned the wave as he passed by the police sedan. In the rearview mirror, Emily checked out the usual assortment of old lawn mowers, trimmers, blowers, and bags of clippings in the bed of the truck.

The detectives drove back toward Sacramento, and Emily reached for the cell phone vibrating in her pocket.

"Hunter here."

"Hi, Emily, it's Sandy," the friendly voice of the Chief's secretary responded. Sandy served as a buffer between the top cop and staff for years. In fact, she outlived the last four Chiefs who left the office for various reasons: drunk driving convictions, shifting political winds, and in one case a bitter divorce case where the Chief of Police torched his estranged wife's Audi.

Sandy told Emily the Chief requested an immediate audience with both of the detectives. She added, "He's really pissed—that's not unusual, but this time the Mayor is taking a very personal interest. You know that's never a good thing for us. Tread lightly when you meet with him, please."

"This is about Lori Townsend, no doubt?" Emily said with a tone of sarcasm in her voice.

"Well it's not about the annual Police Athletic League breakfast."

"What is it with the Townsends and the Mayor anyway?" she asked.

Silence on the other end of the phone.

"Sandy? Tell me, please."

"You know very well Mayor Stone has greater political aspirations. Roger Townsend ranked among the biggest political fundraisers in California. The Mayor hoped Mr. Townsend would back his campaign for a seat in the Senate."

"I thought he learned his lesson when he didn't win in a landslide against political no-names in his mayoral race last year?" Emily said.

"He came out really bruised and hurt after—and now he's on the Chief's doorstep threatening audits and pushing defunding the police initiatives."

"Thanks, Sandy, I really appreciate the heads-up. Let the Chief know Detective Medina and I will drop by and see him in a couple of hours." Emily mulled over the Mayor's unexplained sense of attachment and urgency to this case.

"He wants to see you both right now," Sandy reminded.

"We have a couple of stops to make. It shouldn't take more than a couple of hours, at the most. Thanks, Sandy." Emily disconnected the call and placed the cell on the center console between the front seats.

Javier tilted his head at his partner. "You are determined to get me fired, aren't you? As if Chief Clark and Mayor Stone aren't pissed off enough, you're gonna blow off the meeting?"

"Would you relax? He requested an audience. An audience? Who does that? He's only reacting to the Mayor. It was a request anyways."

"You know better than that! You're as much of an ass as Stone is, you know?"

Emily smiled and replied, "Don't worry. I've got this covered. Besides, I think we have a little surprise in store for our Mayor."

Javier pinched the bridge of his nose where he felt the beginning of a headache coming on. "Oh dear God."

CHAPTER FOUR

THE OFFICES OF Townsend and Associates took up the entire seventeenth floor of the Renaissance Tower, in the heart of downtown Sacramento. The building carried the label of the "Darth Vader" building from its gloomy dark glass exterior and sharp clashing angles. During the construction, the architectural community expressed horror with the contrasting modernistic structure within blocks of the classically designed State Capitol building. Such was Sacramento, a city in search of an identity.

The moment the elevator doors parted on the seventeenth floor, Emily and Javier felt the funeral mood. The receptionist spoke in a low reserved voice and told them Mr. Anderson, the managing partner, would see them shortly. Around them, dark high-gloss wood paneling matched the somber atmosphere. Small groups of employees clustered together in the hallways mumbling about the uncertainty of the company's future, with snippets of phrases like *buyout*, *severance*, and *layoffs* overheard.

Jonathon Anderson emerged from a doorway behind the reception area and appeared every bit the stereotypical investment banker. His crisply pressed dark blue suit, white shirt, and contrasting tie the corporate uniform of the day. His expensively cut, short, dark brown hair retained a smattering of grey at the temples, lending an aristocratic air.

"Detectives, you have me at somewhat of a loss. I wasn't told to expect you today," Anderson said with a slight European accent Emily couldn't quite pin down.

"I apologize for the lack of notice, but we are gathering information about Mr. Townsend as quickly as possible," she responded.

"We are very shaken by his passing. He stood at the very core of this company. He is much more than a name on the wall."

Emily caught the reserved, polite reference to Townsend's death and responded, "*Passing?* Mr. Townsend was murdered, and we are attempting to find out who is responsible."

Anderson glanced around the reception area and said, "Please, let's take this conversation into a more appropriate location. If you would follow me?"

He led them through the same door from which he emerged a few seconds earlier and escorted the detectives into a large conference room. The twenty-foot-long table and thickly upholstered high-back chairs dominated the space. In front of each chair, matching leather blotters and emerald green–shaded lamps marked the workspaces. One person was seated at the table, a smallish man in a white shirt, his tie loosened at the neck. He pored through a pile of documents in front of him and did not appear to appreciate the interruption.

"Detectives, please let me introduce you to our in-house Chief Counsel, Michael Bartson. Michael, they wish to talk about Roger, and it would be appropriate for you to be here for this conversation, I should think."

Bartson pushed back from the table, said, "With Roger's death, we're kind of busy at the moment. Can this wait until a more convenient time, Detectives?"

Emily pulled out one of the leather chairs opposite the attorney. "We're busy, Mr. Bartson. This is about as convenient as it gets."

Anderson positioned himself next to the company's attorney, and Javier parked adjacent to Emily.

"This is a nice place," Emily said as she rocked back and forth in the expensive high-backed chair. "I don't own anything this comfortable at home, that's for sure." Emily pulled the string on the task light in front of her and asked, "How much was Roger Townsend worth?"

"Detective, that is a private matter," Anderson responded.

"Not any longer. It seems to be a very public matter now," Emily said as she rocked back and forth in the chair.

Bartson put both of his small hands on the table. "Roger was very well off, Detective, though the exact amount of his estate has yet to be determined. That's one of the tasks we're trying to undertake. As you can imagine, until we complete that, we are at a loss to manage our assets."

"And I'm sure you're broken up about Roger's murder too."

"Frankly, Detective, I really don't have time for that. This company is my client, not a single man. It's a shame he died, and I'm more concerned about the impact of that loss on the company."

Emily appreciated his brutal honesty.

Javier pressed Anderson, who started to speak and decided against it. "Mr. Anderson, you have something to say?"

"No . . . well, um . . . yes, I do." Anderson leaned forward. "I told you, we were all shaken by Roger's passing. This company ran in accordance with his vision, and because of that vision, he's dead."

Emily asked, "What do you mean?"

"Roger Townsend was a complicated man. A ruthless son of a bitch. If he discovered a way to make a buck off someone else's misfortune, Roger would be there, a vulture, circling in the desert sky. Then, in the same day he'd establish some charity for the disadvantaged."

"Some would call him a modern-day Robin Hood. But, frankly, his charitable activities were becoming a distraction for the business," the attorney added.

"Mr. Anderson, I get the feeling you think there was more to it," Emily said.

Anderson glanced over at the attorney, who cautiously shook his head. "It was not in Roger's nature to wait in the wings and hope a business failed. Roger would make sure it folded. It was like he'd swoop in and collect the smoldering remains and funnel a portion into a nonprofit somewhere."

"Anderson, this isn't appropriate," Bartson warned.

"Screw appropriate! Roger was murdered! He was cutthroat dealing with people who lost everything. He brought this on himself. We are lucky he was the only one killed."

"As counsel for this company, I strongly advise you to shut the hell up!" Bartson said.

"You and I both know what Roger did was wrong. We need to help find out who killed him."

The attorney leaned back in the chair, simmering in anger.

Emily again asked, "How much do you think Roger Townsend was worth? Gimmie a ballpark?"

Anderson thought for a second. "Easily seventy-five million. That's excluding properties and whatever he held in his private portfolio. His personal attorney would maintain that information."

"You have his attorney's contact information?"

"Wayne Corona," Bartson responded hotly.

"Corona? The criminal attorney?" Emily asked.

"The same. For the life of me, I can't tell you why," Bartson said.

"Mr. Anderson, we are going to need a client list for the company," Javier asked.

The attorney stood again. "Absolutely not! That's confidential information and has nothing to do with a home invasion robbery!"

"Mr. Bartson," Emily said. "We are going to obtain your client list. Either you hand it over, or I'll come in here with a warrant, very publicly box up every shred of paper, and carefully go over them for months. That should about shut you down, don't you think?"

"Mr. Anderson, we are also going to need a list of the people and organizations Mr. Townsend contributed to over the past two years," Javier added.

The attorney fumed, but Anderson ignored his antics. "I'll forward the client list to your offices today. Roger's fundraising efforts were held separately from his business with the company. Perhaps his personal attorney can help you with that information."

"Thanks, Mr. Anderson, we appreciate your cooperation. One more thing, could you find us any schedule or list of meetings Mr. Townsend kept?"

"I don't see why not."

"Of course you don't," Bartson grumbled.

Emily stood and told the men they would find their way out. As soon as Emily closed the door behind them, she could hear raised voices from within, the two men shouting back and forth at each other. The receptionist's wide eyes showed her surprise by the noise, and she wasn't sure what to do.

"I hate it when they fight in front of the children," Emily said.

Waiting for the elevator, Javier said, "Our list of suspects got a little bigger, didn't it?"

"Sure did and I don't think we're done yet. We need to head over to Wayne Corona's office. He's gonna know who Townsend funded, and more importantly those who didn't get a piece of the pie."

"We're supposed to meet with the Chief, remember?" Javier prodded.

"How could I forget, but Corona is right on the way. I'm sure the Chief had something more important come up, a pedicure, or whatever it is Chiefs do." She really didn't want to go back and face the Chief. Once politics infects a case, common sense disappears. The longer she could manage to delay the meeting, she hoped other "more pressing" political issues would make Mayor Stone back off. I mean, there should be more pressing issues running a city than micromanaging a homicide case.

CHAPTER FIVE

FADED GOLD PAINT flaked from the three-inch-tall lettering on a J Street storefront marking the law offices of Wayne Corona. Next door to the attorney's suite, the local immigration office held throngs of mostly brown people who waited patiently for visas, green cards, DACA renewals, and citizenship applications. The sign on Corona's door, below his name, advertised he specialized in immigration law, criminal defense, and personal injury. Hardly the offices one would expect of a high-powered attorney who managed the personal affairs of the seventy-five-million-dollar Townsend estate.

"This isn't how I pictured it," Javier said while navigating through the clusters of people outside the immigration office.

"Don't let this quaint, homey setting deceive you. Corona is a good defense attorney; he's a snake, but he's the attorney I'd want if I were guilty of something," Emily said as they paused at the street level door.

"He's a lowlife defense attorney. Why would Townsend use a guy like Corona for his personal work?" Javier pulled on the door and found it locked.

"He's got a sketchy network of people who work for him, informally. Paralegals, he calls them. Thugs, really. I faced off with

Corona a few years back, and his people got to the witnesses in a gang shooting. We had the guy dead to rights, in possession of the weapon, and ballistics matched. When it came to the trial, the victim said he was depressed and tried to shoot himself. He claimed the gangster stopped him and ripped the gun away from him at the last second. The shooter walked out of the courtroom with the jury thinking he was a hero.

"Corona's paralegals pressured witnesses in a dozen cases I know of. But Corona always seems to keep his hands clean."

Javier rattled the door. "It's all locked up." He tapped his watch face as a reminder of the meeting with the Chief.

"No, it's not." Emily pushed around Javier, pulled hard enough to bow out the cheap aluminum frame on the outer door, and popped the electric lock free.

"Oh Jesus, I'll add breaking and entering to my resume," Javier said.

He followed Emily up the narrow stairwell to the second-floor landing. The heavy wooden door to the attorney's office stood ajar. Emily pointed to chipped wood near the lock, a sign of forced entry. Both detectives pulled their weapons, and Emily used her left hand to push the door open. Javier made sure no one came down from the third floor behind them.

The outer office was vacant; no secretary waited to greet potential clients. Emily motioned Javier to follow her into the inner office as she slowly slipped inside.

Someone had turned the place over; file cabinets knocked on their sides, books thrown from the shelves, and piles of legal papers were strewn on the floor. Emily caught a scuffling sound, and with a finger to her lips, she nodded at an inner office door.

A faint high-pitched whine came from behind the wooden door. Javier regripped his Glock in both hands and nodded. Emily pulled the door open with a sharp tug, and Javier entered the room with Emily close behind.

A young Latina woman and a barrel-chested Black man were bound and gagged at a small conference table. They were trussed with layers of duct tape, securing them to their chairs. The young woman's eyes were wide with terror.

"It's okay now. We're the police," Javier told her softly.

The man appeared in his early thirties and muscled. Emily assessed the man's build as prison yard bulk—heavy on top and spindly legs. He bled from a gash on the back of his head and wheezed through the duct tape across his mouth. Emily pulled a pair of latex gloves from her back pocket and ripped the tape from the man's mouth along with a few strands of his thin mustache.

"Awww . . . man, why you'd do me like that?"

"Do you want me to put it back?" Emily held the tape up.

"No . . . no . . . man, it's cool. Get me outta here."

Emily removed the duct tape and a set of phone cords from the man's thick arms and asked him, "What happened here?"

"A couple of white dudes came in, and one pulled a gun on Rebecca, grabbed her by the hair, and pushed her into Wayne's office. I was in the office picking up a file Wayne wanted me to work on."

"You one of his paralegals?" Emily asked.

"Yeah, my ID is in my back pocket." He rubbed his wrists where the tape cut into his skin. "I've been working for Wayne for about three years."

Javier gently removed the tape from the frightened woman's face as the tears flowed from her dark brown eyes, streaming mascara halfway down her cheeks. "I thought he was gonna kill me."

"Have you ever seen them before?" Javier asked.

She shook her head nervously. "No, I've never seen either of them before. I don't think they were Mr. Corona's clients."

"What did the man with the gun say to you?"

The young woman pulled at the hem of her dress nervously and replied, "He grabbed me and pushed me into the office. All he ever said to me was to sit down and shut up, or he'd kill me. I believed him."

Emily asked the man the same thing, and the paralegal said, "Before they said a word, one of them clocked me on the back of the head. He shoved a gun under my nose while I was on the floor and told me to find a file for him. When I gave him what we have, he got pissed and wanted to know where Mr. Corona was."

"Where is Mr. Corona?"

"He was going to work from home for most of the day. I didn't tell them, though. I just said he was out."

"The files, which ones did he ask for?" Emily asked.

The large man rolled his neck from shoulder to shoulder, and a snapping sound came from the effort. "Oh, that's better. Dude wanted a file on Roger Townsend."

"Did you give it to him?"

"Hell yes! I'm not about to get killed over some paperwork." The man smiled softly and continued, "But, he didn't find the whole file."

Emily waited for him to finish.

"All we keep here are active legal files for our clients. Documents he hadn't worked on for a few months, or relating to Mr. Corona's political action committees, are stored at his home."

"So he didn't find what he came for?" Javier asked.

"I don't know what he came for, but he only stole a fraction of the work Mr. Corona did for Mr. Townsend. A copy of a prenuptial agreement, his will, and some new property acquisitions were the only things in the file here."

"Can you tell me more about them?" Emily asked both of them.

Shaken, the woman's memory was a blank beyond being snatched by the hair. But the fire in the man's eyes told a different story.

"What is it?"

"There were two of them. The one with the gun, he looked like a guy I know I've seen a couple of times. Tall white dude, yoked, short light brown hair, and prison tats on both arms. The other guy was your standard skinny-assed white boy tweaker. Never seen him around before."

Emily jotted down the information and asked, "When and where did you see the first guy?"

The man's eyes flickered for a brief moment until his expression turned hard and cold. "Last time I saw him was about three years ago at Pelican Bay State Prison."

"You remember him from there?"

"Not much else to do walking on the yard other than study the other men. I remember him 'cause he was one of the nuts they locked away in the PSU."

Emily asked him, "What's that? What is the PSU?"

"It's the place where they put guys who hear voices, try to cut themselves, or howl at the moon. You know the kind. They're always getting into trouble with other inmates and push it too far with the cops—stabbing people and shit. The PSU is the Psychiatric Services Unit."

"PSU? What's wrong with this guy?"

"No telling. I heard he couldn't take being locked up in his cell no more. That happens, the isolation gets to 'em. He tried to drown himself in his toilet. You'd be surprised how many guys try that one."

Emily put away her notebook and asked the man, "When did you parole out?"

"From Pelican Bay? About three years ago. I did a hundred and twenty days for a bullshit violation about a year and a half ago and got discharged from parole about six months ago." He pulled a small paper card from his wallet and passed it to Emily, which identified him as Benjamin Tooker, discharged from parole supervision.

Javier helped the woman make a phone call to her parents, and they were coming to pick her up. "Are you sure you don't want me to call an ambulance for you?" he offered.

"No. I want to go home. I don't want to see this place again."

Javier turned to the big man and asked him if he needed someone to look at the gash on his head. Tooker removed a handful of paper towels from the back of his head and noticed the blood flow had slowed.

"I'm all right. I been hurt worse."

"Still, I'm gonna ask the EMTs to check you out before you skip," Emily said.

Tooker nodded and pressed another paper towel to the gash on his head.

As the crime scene technicians arrived, Emily directed them to the likely path of suspects and what they came in contact with while ripping through the law office.

The young crime tech nodded and focused on his work while Emily wondered when they started hiring straight out of high school. The tech's youthful face bore no trace of visible facial hair and not even the shadow of a wrinkle. Emily recalled a much different view in her own mirror this morning, and this pup in his ill-fitting jumpsuit made her feel even older.

Javier caught Emily staring at the younger man, and he said, "Were we ever that young?"

"Speak for yourself, I'm still young. I spend half my paycheck on toners, concealers, scrubs, washes, and pore minimizers to make damn sure. You . . . you were born old."

After Tooker and Rebecca were given a once-over by an EMT, Emily gave them her business card and told both of them to call if they thought of anything else.

Finished with their initial walkthrough, Javier followed Emily down the narrow hallway to the street.

Emily strapped into the Crown Vic and started the engine. "What did you make of Tooker's account of the two white guys— one with a Pelican Bay pedigree?"

"I don't know. He said he recognized the guy. Think he knows more than he's saying?"

"It's hard to say, but it gives us a thread to pull on, which is more than we had an hour ago. We can drop in on Corona and start the computer searches going after we're done with the Chief."

They rode in silence for the ten-minute trip to the Police Department headquarters on Freeport Boulevard. Small light industrial and commercial establishments were open for business, and traffic in the area congealed considerably. Finding a vacant parking space in the police lot near the back fence, Emily pulled into the rare empty slot. As she entered the chief's office suite, the chief's secretary, Sandy, glanced up and smiled.

"Well, you took your sweet time, didn't you," she said.

"Something came up," Emily replied.

"Doesn't it always?" Sandy peered over her reading glasses at the detectives. "He's in a meeting now and running late. When he opens the door, I'll let him know you were here."

"Thanks."

Sandy stopped them before they left. "Detective Medina, we have the highest expectations you will keep Detective Hunter out of trouble," she said.

On the way back to their desks in the detective bureau, Emily opened a training room where a class of more young faces was deep into a refresher course on sexual harassment. The department settled a couple of damaging cases quietly, and as part of a confidential settlement agreement between the parties, all officers received the training. Emily crept into the classroom while the sergeant read from the lesson plan. Emily pulled a whiteboard from behind the instructor. The wheels locked and scraped across the linoleum surface with a piercing shriek. All the faces turned in her direction as she unlocked the wheels.

"Sorry," Emily said, and she rolled the whiteboard from the room.

Javier shook his head, held the door for her, and helped roll the board into the detective bureau near their desks. Emily picked up an eraser from the tray at the bottom of the board and wiped off the training outline for the class she interrupted. With a marker, she made a series of notes on the board.

"Okay, we start with the murder of Roger Townsend and the assault on Lori Townsend in their home."

"Then today, the break-in at Townsend's attorney's office and two employees held at gunpoint while our guy searched for a legal file on Townsend," Javier added.

"Townsend's legal work, or the money he tossed around to fund politicians, could be the common ground."

Javier asked, "Where does the ex-con from Pelican Bay fit in?"

"Which one, the crazy white guy or Benjamin Tooker?"

"Well, both actually. Corona hired Tooker on as muscle, right? Could be Tooker identified Townsend as a target for the home invasion for his prison pal."

Emily added another circle to the board. "Let's not forget what Anderson told us at Townsend's offices. A combination ruthless businessman and charitable donor. The client list may put another piece of this puzzle together."

"What are we left with? A nutso ex-con from Pelican Bay who gets a tip from Tooker that Townsend was ripe for the picking? Or, a business rival puts out a hit? That I get. But what would either guy want with legal files?"

"I don't know . . . blackmail maybe?"

"You can't blackmail a dead guy."

Emily reached for the desk phone when it rang. "Hunter here."

"Detective Hunter? It's Benjamin Tooker. We met at Mr. Corona's office."

"Yes, Mr. Tooker, I remember," Emily said and pointed to the phone extension on Javier's desk. He slowly lifted the receiver and put it to his ear.

"Detective, I got to thinking about the files Mr. Corona kept at his home. I dropped by and . . . Detective, I swear it wasn't me. He was dead." Emily heard the panic in Tooker's voice.

"Okay, calm down, where are you now?"

"I'm sitting in my car in front of Mr. Corona's house. He's dead. You gotta believe me. I didn't do this."

"What's the address? We'll send someone there as soon as possible."

"It's on Fair Oaks Boulevard, 2600. It's got a big white gate. It's still open. I don't want to be here when the cops show up."

"Sit still. Detective Medina and I will be right there. Hang tight." Emily disconnected from the call and Javier was already on the line with communications to dispatch units to the location Tooker mentioned.

Emily snatched her jacket from the back of her chair and stopped in front of the whiteboard. She drew another circle and wrote "Corona" in the center. She traced a line from the circle to "Roger Townsend," intersecting with a circle that said only, "White man, tattoos, mentally ill, Pelican Bay."

"Let's go before Tooker gets cold feet and disappears. He knows more than he's telling."

CHAPTER SIX

OF ITSELF, the death of a defense attorney was nothing to cry over. One less client for the local bail bondsman, and fewer witnesses threatened. An old joke ran through Emily's mind: *What do you call a dozen lawyers on the bottom of the ocean? A good start.* Emily's gut told her Corona's death would send shock waves through the city. The attorney's connections and the money funneled to and from clients made up a veritable who's who of the power brokers in local and state government. If the money trail from Townsend's coffers went public, there would be more than a few uncomfortable prominent politicians scrambling to explain their campaign contributions. Desperate enough to eliminate Corona and the paper trail.

A police unit's lights marked the Corona driveway. Emily waved at a familiar face in the sedan that blocked access to the residence. The officer nodded and pulled his car forward to let Emily pass. The attorney's home was an L-shaped affair with a six-bay garage to the right side of the two-story main building. The Tudor design felt disconcerting, with its angles, slats, and cupolas. The knot of police vehicles in the driveway did nothing to soften the effect.

Emily spotted Benjamin Tooker in the rear of one of the patrol cars. Javier got out of the Crown Vic and approached the window of the patrol car. He spoke with Tooker while Emily found a pot-bellied sergeant sitting on the hood of his patrol car, his stubby legs dangling off the side.

"Hey, Hunter. This one your case?"

"How come you're not inside contaminating my crime scene?"

"Come on! I only did that once. How's I supposed to know that sucker kept body parts in his refrigerator. I was thirsty. Anyway, my feet are killing me, so I've got the kids out securing the crime scene and perimeter."

"What about the guy in the back of the car?"

"He's been cooperative. We needed to verify his identity and his story before we cut him loose."

"Did he check out?"

"He does. Ex-con, but he's been clean a while, and he didn't have a drop of blood on him. And whoever did this—" the sergeant pointed toward the house—"would be covered in the stuff."

Emily nodded. "Crime scene techs been called?"

"Hey, I didn't fall off the truck yesterday, Hunter. Yeah, I called them and the ME's bag boys."

Emily approached the wide steps to the front door. Someone had knocked over the pathway lighting and removed the cover from the porch light. The bulb wasn't in the socket. Emily felt a twinge of guilt over unscrewing the neighbors' lights, but this harkened a darker, more sinister vandalism. It also meant the attack occurred before dawn. She found the bulb intact in the nearby rose bushes. She made a mental note to ask one of the crime scene technicians to collect it and try to lift a print.

Javier joined Emily at the home's threshold. "Wow," he said. The attorney's art collection, wine room, and expensive ebony wood furniture glistened steps away from the entrance. "I guess this makes up for the crappy little downtown office."

Emily stopped at the glass front of a temperature-controlled wine room, where Corona amassed at least two thousand bottles in his collection. A twinge of jealousy struck Emily. Unlike her, Corona didn't wait for a buy-one-get-one-free sale at his local wine shop.

Javier noticed his partner admiring the wine collection and said, "You need to go to a twelve-step meeting, Hunter?"

"Probably," she said before he broke her connection with the wine collection and continued deeper into the home.

An upended hallway table marked the first sign of disorder in the obsessive-compulsively arranged residence. One of the table's slender tapered legs was broken off and missing. An expensive flower arrangement lay strewn on the floor, with wet footprints trailing deeper into the residence. Down a wide hallway from the great room, an officer leaned against an open doorway. Emily noticed a few drops of spattered blood on the hallway wall. She wouldn't have noticed the small stain if it hadn't been for the overhead light focused on an oil painting.

The officer stood stiffly and sucked in his slight belly. Emily had that effect on men but was usually oblivious to it. Long ago, she promised herself not to date anyone she worked with. However, work ate up her free time, and the men she found interesting off the job were not interested in her, or were intimidated because she wore a badge.

Emily started to think, at thirty-six, she might've carved a path to be the old woman on the block who talked to her cats. She had a head start with her "not my cat," with whom she confided her deepest secrets. So far, the cat hadn't betrayed her trust. The trespassing cat was the one male in her life who hadn't caused her heartache or pain. She reflected once that Javier hadn't either, but he was her partner and was held to a higher standard.

"Were you the first on scene?" Javier asked.

"Good afternoon, Detectives," the officer on post in the hallway said in a deep voice. He never took his eyes off Emily and didn't catch the question Javier asked.

"Um . . . I'm sorry, Detective, what?" The man's face blushed slightly.

Javier sidestepped between the officer and Emily. "Were you the first officer on scene?"

A bit embarrassed, the officer responded, "Yes, I was. Officer Petty took custody of the guy in the car out front."

"Did you enter the room here, Officer?"

"Conner, ma'am. I did, to check if the victim had a pulse. I went for his carotid artery, but with his neck sliced open, I backed out and called it in."

Emily noticed the officer donned blue elastic shoe covers to prevent evidence contamination. "Were you wearing those when you entered?"

"Yes, Detective. I carry a set with me. I get called the booty bandit."

"Good move, Officer."

Emily tucked her hair behind her ears and followed Javier into the room with Wayne Corona's body.

Javier used caution, careful to stay along the wall as he observed the body at different angles. He paused and asked Emily, "Look familiar?"

Javier focused on the wounds. "That is kinda strange. I don't want to use the C word, but what a . . ."

"Coincidence . . ." Emily finished.

"Let's take a closer look at him. Watch your step—there's a big pool of blood over along the wall. Why it's over here four feet from the body is another question." Emily inched toward the body, careful not to disturb the scene until the ME and crime scene techs documented everything. One slip up could be enough to lose a case, tossed on a technicality.

"We got a shoe print in the blood over here," Emily said.

"Over here too," Javier said. "The killer rummaged through files in this cabinet."

Blood stained the glossy maple handles of the four-drawer filing cabinet. A pile of file folders lay in disarray on the floor nearby. More blood spatter fell in large drops on the files themselves. Javier found a wet blood pool on the top of the cabinet in the shape of a knife.

"He laid the weapon down here while he searched the files after he cut our victim."

"Cut from ear to ear resembling Townsend. I don't see a gunshot wound though," Emily said.

"He got what he came for." Javier held an empty, blood-smeared file folder with the name TOWNSEND inscribed on a label.

A noise and rattle from the door marked the arrival of the crime scene technicians and the medical examiner's team. Camera strobes lit up the hallway as they documented the scene. Emily scribbled a rough diagram of the position of the body relative to objects in the room before the techs started their precise documentation processes.

The detectives backed out of their way and let them work, Emily lowered into the chair behind Corona's desk. It appeared thick and plush, but she was a bit surprised it came off stiff and very uncomfortable. She pulled open desk drawers stuffed with the usual desk clutter, paper clips, notepads, and pens. The bottom drawer didn't pull smoothly and stopped an inch or two out. It had fallen off the rollers and bound up against the track. A quick, hard jerk loosened the drawer, and Emily pulled it all the way out.

On the back of the drawer, heavy layers of duct tape secured a .38 caliber Smith & Wesson Model 10 revolver.

"What do you wanna bet that this is the gun used on Roger Townsend?" she said.

"You saying Corona was the shooter? Then who crept back and cut his throat?"

"Corona could have been a loose end."

Emily motioned for a tech to take photographs of the firearm.

"Check that out," Emily said. "Looks like dried blood on the trigger guard. Need to make sure we match it. Bet you it's Roger Townsend's."

"Whoever taped the gun to the cabinet did it fast and misaligned the drawer when they slid it back," Javier said.

She pointed at the multiple layers of tape holding the weapon. "This guy likes his duct tape. I bet we'll also find this tape came from the same roll used to bind Tooker at the law office."

Kneeling down near the drawer, Javier observed, "There's no blood on the tape whatsoever. The rest of the place is covered with the stuff. No telling when the weapon was ditched here."

"If it's our weapon, it could've been hidden any time after the Townsend murder. Makes Corona seem involved, doesn't it? In spite of how this looks, I can't picture Corona as a trigger puller in the Townsend killing, can you? He hired a gang of paralegals to do his dirty work," Emily said as she turned away and surveyed the photographs on the wall behind the desk.

She'd seen ego walls before, but this one established a higher level of self-appreciation. Corona's smiling face featured among three Presidents, a half dozen Senators, six Governors, and a sea of executive types in expensive suits with other faces she didn't recognize. Assuming Corona helped fund even half of the political campaigns represented on the wall, it meant he lived in a lot of deep pockets and was privy to their darkest secrets. Emily wondered which secret cost Corona his life?

After three hours, Emily left with a small box of the dead attorney's possessions that she and Javier would go over tomorrow. They found the last three months of phone bills, Corona's cell phone, a Rolodex, and a black leather planner. Every item was meticulously cataloged, placed into evidence envelopes, and loaded into the box along with a laptop computer from the dead man's desk. Emily planned for a warrant to access the computer files because of the attorney-client privilege issues. She thought about searching first then asking for a warrant if she found something. They might need a Special Master to review the laptop content to make certain the attorney-client privilege followed Corona to the grave. If a defense attorney discovered a breach outside the lines, any evidence would be lost. More than that, Emily played by the rules.

By the time Emily loaded the box into the Crown Vic, the Medical Examiner's team wrapped and packed Wayne Corona's body, and the techs tagged and bagged the fibers and blood evidence. Benjamin Tooker didn't waste any time leaving the police-filled location after they cut him loose. Not a safe space for a Black ex-con.

Local interest in the spectacle died away as the hours passed, replaced with the more typical indifference from the cocoon-centric lifestyles of the locals. One patrol car remained at the gate to keep the remaining curious few away from the residence.

Emily checked her watch. "Well, Howard didn't receive his report for the mayor today. He's gone by now."

Javier settled into the passenger seat and buckled in as he said, "Do you try to piss him off, or does it come naturally?"

"I think of it more as a gift only to be used to help mankind. Besides, the guy is an empty uniform and completely useless."

"Useless or not, he's gonna own our asses tomorrow. You know somebody's got to do that job, dealing with the administrative and political bullshit," Javier said, shielding his eyes from the setting sun.

"You getting soft on me, Medina? Are you actually defending Captain Howard?"

"No, it's not that. He's not evil."

"I'm not saying he's the Antichrist, but he's a shitty human being."

"Not to change the subject, but you know what you need? I'll tell you. You need to call up Officer Booty Bandit back there, let him buy you a drink, and let nature take its course."

Emily reached over and slugged Javier in the shoulder before the words dried on his lips. "Asshole!" What bothered her most—maybe he was right—but she didn't need his help to get laid. "I can do fine without you pimping Officer Booty Bandit and his cute little smile," she huffed.

"Noticed the smile, did you?"

"Asshole!"

Minutes later, the sedan pulled into the nearly vacant police department parking lot, and Emily let Javier out at his car. "I'll see you in the morning, Em."

"I'm gonna log this stuff in and head out too."

Emily carried the box inside and dropped it on an empty patch on her desk. No lights were on in the detective bureau, so Emily turned on her desk lamp, grabbed an evidence form from the box, and confirmed the items secured from the crime scene were accounted for. She checked them off once more and logged them into an evidence locker.

Before she shut the locker, Emily picked up the plastic envelope containing the victim's cell phone, a standard, no frills phone. The kind you used to pick up from the wireless company when you signed up, rather than the bells and whistles phones most attorneys carried around as status symbols. In fact, she remembered an occasion last year where she ran into Corona entertaining a client, and the attorney answered a different, much more expensive big-screen model. Why would he carry this one, Emily wondered, a replacement, a burner phone, or a backup number?

Through the plastic, Emily hit the MENU button, a bit surprised an attorney of Corona's stature wouldn't use a phone with password protection. She scrolled down to the list of recent calls. On the display, the last four names hit Emily hard. The green illuminated letters spelled out Lori Townsend, each time.

CHAPTER SEVEN

EMILY PULLED OUT of the department parking lot, her phone chirping as she merged into traffic. Her knuckles tightened on the wheel. She was drained, both her and the car; it was as if the glowing red light on the dash forecast her energy reserves too. The early hours on any case were frantic, a race chasing down fresh leads that would evaporate as time elapsed. From experience, Emily knew the trail to the truth was vulnerable to the drifts of time.

She drew a deep breath and picked up her phone. A call from the lab could wait until tomorrow, but if the call announced another death tied to the Townsend case . . .

"Hunter." Her tone warned, *Don't fuck with me and this better be important.*

"Miss Hunter?"

"Who's this?"

"Miss Hunter, this is Tailia at Senior Care Solutions."

Emily's throat tightened. Sheila was with her mother. Did Connie slip out again? Was she hurt?

"Is everything okay?"

"We've had an incident, Miss Hunter. I'm afraid we'll no longer be able to provide services for your mother."

"Incident? What kind of fucking incident can a seventy-year-old woman get into?"

"Can you or another family member come over and tend to her?"

"What's going on?" In her mind, dark scenarios flicked past. Mom torched the kitchen again—no, she couldn't do that again because Emily shut off the gas to the stove, and Sheila was there to supervise. If her mother wandered off, Emily would receive an alert on her phone from the pendant she'd made Connie wear.

"Mrs. Hunter physically assaulted her caregiver—"

"What? Mom assaulted Sheila? She loves Sheila. What happened?"

"I'm getting the details from Sheila and from the doctor—"

"Doctor? What exactly happened?"

"I don't know why—or what transpired before the attack—but Mrs. Hunter became confused and started hitting Sheila. She threw a dish, and it cut Sheila's cheek."

"Sweet Jesus. Is Sheila all right?"

"The doctor didn't need to stitch it up. She's quite upset, as you can imagine. We can't allow any of our staff to be treated in this manner. I'm sure you understand."

"I do. But I don't understand why this happened. Did Mom say anything?"

"I don't know. The police are interviewing her now and—"

"You called the police on my mother?"

"I don't have a choice, Miss Hunter. We're required to report assaults on our staff members. Can you or a family member come and see to your mother?"

Emily closed her eyes and leaned back in her seat. "There is no one else. I'll be there as soon as I can."

She disconnected the call and tossed the phone in the seat. "Shit, shit, shit!" Her voice echoed off the windows in her car. Calling the cops on an old woman. Emily pressed the gas pedal a little harder and fumed on the drive home.

Emily's jaw tightened the moment she pulled up to her place behind a black and white Sacramento patrol car parked at the curb. *Dammit! If they have her in handcuffs, someone else is going to the hospital.* Emily threw open her car door and stormed to the house. Once in the front door, she found an empty living room, but there were voices and clicking sounds from the kitchen. Emily shot around the corner to the kitchen and found Connie Hunter having tea with Officer Conner—Officer Booty Bandit.

"Mom?"

Connie Hunter glanced up from her teacup. "Oh, hello, dear."

"What's going on?"

"I'm having tea with my new friend, Brian."

Officer Conner raised his teacup to Emily. "Evening, Detective."

That smile again. Emily slid into a seat next to her mother.

"Mom, can you tell me what happened tonight?"

"Whatever do you mean, dear? Brian and I are having tea, dear."

"I heard there was a problem with Sheila?" Emily asked.

"Sheila said some mean things. I don't think I want her here anymore."

"I don't think that will be a problem, Mom. Did you guys have an argument?"

"It's not important. Brian and I are having tea. Would you care to join us?"

"Detective, she doesn't remember what led up to the altercation. She was a bit agitated when I got here, but she's very mellow now. She ever have issues getting physical with her caregivers before?"

"No. Nothing before this. Thanks for sitting with her and calming her down."

"I've seen this happen. My mom was diagnosed with dementia at first, then the Big A."

"Alzheimer's?"

Brian nodded.

"I'm sorry."

He shrugged. "It's all part of life, I suppose. Anyway, this is familiar territory. Is her doctor working with you?"

"They haven't been concerned about her cognitive decline. At her last appointment, the doctor told me she was within normal limits for a woman her age. This—this isn't normal." Emily wiped a tear away with the back of her hand.

"It's normal for someone with memory or dementia issues."

During the conversation, Connie sipped away at her tea, oblivious to the nature of the discussion around her.

Emily put her head in her hands and propped her elbows on the table. "I thought I'd have more time, before—"

"We all wish we could plan for this more. Life has other ideas."

"I'm sorry you got called in for this, but I'm glad it was you."

"Anyone would've been fine. Connie's very pleasant company."

Connie Hunter pretended not to overhear Brian's remark, but a slight smile crept on her face.

"Tea, dear?" Connie reached for the teapot.

"Let me," Brian said and refilled their cups. "Want a hit, Detective?"

Emily plodded to the cupboard, removed a cup, and returned to the table. She watched as Brian poured her cup with a steady hand. She allowed herself to breathe in the fragrance of her mother's favorite chamomile tea blend.

"Good choice on the tea," Emily said. She shook her hair out of the ponytail and let it fall.

Brian smiled. That damn smile again. "I figured it might be a good idea to avoid caffeine tonight."

"Mom, we need to find someone to come and stay with you."

"I'm not a child. I've lived on my own for—I don't need a stranger barging in and telling me they know what's best."

"Sheila wasn't a stranger."

"I never liked that woman. Bossy little know-it-all."

Emily reached for her mom's hand. It felt soft and vulnerable. "I thought you and Sheila got along."

"I only said that for you. I know that's what you wanted. I don't need a babysitter, Emily."

Her mother kept her eyes cast down at her teacup. "I don't want to be a burden."

"You're not, Mom. I need you to be safe."

"I'm fine on my own."

Brian cleared his throat, getting Emily's attention. He tilted his head toward the living room. "Mrs. Hunter, I've got to go now. It was very nice to meet you."

"I hope I see you again," Connie said.

Brian flicked his eyes in Emily's direction. "I hope so too."

"Mom, I'm going to walk Brian out. I'll be right outside, okay?"

Her mother didn't answer and sipped her tea.

"Brian, thanks for being so nice to Mom. It made a world of difference," Emily said when they were in the living room.

He shrugged. "I get it. I've been there. I think I kept a list of agencies and facilities offering memory care services."

"I'm not sure what to do now. Senior Care Solutions—they were one of the few willing to work around my schedule." Emily's mind flooded with questions with no simple resolution. When it came to the care of someone in the twilight of their life, she'd seen so many older people cast off and abandoned in nursing homes, or left to languish perilously on their own until an accident hastened their end.

"Let me put together some names and some contacts, for a place to start."

Emily nodded. "That would be great, thanks. How's this going to work? You need to file a report and refer this mess to the district attorney. We'll do what we have to. I don't think she'd understand getting booked and fingerprinted."

Brian waited until Emily paused. "The caregiver's employer is a mandatory reporter—they are required by law to report any physical assaults involving patients under their supervision. They did that. They reported it. I responded. It's within our discretion to take it from there. Nothing would be served by pushing this any further. Connie's a sweet woman and she 'had a moment,' as my mom used to say."

"I can't ask you to give me a break because we both wear the same badge."

"No professional courtesy here. Only doing what's right."

The crackle of static and a dispatch call came from his radio. He keyed the microphone on his shoulder. "Charles-31, responding." Then to Emily, he said, "I need to take this. Can we have coffee sometime?"

"I'd be up for that, sure."

He gestured to his uniform. "Well, you know where to find me. I'll get those memory care agencies and contacts to you tomorrow, okay?"

"That would be a big help, thank you."

Once Emily closed the door behind Brian, she let her mind wander to what might be—an easy casual meetup with Brian. No strings, no preconceptions, simply being there with another person. That evaporated with the sound of a crash from the kitchen.

Emily rushed to the room, and her mother stared, nonplussed over the shattered remains of her cup on the floor.

"Mom?"

"Yes? Oh, I must've bumped my teacup." She started to press up from the chair, but Emily placed a gentle hand on her shoulder.

"I'll take care of it, Mom."

Emily swept up the sharp ceramic shards, dumped them into the trash, and returned to her mom.

"We need to figure out how to find the help you need," Emily said to herself as much as she did for her mother.

"I don't need anyone. I have you."

Emily patted her hand. "I'm not here all the time. I don't want you to have an accident."

"Nonsense. When you get home from school, you can help me with whatever needs doing."

"School?" That icy paranoia cranked up once more.

"When will you graduate again? Why does Kennedy High hold the ceremony outside on the football field? Doesn't seem very dignified to me."

"Mom, I've been out of high school for a while now."

A confused look spread on Connie's face. Then an abrupt change of topic. "I'm going to bed now."

Emily assisted her to her room and got her settled in bed. She kissed her on the forehead. "'Night, Mom."

"Goodnight, dear."

Emily left the door open a crack and retreated to the living room. She collapsed on the couch, and the situation fell upon her. How could she take care of her mom and hold a job, especially one as demanding as a police detective? There was no other family to share the burden. Emily didn't really mean *burden*; her mom wasn't that at all—she needed a little extra attention. Maybe she could ask for a little time off until she could fix everything. Who was she kidding? This wasn't some midlife crisis speed bump and a time-out wouldn't make it better. Some things weren't fixable. Emily knew this was life changing—for her mother and for herself. Her mom had reached the stage where continuing care became inevitable.

She catnapped on the couch and snapped awake at any sound, glancing down the hall to check on her sleeping mother. Emily imagined this is what being a parent of a toddler felt like—worry, fear, and dread of what would happen next. Some mothers called this constant feeling of dread the "joys of parenthood." Yet another reason Emily wasn't on the baby train.

As dawn started to blush the living room windows, Emily called Javier. Her mom couldn't be left alone, not in this condition.

"What's up? We pick up a new case?" Javier asked.

Emily bit her lip for a moment, wondering how she could tell her partner she needed to abandon him in the middle of a high profile case. "Javi, it's Mom. She's—shit, I don't know what to call what happened. An episode."

She recounted the dish throwing, the caregiver walking out, and the call to the police.

"Wait, what? They called in for your mom? What were they expecting? Someone was going to perp-walk your mom to jail? Good God, Em, what is it with these social worker types? They're helpful and kumbaya until shit gets real, then they turn their backs on people when they need it most."

"I don't know what I'd have done if Stark or one of those knuckle-dragging assholes had taken the call." Emily experienced more than her share of run-ins with Officer Stark, a twenty-year patrol veteran who believed women couldn't pull their weight and shouldn't be given "cushy" detective assignments.

"Wait, you're telling me a patrol unit was dispatched to your mom's place?"

"Yeah, I was lucky it was Brian who took the call. He calmed Mom down by the time I got there."

"Brian?"

Shit. Her partner was not going to let her live this down.

"Brian Conner. I think we met him at Corona's place—"

"Oh, I remember Officer Booty Bandit and his cute smile, I think you called it."

"I did not!"

"Own it, Emily. Conner is good with the older ladies?"

"Turns out his mom has similar issues with dementia and Alzheimer's. He knew what to say to help her calm down. They were having a flippin' tea party when I got here."

"Alzheimer's? I've never heard you say that before. Is your mom—"

"No, no, she's not there yet. But this gave me a wake-up call that she needs more attention than a drop-in caregiver service can provide. I need to find someone to move in with us or get her into a place where she'll be safe. That will be a nightmare. Brian said he'd help me with finding a place."

"I'll bet he did," Javi said.

"Don't be a dick. That's kinda why I called. I need some time to figure this out. I can't leave her alone."

"I'm sorry, Emily. Hey, how about my mom? She's worked at an assisted living facility. She could spend the day with your mom. I know she wouldn't mind. They know one another. Connie wouldn't have to get used to a new person in her life."

"Would she be willing to do that? I mean that's a lot to ask. It would be temporary until I can figure out what to do."

Javier said he'd call his mom and, forty-five minutes later, Lucinda Medina arrived at Emily's doorstep.

Lucinda didn't look sixty-five years old. Javier told Emily how her family had emigrated from central Mexico before they adopted him, but the smallish woman in front of Emily didn't show the scars or deeply held fear crippling many who make the crossing. Lucinda considered herself an American and endured through the laborious, bureaucratic process to become a citizen. She held fast to some traditions but adapted well to the fast pace of life in the California Central Valley.

"Lucinda, I can't thank you enough for spending time with Mom."

"It's my pleasure. I'll make her comfortable, and I'll be here for her as a friend. She won't want to think you arranged a babysitter. As far as she's concerned, I'm here as a family friend."

"Thank you, and I'll pay you for your time."

"No, you won't. Didn't you hear what I said? I'm doing this as a family friend." She put her hands on slim hips, a pose of motherly defiance.

Emily hugged Lucinda. "We'll talk about how I'll make this right for you later. Thank you."

"You go and keep my son out of trouble. Connie and I are fine, and we'll do something fun today. I'll call you if anything comes up—which it won't. Don't worry."

Lucinda shooed Emily out of the way.

Maybe things were going to work out.

CHAPTER EIGHT

EMILY GOT A quick shower and change of clothes and headed back to the detective bureau. She couldn't keep her mind from ruminating over her mother's confusion and the calls between Lori Townsend and the dead attorney. On the drive in, she pulled up to a drive-through coffee shop and ordered two large black brews—one with stevia for Javier.

When she called Javier's desk number, he picked up on the first ring.

"I know you followed my advice and got loose with Officer Booty Bandit," he said, recognizing her phone number.

"Very funny, smart-ass. I'm on my way in, and I'll pick you up in the parking lot. And your mother is a saint."

"What you got lined up for us?"

"We need to hit Lori Townsend again." Emily explained the sequence and suspicious timing of the phone calls from the attorney. "I need to find out where she is this morning before we make the drive out to Granite Bay."

Emily agreed to meet Javier in front of the police department building in fifteen minutes.

"Heads up, Captain Howard jumped me this morning about not getting to his briefing yesterday."

"Great. See you in a few."

She hung up and from her case notes dialed the Townsend home in Granite Bay.

"Hello, this is Detective Hunter."

The Hispanic housekeeper's delayed response betrayed her fear of the police. "Yes—I remember."

Emily spoke carefully so she didn't spook the housekeeper. "Can you tell me where I can find the lady of the house?"

After a pause, the housekeeper provided the information to the detective and hung up as quickly as she could.

Javier waited in the parking lot and jumped in the car when Emily pulled up.

"Where's Mrs. Townsend?"

Emily handed him his coffee.

"The housekeeper said she left for an aerobics class that's supposed to go from eight to nine thirty this morning. She gave me the address out by the university, on Carson Drive."

He nodded and took a sip. "Ah, you remembered the stevia."

"That's plain nasty tasting stuff. Years from now they're gonna find out it causes mutations and shit."

"Hey, a third eye could come in handy."

"Shut up and drink your poison."

"Oh, by the way, my mom says it's time you came by the house for dinner. You've been my partner for six months, and she wants you and your mom over for a proper dinner. You should bring a date, maybe give that young officer a test drive."

"You're impossible. If you're gonna feed me, I think we can make that happen. Besides, I'm gonna owe your mother big-time for bailing me out."

"Be on your best behavior. She's a little old-fashioned."

"I'm always a pillar of virtue," she said.

"When you're not f-bombing the countryside."

The address the housekeeper gave them led to a nondescript commercial building behind the Scottish Rite Temple. The only indication of the nature of the business came from a small sign on the smoked glass door proclaiming ROBINSON PERSONAL TRAINING.

Emily pushed the door open, and they entered a huge open space divided with a short wall down the center. One side held a small assortment of exercise machines with cables, pulleys, and weights which, to Emily's eye, resembled medieval torture devices. The other half of the business consisted of a glossy wooden floor where a dozen women paced through an exercise routine. Among them, Lori Townsend bent, skipped, and twisted to loud thumping music. Lori noticed the detectives enter from their reflection in a mirror hanging along the far wall.

Emily sensed Townsend wasn't startled or surprised when she noticed them. In fact, Lori got an extra bounce in her step. She was performing.

Javier approached a young woman camped at a small desk deep into her celebrity gossip magazine.

"What is this?" he asked, pointing to the strutting women.

"It's a low impact hip-hop Zumba class," she responded while tucking her feet under her butt.

"They look pretty high maintenance," Javier said. The two-hundred-dollar hairstyles, full makeup, jewelry, and skintight designer clothing didn't scream cross-fit boot camp.

"Tell me about it. There's enough Botox in there to smooth out the Grand Canyon."

"Do you keep track of who attends these classes?"

"Yeah, that's how we charge them, by the class." She reached for a binder and opened it to the class in session. She leaned toward

Javier. "Between us, we call them the Gold Diggers. I swear they keep a scorecard for the rich married men they bag and tag."

The music stopped, and the women milled about giving one another hugs and air kisses. Lori Townsend removed a fresh towel from the table near the back of the room and walked, or rather slinked, to where Javier stood with the young woman.

"Rachel, a cold water, if you please," Lori said in a condescending tone, more of a demand than a request.

Rachel rolled her eyes at Javier and got up from the chair to fetch the bottled water from the refrigerator behind Lori.

Lori stepped closer and dabbed the glistening perspiration from her chest to her neck, being careful not to wipe off her makeup. "I didn't expect to see you so soon, Detectives. Do you have some news for me? Find out who killed my husband?" Lori turned and grabbed the bottle of water from Rachel without a word of thanks.

"Detective Medina and I have a few more questions for you, Mrs. Townsend."

"Really? I thought we were done. Johnny said you wouldn't need to bother me anymore."

Javier ignored her and asked, "Do you know Wayne Corona?"

"Of course. He's Roger's attorney."

"Was he your attorney also, Mrs. Townsend?"

"He handled Roger's finances, so yeah; I guess that would make him mine also. Why do you ask?"

"When did you last speak with Mr. Corona?"

"What are you getting at, Detective?"

Emily paused. "Wayne Corona was murdered yesterday, and we know you called him a few hours before."

Lori's mouth hung open, surprised by the revelation of the attorney's death. "I—I needed to make arrangements with Wayne to bury Roger. He has—he had Roger's Last Will and Testament and Roger's wishes for his funeral. Are you certain? Wayne's dead?"

"We are. Care to explain the calls to Wayne in the days before your husband died?"

Small beads of sweat, not from the aerobics class, broke out on Lori's forehead and she didn't take her eyes off Emily. After a brief silence, Lori said, "Because I was sleeping with Wayne."

"How long had that been going on?" Emily asked.

"A couple of months, I guess . . ."

"Did Roger know you were seeing Wayne behind his back?"

"Really, Detective, don't make it sound dirty. No, Roger had no idea—he was clueless when it came to these things. Wayne and I were discreet. My husband had his distractions, and I had mine. We had an arrangement." Lori paused to put a thin wraparound skirt low around her hips and said, "Now if there's nothing more, I really must go. I have a husband to bury."

Lori strode out the smoked glass door and got behind the wheel of a brand new emerald green Porsche 911 GT3 RS. The four-hundred-fifteen-horsepower engine rumbled, and the sleek sports car backed out of the parking slot. Lori glanced back at the glass door, made sure the detectives watched her as she gunned the powerful engine, spun the tires, and shot out of the parking lot.

"She really handles the grieving widow role well, doesn't she?" Emily said.

"Everybody deals with it differently. She might be a gold digger, but I can't picture her cutting her husband's throat."

"The new car must be a way of channeling her misery."

"I can run the registration, but it probably belonged to her husband," Javier said.

The detectives stepped outside, surprised by a patrol car parked next to their Crown Vic. A uniformed officer leaned on his car and waited for them. Emily recognized the officer as Ron Johnson, a ten-year veteran of the department.

Johnson put his hands up and said, "Hey, Hunter, don't kill the messenger. I'm here to escort you to the Mayor's office."

Javier muttered, "Oh shit."

Emily smiled at her old friend and asked, "And if I refuse?"

"I gotta shoot you, I guess," Johnson said while he shrugged his shoulders.

"I've seen you shoot; I like my chances."

"Come on, Emily, let's go," the officer pleaded as he got back into his patrol car and waited for Emily to sit in her Crown Vic.

It wasn't exactly a slow-speed chase in a white Ford Bronco, but the two police vehicles slowly made their way to City Hall. At the curb, Officer Johnson waved goodbye and sped off for his next call.

Captain Howard waited at the door for the detectives. "The Mayor is expecting you." The Captain turned and led them to the Mayor's office; the shiny worn fabric across the back of Howard's pants glinted as he shuffled, a dead giveaway of too much desk time.

The Mayor's secretary pointed to the inner office door and said, "He's ready for you."

Nothing was ever out of place in Mayor John Stone's office. Stacks of business cards dotted the desktop. Emily swore the same impressive looking files permanently lived in the politician's in-basket, props to portray him as the connected, detail-driven city administrator. They were arranged to impress his visitors who didn't know better. The Mayor didn't look up and ordered the detectives to sit in the chairs positioned in front of the desk. Captain Howard watched too many gangster movies and stood behind them playing the part of the enforcer.

"Detective Hunter," the Mayor began. "I thought I made myself very clear. I told you not to bother Lori Townsend with your questions. She's gone through quite enough already, wouldn't you agree?"

"Let me guess? The woman calls and cries to you?"

"She called to complain about your harassment. After I ordered you to stay away, did you actually go to her home and interrogate her? What's this I hear about this morning at a fitness class session? You corner her and embarrass her in public?"

"No," Emily replied simply.

"Don't bullshit me, Hunter. I know you were at her home because she called me in tears over the way you treated her."

"We didn't interrogate or embarrass her if that's what she implied. If I wanted to sweat her, I would drag her in and sit her ass down in an interrogation room for a couple of hours."

"You deny going to her residence?"

"No, I dropped in on her."

"And you harassed the woman the day after she suffered a beating and her husband was murdered?"

"The Chief directed me not to question her, so I didn't. I ordered Detective Medina to speak with her. You know, I find it strange the woman didn't know her husband sought medical treatment because he was dying from cancer. Tells me maybe their relationship wasn't what she wanted everyone to believe."

"Cancer? Roger had cancer?"

Emily nodded.

The Mayor shook his head. "Mendez—you questioned this woman and felt compelled to treat her as a common criminal?"

"Medina," Javier said.

"Whatever."

Medina leaned forward in his chair and responded, "Mr. Mayor, it is telling she didn't know her husband was terminally ill. I followed up with her to ask if she'd put together a list of people she'd seen her husband with and a list of property she found missing for our follow-up."

"Explain why I got a phone call from her this morning in hysterics you were trying to tie her to the murder of that dirtbag attorney, Corona?"

"She wasn't emotional when she left us," Emily said.

"You're out of your minds if you think she was involved in Corona's murder. I should suspend you both—"

"That's not your call," Emily baited him. "But while you try, explain why Corona and Roger Townsend were killed in the same manner and why Townsend's legal files were stolen from the attorney's home and office."

"What sleazy business dealings Roger and this Corona fellow were into have nothing to do with Lori."

"Maybe not, but what about Lori banging Wayne Corona? You think there's a connection to the murders? I've gotten convictions with less of a motive. Someone got jealous Lori was—"

"No way! You've gone too far. You drop this right now. Both of you. No contact with Lori Townsend from this point forward. She is a victim, and you're dragging her around as if she's a suspect. Lori is an upstanding woman in this community, and I won't have her subjected to this kind of treatment from a nothing woman like you." The Mayor stood behind his desk and leaned forward with both hands white-knuckled on the edge. "Is that clear enough for you, Hunter?"

Emily remained in her chair and responded, "Sure, I understand. You don't want me to reveal your little friend's indiscretions. I get it."

"Get out of my sight." The Mayor stuck a thumb out toward the door.

Javier hooked Hunter under the arm, pulled her up from the chair, and moved toward the door. She turned back as the Mayor called her name.

"Hunter, you're hanging by a thread here. Watch yourself, or your career is over."

Javier tightened his grip on Emily's arm and led her out of the office. They heard Mayor Stone pick up the phone and say, "It's taken care of, Lori. They won't bother you again."

Howard closed the door in their faces and remained inside the Mayor's inner sanctum.

The detectives went without speaking for a moment until they heard a shuffling from behind them.

"You're a virus, Hunter." Howard caught up to the detectives on the street. Before Emily could reply, the Captain tossed the morning's newspaper at her. She caught it against her chest and glanced at the headline. A full half-page article above the fold described the brutal slaying of prominent attorney and fundraiser Wayne Corona.

"The Chief wants you to call this reporter and give him a statement about the Corona murder. Along the lines of, 'The murders of Corona and Townsend do not appear to be related. You are following up leads which indicate a disgruntled client may have killed the attorney.'"

"The Chief wants, or is that coming from your buddy the Mayor?"

"Does it matter? You have your script. Anything more and I'll have your ass."

"There isn't much left anymore," Emily replied as she left the Captain standing on the sidewalk.

She mulled over what else could go wrong; her mother's dementia progressed rapidly, the investigation got more and more muddled in a political web of shit, she got to feed bullshit to the fucking media, and now a no-contact order on Lori Townsend, the one person who could unlock the secrets at the center of the murders. Emily's mood sank from bad to worse at the sight of Jonathon Anderson, the Managing Partner of Roger Townsend and Associates, waiting for her at the detective bureau.

CHAPTER NINE

ANDERSON WAITED IN a cheap metal chair near the door leading into the detective bureau. The executive's eyes darted between each officer who passed near him. He was rigid and out of his element in this noncorporate environment, where grim people carried guns around him. He wore another dark blue suit with a starched white shirt and kept his hands in his lap to avoid touching the uncivilized surroundings. As she drew close, Emily recognized what lay at his core—fear. Dark circles under his eyes, a tight jaw, and tense shoulders betrayed Anderson was afraid.

As the detectives approached, Anderson rose from his seat and extended his hand. "Detectives, I hope you don't mind me dropping by, but I felt it important we speak." The words came out in a rapid stream.

The executive's hand was limp and clammy, a change from his confident bearing in the office yesterday. "Why don't we go someplace we can talk." Emily motioned toward a room with a simple metal table and three chairs.

Anderson followed the detectives into the room and looked like he expected a wall of one-way glass or small cameras tucked into a corner as seen on television drama shows.

"Is this where you beat confessions out of people?" Anderson asked with a nervous scratch in his voice.

Emily sat down across from him and unbuttoned her jacket. "No, we do that down in the basement."

For a second, Anderson didn't get the joke. He broke the tension and passed a manila envelope to Emily.

"This is the client list you wanted. The firm asks you to respect our client confidentiality. If our list got out, it could be most detrimental to our business."

"I understand, Mr. Anderson. We'll keep this as quiet as possible." Emily sensed Anderson wanted to say more, so she waited and allowed Anderson to fill in the silence. A simple interrogation technique, yet amazingly effective. Emily often used it in her relationships with men. Perhaps another reason they didn't last very long.

"The second document is a list of assets and holdings for Roger Townsend at the time of his death. Our accounting review discovered company funds were transferred to offshore shelters, newly created accounts, or withdrawn altogether." Anderson wrung his hands together, uncomfortable with the information he revealed.

"How much are we talking about?"

Anderson cleared his throat and said, "Over the past eleven months, the accounts are missing millions of dollars."

"And you have reason to believe Roger Townsend made these transactions?"

"Yes. Each electronic transfer originated from his office, or from his home computer. Every transaction required his personal code."

Emily studied the list of transactions, and the last one made the hair on her neck stand on end. The date Roger Townsend died.

"This last transaction for one hundred thousand dollars? What can you tell me about that one?"

"The transaction moved funds to a newly established private account in the name of a shell company, Community Growth. At first, I thought it might be one of Roger's community foundation projects. Our people found the signatories on the account don't exist. It was a false front." He shifted in his seat. "The one hundred thousand hit the account and was withdrawn within an hour. It's gone and untraceable."

"Any of these accounts in his name?"

"One or two. The rest are numbered accounts. It will take some time to drill down to find out who's on those accounts. Assuming we don't run up against international banking regulations."

"How much did Roger Townsend siphon off to these accounts, altogether?"

"Four million even."

"Jesus. And no one noticed this money missing?" Javier asked.

"It's not as easy as that. We channel millions to our projects and fundraising efforts. These were hidden in a batch of other transactions. It wouldn't be discovered until our annual audit. The audit would identify transfers to improper or unusual accounts, and the red flags would've gone up."

"Roger knew the audit would take place, I would imagine?"

"Of course he did. There is no way this list of transactions would have been missed. It's almost as if he wanted us to find them. He couldn't have drawn a clearer road map."

Emily let the thought percolate for a few seconds. What was Townsend trying to tell them? What was he pointing at?

"You said before, Roger was a complicated guy," Emily said.

"Right . . ."

"Who would benefit the most from his death?" Emily waited for Anderson's reply. The man fidgeted around in the chair, and his face slowly turned a darker shade.

"I don't know how his personal finances were structured. You'd need to obtain that from Wayne Corona, or Lori. But, I got the impression Roger didn't share too much detail with Lori."

"Who stands to gain the most at Roger Townsend and Associates?"

Anderson's face bloomed fully red now, and he said, "I would," in a low tone.

"How's that?" Javier said.

"His interest in the company shifted to me upon his death, a provision of the corporate charter. The same thing if I died first, he would take over my part of the company."

Anderson received a huge windfall following the death of his partner. Emily didn't make this guy out as the murdering type. Rob you blind behind your back, maybe, but murder—she wasn't convinced. But, stranger things have happened and for a shit-ton less money.

"I've gotta ask. Where were you the night Roger was killed?"

"You've got to believe me, Detective. It wasn't me. I didn't kill him!" Anderson stiffened at the thought. He started to hyperventilate. "I was home with my wife—you can call her to verify it."

"We will, Mr. Anderson. She'll tell me you were home all evening?"

"Yes—I—I got home around nine."

"And before that?"

Anderson fell silent, his shoulders slumped forward.

"Mr. Anderson?"

"I was with Lori. We've . . ."

"Go on."

"I've been sleeping with her for the last three months." He drew in a ragged breath and whimpered. "Please, you can't tell my wife."

"I'm not your priest, Mr. Anderson. But this doesn't put you in a very good light, does it?"

He shook his head slowly and then said, "You have to believe me—I had nothing to do with Roger's death."

Emily put up a hand, silencing the man. "Let's see if I have this right. You've been screwing your friend's young wife, and you seized control of the company after he died. Does that about sum it up? Why should I believe you didn't have a hand in getting Roger out of the picture?"

Anderson began to quiver. The façade of the in-control business power broker shattered. "It wasn't like that."

Emily leaned forward over the table and rested a hand on his. "Tell me what happened."

Anderson pulled his hand away from hers and wiped the tears from his reddened cheek. "She made me do it—I didn't want to— but she told me if I didn't have sex with her, she'd tell Roger I stole from the company."

"You're telling us Lori Townsend forced you to have sex with her?" Javier said.

Anderson raised his tear-streaked face; the embarrassment turned his neck crimson. "Yes—no—I didn't want to, but she made me. I'm sorry, I didn't know what to do."

Javier shook his head.

"Let me get this right. Lori Townsend forced you to have sex with her. Did she hold you down?" he asked

"No—no, it wasn't that. At first, it was mutual. She let me know she was available and willing. I thought it would be a onetime thing. Then she kept coming back. I told her I couldn't do it anymore. Lori got angry. She said she'd tell Roger I embezzled from the company."

Emily tapped a finger on the accounting sheets in front of Anderson. "Which of these accounts is yours?"

His head snapped up, and a hurt look came over his face. "No, none of them, that's the point. I think she knew about these transactions and wanted to blame me for them. You have to believe me—none of these are my accounts." His eyes switched between Emily and Javier, hoping for an understanding look. When none came, he lowered his head.

"Mr. Anderson, I think that's all we need from you today. We'll call you if we need to talk to you or Mrs. Anderson." Emily stood up as a signal for the broken man to leave.

The executive wiped his eyes, nodded silently, and left out the door from the interview room. Anderson slouched as if everyone in the detective bureau judged him as he crept toward the lobby. In reality, no one had the time to watch him leave the building.

While they returned to their desks, Emily said, "He gets the company, and Lori. That's a pretty good motive for getting Roger out of the way."

"Unless he's one hell of an actor, Anderson doesn't strike me as our cutthroat killer. But I think he knows more about Roger's shady business dealings than he's telling us."

"You're thinking if we sweat him, maybe he'll give us some dirt on Roger's money trail," Emily finished the thought.

"Something along those lines, yes."

Emily laid the stack of accounting paperwork from Anderson on her desk and picked up a pile of message slips. One from Sharon Pixley; the chief forensic pathologist; one from David Black the supervising crime technician; one from Lucinda Medina, with a one-line note saying everything was okay on the home front. On

the center of her desk lay a sealed envelope addressed to Detective
Hunter, written in neat cursive handwriting.

Emily slipped the phone technician a few bucks to disable her
voice mail because she didn't trust voice messaging and preferred
her messages the old-fashioned way, on a slip of paper. She didn't
hold a good feeling about any of the calls she needed to return, but
stopped on the message left by Javier's mom and dialed the
number.

As she waited for the call to go through, she told Javier, "I'm
calling your mom to tell her you were a little too friendly with that
counter girl at the aerobics studio."

"Yeah, right."

"Hi, Lucinda, it's Emily. I wanted to call and check in. How's
everything going?"

"Oh, Emily, I didn't want to bother you at work. That's why I
didn't call your cell number. I only wanted to check in, and I told
the nice man who answered the phone we were okay."

"How is Mom this morning? Did she mention the spat with her
caregiver yesterday?"

"Connie is fine this morning. In fact, we just got back from a
nice walk around the neighborhood. We did talk about what happened yesterday. I think Connie may have been right."

"Right? About what?"

"I wasn't there, but Connie feels this Sheila person gave her no
choice. She thinks the woman pushed and threatened her."

"What? Why wouldn't she tell me if that happened?"

"She said you would be disappointed and blame her for not
getting along with Sheila. To me, Sheila got what she had coming. If she did half of what Connie says, that is abuse. The dish
wasn't thrown at Sheila. The woman pushed Connie while she
stood at the sink, and Connie dropped the dish on the counter.

A sliver of the broken dish flew up and caught Sheila on the cheek."

"Sheila and her employer made up a story to cover her ass."

"So it seems. I'm afraid to say it, but Connie is showing signs of early-onset Alzheimer's, and you should make an appointment with her doctor for an evaluation. I've seen this many times, and there are some medications to slow the progression of the disease. She needs supportive care. Worth thinking about."

Emily sighed. "Thank you for being with her. I really appreciate it. Now, if you could speak with your son about flirting with every woman he meets on the job."

Emily handed the phone to Javier, who took the phone as if it were radioactive.

"What's wrong with you?" he whispered to Emily.

"Hello? Javier?" his mother's voice rang through the phone.

Javier shook his head, and Emily waved the phone in his face. Finally, he snatched the phone and turned away from his partner.

"Hello, Mama."

Javier leaned away with the phone, doing more listening than speaking.

Using her cell, Emily called the crime lab supervisor who quickly told her the .38 caliber revolver they found taped to the drawer in Wayne Corona's home was the weapon used in the Townsend homicide. The medical examiner found no traces of nitrates from gunpowder residue on Corona's hands. The smattering of blood on the weapon was pending.

Emily reached Sharon Pixley's voice mail and told her they would stop by the Coroner's office later this afternoon.

Finally, Emily held the plain white envelope and noticed a smudge of light pink lipstick on the back. She waved it at Javier because she picked up a bad feeling from the envelope and wanted him to witness her opening the mail.

Javier, grateful for the rescue, begged off from his mother and hung up. "I owe you one for that move. You know my mom is very traditional and thinks I should be married by now. She wanted to know who this woman was you said I'd been flirting with and when she was going to meet her." He glanced at the lipstick-smudged envelope.

"A girlfriend, Emily? You holding out on me?" Javier baited her.

She used a letter opener and sliced through the upper edge of the envelope. No white powder, no hazardous material; the envelope held only three folded pieces of expensive stationery. The same neat handwriting from the outside of the envelope was also found on the note inside. Emily opened the stationery and read.

Dearest Detective Hunter,

I've enclosed a list of people Roger met with in his home office in recent weeks. Secondly, I've prepared a list of items missing since the robbery. I promised these two items to you, and I'm a woman of my word. If I promise something, I mean it, Detective. Do you? You told me you'd find my husband's killer. Leave me alone and go do your job.

Love and Kisses,
Lori.

"Wanna bet she sent the Mayor a copy?" Javier said over Emily's shoulder.

"I'm surprised I haven't gotten another call from Mayor Stone. He's awfully quick to come to her rescue. Makes you wonder why."

"Same reason as Jonathon Anderson, maybe? Think they're involved too?"

"Wouldn't shock me. The Mayor has a reputation as a bit of a skirt chaser—but, I'm starting to see Lori Townsend isn't a shy stay-at-home type either."

Emily pushed back from her desk and stuffed the inventory Lori provided in her jacket. "Let's show these property descriptions around at the usual pawnshops and burglary investigators. Then we can drive over to the Coroner's Office and see what Sharon has for us. We need a break on this investigation soon, or the Mayor will force the Chief to pull us off the case."

"Would that be a bad thing?" Javier asked.

"If it means the Mayor gets to tell us how to do our jobs, then yeah, that's a bad thing. So, let's get moving."

CHAPTER TEN

THE FIRST BREAK came quickly. The two detectives entered a dirty storefront into a popular pawnshop on 11th Street. No sooner than they entered, two scruffy-looking white men in their late twenties ducked their heads and quickly swept up the items they had put out on the counter. The taller of the two men shoved a gold necklace into his filthy jacket pocket and rubbed his nose with the other hand.

"Good morning, Detectives," a tall thin Black man called out from behind the counter.

The two men took their cue from the pawnbroker and quickly trotted out of the store, away from any conflict with the police over the questionable provenance of the jewelry in their possession.

The owner smiled, shook his head, and said, "Hunter, you're bad for business." Nathan Cole had worked the pawn business for over twenty years in this downtown Sacramento location. On occasion, he advised Emily of the arrival of unusual items pawned at the shop. When a customer wanted to dump guns, knives, or high-end jewelry too quickly, Nathan wasn't one to shy away from picking up the phone if a transaction didn't feel right.

"I suppose those two guys recently got Grandma's necklace in her will," Emily said, hooking a thumb at the door where the pair left.

Nathan chuckled. "They had no idea what they were doing. They wanted two grand in cash for a chain worth only a hundred at best. You coming in when you did was the best thing that could've happened to them."

The owner put away a dark blue felt tray behind the counter and wiped the glass top with a rag smelling of harsh disinfectant. He wiped and asked, "What do you have for me, Detective?"

Javier pulled the list of missing items from his jacket pocket. "These were reported stolen following a home invasion." He handed it across the counter to Nathan.

The thin, dark-skinned man pulled a pair of reading glasses from the pocket of his baggy white linen shirt. He tipped his head back, holding the paper at arm's length, and examined the items listed. Lori Townsend reported two men's watches, gold coins, and two men's gold rings with diamonds and emeralds.

Nathan turned serious. "When were these items stolen?"

"Two days ago."

"Hmm . . . come with me." Nathan directed them to the counter on the backside of the open showroom filled with expensive watches and fine jewelry. Lighting under the countertop reflected against a dozen diamond studs and a sea of engagement rings from scores of broken promises and canceled dreams.

"One of the watches on your list matches one we took in yesterday." He scanned down the counter until one caught his eye. "Here it is, a Rolex Cosmograph Daytona." Nathan removed it from the case and put it on the counter.

Javier studied the onyx face with three inset small dials and tachymeter bezel. "How much is this worth?"

Nathan pulled the number out of his pawnshop owner's memory. "The list price is around twenty-eight to thirty thousand."

"It's only a watch, right?"

"It's a very good watch," Nathan responded with a smile while he pulled a thick catalog from a shelf under the counter. He flipped the pages until he found the entry he wanted. He made a show of stabbing the page with his finger. "This is the other watch on your list, a Vacheron Constantin Malte." The crystal face of the watch revealed the gold and sterling silver workings within. "This one lists at four hundred thousand."

"For a watch, really?" Javier asked.

Nathan put the catalog away and answered him, "People who buy these think of them more as a status symbol. They don't worry about money and really don't care about the price other than they own one and you don't."

Emily picked up the Rolex and turned it over in her hand, heavier than she expected. She caught a small inscription, "To R from L."

"When this Rolex came in yesterday, did you get a look at who brought it in?" Emily asked. She felt the anticipation on the back of her neck.

"I wasn't in yesterday, so I didn't put my eyes on the seller."

Emily felt the air leave her lungs in frustration.

"But let me go pull the tapes for yesterday."

Nathan disappeared into the back, and a moment later, the front door chimes sounded. A sickly thin man with a bad case of the shakes staggered through the door, with a beat-up stereo system, the kind street kids carried over their shoulders with the music blasting three decades ago. The man's glassy eyes settled on Emily, and a lecherous smile revealed yellow stains on the few teeth that remained in the junkie's head.

"Hey, mama," the junkie said as he swerved into a counter. "Oh, baby, where you been all my life?"

Emily ignored the man until he pressed close enough to make her stomach flip from his hot, sour breath. She turned abruptly, surprised he stood over three feet away. He smelled much closer.

"Back off," she said.

The junkie pretended she'd hurt his ego. "Why you gotta go and be like that?" He got over the rejection quickly and put the battered stereo on the edge of the glass counter. The black plastic box teetered on the edge of the counter until he noticed his prize threatened to topple to the floor. "Whoa . . . whoa . . . whoa." He hugged it with both hands and nearly fell himself.

Nathan shook his head in disgust. He set a handful of compact videotapes on the counter. "Buster, what have I told you? I don't want anything from you. Now get!"

"Nathan, dude, give me a hundred, and I'm gone." He pushed the stereo to the center of the counter and beamed with junkie pride.

Nathan turned to the detectives and said, "Give me a minute, please." He pushed the tapes aside and tapped a finger on the cracked and battered black plastic box. "Where'd you find it, Buster?"

"It's mines."

"Really? Does it work?"

"Yeah, yeah, yeah. Seventy-five bucks."

Nathan picked up the box in his large hands and turned it over. He gave Buster a narrowed eye. "You see this?" He pointed to a rough engraving on the back. "P04869 FSP. Buster, that means this belongs to someone who paroled from Folsom State Prison."

Nathan pointed out the red wax melted over the screws on the back of the stereo, placed there by prison staff to alert them if someone tampered with the appliance, tried to make weapons from the plastic, or hid contraband inside.

The junkie wasn't ready to give up yet. "Fifty bucks, Nathan."

Nathan pulled a five-dollar bill from the till and slid a food coupon for a nearby McDonald's under the currency. "That's all I got for you, Buster. Now, on your way."

Buster snagged the five dollars and the food coupon, giving Nathan a nod. "Thanks, dude." He swerved out, but not before he told Emily, "Baby, you ready for a good time, you come find 'ol Buster . . . aaight?"

"I can't wait," Emily responded.

Nathan snagged the worthless ghetto blaster and tossed it in an electronic recycle bin. He returned to the counter and popped the first store surveillance tape into an old compact tape player. The player connected to one of the large-screen televisions on the wall behind the counter. The screen brightened and grew into an image of the interior of the pawnshop above the cash registers.

Emily turned and observed the camera in a small grey armored box near the ceiling. The video display ran forward with a time-stamp slowly ticking in real time. From the moment the bars pulled back from the doors, it showed a slow, steady stream of sellers and shoppers searching for bargains on the video screen.

"Can we speed up this tape? We'll be here all day," Emily said.

Nathan hit a button on the remote, and the tape flowed forward, transforming the orderly pawnshop into an ant maze. New property came in, and only a few sales left the premises. The time-stamp read 11:45 and Nathan froze the image on the screen. A thin white man, in a grey hooded sweatshirt, stood at the counter in the area where the shop displayed their watches. From under the sleeve on his right hand was a large bright gold watch similar to the stolen Rolex.

"Let me advance this frame by frame and see if our boy here lets us take a look at him," Nathan said.

The man kept his back to the camera, careful to stay out of the frame. Emily figured he'd been in the shop before and knew the camera placement. Slowly they watched the man in the hood talk with one of the store employees. He unbuckled the watch from his wrist and slid it out on the counter.

"Can you freeze it there?" Emily asked.

Nathan hit a button, and the tape stopped at the frame. "Too bad I can't zoom in on the watch."

"We'll do that later, but the outline of the watch sure resembles this one," Emily replied as she examined the Rolex in his hand.

The tape rocked forward, and the man made a sale. The pawn-shop employee examined the watch and motioned the man to the cash register. The hood stayed in place while the man passed in front of the camera, and he kept his head low, out of view.

The cashier placed the Rolex on the counter behind the register and pulled out a book to record the sale. At one point, the man in the hood responded for a request for identification, and he awkwardly pulled out his wallet. He fumbled through cards until he pulled one out and handed it to the clerk. The employee held it up and tried to compare the picture on the driver's license to the person, and after some discussion about the identification, the seller gave in. With a quick frustrated movement, the seller threw back his hood allowing the cashier to verify his photo identification.

Nathan froze the image. The man didn't want to show himself and tried to turn away from the camera, but his full-face image showed clearly.

"There's our boy," Emily called out. "You seen him before, Nathan?"

"Not that I recall."

The tape rolled on, and the clerk handed the driver's license back. The hood went back up, but the man's narrow eyes glanced up at the camera lens. Finally, with the transaction complete, the man signed a receipt and ambled out with a wad of cash. While this last bit of tape rolled, Nathan retrieved the records for the transaction.

"Here we are. James P. Malcolm; he's got a Stockton address. It's most likely bogus. But he did give a local phone number; that's odd. Mr. Malcolm received one thousand dollars for the Rolex Cosmograph Daytona."

"Nathan, we gotta take the watch, tape, and the receipt."

"Like I said, you're bad for business, Hunter."

Nathan handed over the watch. He also passed a receipt book across the counter. The businessman prepared a new receipt turning over the Rolex to the Sacramento Police Department. The receipt valued the watch at the twenty-eight thousand dollar price.

"I need my tax write-offs. I'll email you the video clip."

Javier followed Emily out the storefront door where the afternoon sky started to darken; a collection of puffy grey clouds blotted out the sunlight. The clouds somehow matched their mood.

While they had a face, they were given nothing else to go on. The name and address were probably from a phony ID, but they'd follow through anyway.

Javier dialed up the department's Communications Division on his cell. "This is Detective Medina; I need a reverse directory listing for a phone number." He gave the dispatcher the phone number the hooded man had left at the pawnshop. He didn't expect the response.

"You're sure about that?" Javier hung up and shoved the phone back in his pocket. "So much for that lead . . ."

"What'd you find?" Emily asked.

"The phone number is real. It traced back to 1357 46th Street, here in Sacramento. Sound familiar?"

"The Townsend house?"

"The very same. Our pawnshop boy sold the stolen property and used the phone number from the crime scene."

Emily felt a raindrop on the back of her neck and motioned Javier to their car parked at the curb.

"We have a face. We need someone to ID the guy on that tape. He's the key to this whole thing. If he's not the killer, he knows who is," he said.

Emily nodded and started the Crown Vic. "After we finish with Sharon at the Coroner's Office, we need to put photos of this guy's face out there and see if we get any bites."

She pulled into the downtown traffic and thought aloud. "We need to hit the local probation department and state parole offices. I have a gut feeling he's been in the system. You think—"

"Corona's guy, Benjamin Tooker, mentioned a guy from Pelican Bay."

"Maybe. Tooker said the guy who came after him was tall and tatted up. We couldn't see if he had the tattoos under the sweat-shirt. The guy in the pawnshop didn't strike me as tall."

"I'd say he went five-six, maybe five-eight at best." He thought for a few seconds while the sedan cruised through the light traffic. "You thinking a second guy?" Javier said.

"We need to show the picture to Tooker and see what he says, but yeah. I think we're looking for two guys," Emily said.

CHAPTER ELEVEN

SHARON PIXLEY HUNCHED over her desk when the two detectives arrived at the Coroner's Office. The name on her door read simply, CHIEF FORENSIC PATHOLOGIST. She was the most competent person Emily had worked with in her years dealing with autopsies, determining cause and manner of death, and bringing the forensics together for prosecution. On several occasions, she had proved a formidable prosecution witness because she broke through the technical jargon and let juries know the pain and trauma the victims suffered in their last moments on this earth. Most often now, defense attorneys simply stipulated to her findings, without the jury hearing the gruesome details.

This afternoon she leaned over her desk and signed a stack of death certificates. Sharon removed her reading glasses and rubbed her eyes. "Please tell me you didn't bring me any more business, Detectives."

Emily put her hands up. "No—we come in peace."

Sharon motioned to the chairs across from her desk.

"I left you a message that Javier and I would be by to see whatever you were going to show us."

Sharon noticed the light on her phone blinked red. "I haven't had a chance to clear my voice mail." She leaned back in her chair, loosened her lower back. "I was going to show you a comparison of the wounds on Roger Townsend and Wayne Corona. All indications are it was the same weapon."

"Let's check it out." Emily turned for the door.

The Chief Forensic Pathologist didn't move from her chair. "I can't. Roger Townsend's body was released to the funeral home an hour or so ago."

"What? We're still investigating his murder. Why'd you kick him loose so soon?"

Sharon's face flushed a shade of pink. "I didn't make that decision, Emily. I got a call from the Board of Supervisors office telling me to release the body." She circled around her desk, leaned against it, and crossed her arms. "They actually told me I needed to release Townsend's body to the funeral home, or they would review my budget and make recommendations for a staffing reduction."

"Who threatened you from the Board?" Emily asked.

Sharon avoided eye contact. "If you'll excuse me, I need to get back to signing these."

"Sharon, who pressured you?" Emily asked again.

She sighed. "Stephen Lawson, District 3 Supervisor." She pointed a finger at Emily. "You leave it alone." She picked up a file and handed it to her. "That should be all you need. I managed to take photos comparing the neck wounds of both victims. As you can see, they're identical in depth and length. Townsend bore one hesitation mark, none whatsoever on Corona. I can testify to these findings."

Emily flipped through the file quickly. "Same method and manner?"

"Both victims were facedown. Our suspect pulled the heads up by the victims' hair. A couple of photos in there show bruising and patches of missing hair. The heads were pulled back, and each victim suffered a left to right laceration with a sharp bladed instrument, approximately six to eight inches in length. The blade needed to be repositioned during the cutting."

"What does that tell us about our suspect?" Emily followed.

"Well, from the angle of the wound, he's tall and right-handed. He'd need to be fairly strong to pull the head back and cut this deeply, especially if the victims resisted at first."

Javier asked, "No gunshot wound to Corona?"

Sharon shook her head. "No, only the laceration to the neck, but it appears he suffered a broken nose in a struggle before death."

Emily nodded and considered the partial profile Sharon offered, matching with the information Tooker provided about the crazy tall white man from Pelican Bay.

"Which funeral home picked up Townsend's body?" Emily said.

"Markus and Son's, why?"

"Snatching the body this quickly bothers me," Emily responded and headed for the door.

"Emily, please be discreet with this one. Some very powerful people want this case to go away quickly and quietly."

"When have you known me not to be discreet?"

Javier stopped in his tracks, and Sharon's head shot up from her desk at the comment. They both simply stared at her.

"What?" She pretended to be hurt by their lack of faith. "Okay—I'm a work in progress, gimme a break."

Javier and Sharon exchanged a grin.

Emily checked her watch and thought it was time to hit the funeral home before calling it a day. She didn't usually leave early, but she wanted to go home to see what trouble her mother managed to find today.

Javier asked, "Have you been to the Markus and Son's Funeral Home?"

She started the car. "I've driven by a dozen times, but I've never been inside."

"You've never seen the likes of it. That's the place the elite go to be sent on to the afterlife. Should be interesting, as long as you're appropriately discreet."

"Discreet, my ass."

"See, that's the kind of thing you shouldn't say while we're there," Javier said.

The funeral home's location in a middle-class East Sacramento neighborhood offered a comfortable commute to a memorial service for the elitists, but the nasty bits of embalming and the rest of the mortician's dark arts remained tucked away behind a red brick and mahogany trimmed face.

Emily found a parking spot near the front door and the instant she turned off the ignition, she said, "Oh shit!"

"I see it," Javier responded, looking out the passenger window at an emerald green Porsche 911 tucked around the corner of the building.

Emily got out, stood outside their car, and surveyed the grounds of Markus and Son's. The funeral home was the most extravagant thing in a neighborhood priding itself on indulgence. Carefully maintained gardens and topiary sculptures of winged cats and unicorns dotted the landscape.

From behind a set of large double wooden doors, a middle-aged man came to greet them. His demeanor stiffened as he sensed the detectives were not a bereaved couple, or, more likely he assessed their inability to afford the exclusive services offered at Markus and Son's.

"How may I help you?" the man said professionally, but coolly.

Emily identified herself and Javier, then asked the stiff if she could ask him a few questions.

The man held no expression on his face as he replied, "No."

"No? What are you hiding?"

"No."

"What's your name, sir?" Emily asked, with a show of bringing out her notebook, pen in hand.

"Do you have a warrant, Officer?"

"Do you want me to call for one? It'd be a shame to disrupt your services while we tear this place apart."

Again, no reaction from the man. "Then I suppose we will find out, won't we?"

"What are you hiding?" Javier asked.

"We preserve the privacy and confidentiality of our clients, above all else."

"Why the rush to remove Roger Townsend's body from the Coroner's Office?" Emily asked.

The man's stone face remained unchanged. He wasn't angry or upset; he simply wasn't going to answer any questions.

Emily, on the other hand, wasn't as stone-faced and was getting angrier by the passing second. "Pal, are you gonna answer the question?"

"No."

Emily strode up the steps, closer to the Markus and Son's front man who showed no signs of giving ground. As she prepared to threaten the man with obstruction charges, the wooden door opened once more, followed by the sound of Lori Townsend's heels as they clicked on the marble floor.

Lori Townsend stepped carefully down each granite step. Her four-inch red heels matched her short red dress along with a red ribbon securing her blond hair. As she reached the step where Emily and Javier dealt with Mr. Stoneface, she said, "Detectives, you have news for me on the investigation?" A pair of oversized designer sunglasses hid the widow's eyes. The lenses reflected a polished bronze-hued box in her hands.

Lori Townsend held the ashes of her late husband. The quick cremation meant the evidence the body held went, literally, up in smoke.

"Mrs. Townsend, this is very sudden," Emily said.

"What's sudden is having my husband taken from me. What are you doing about it?"

"We're looking at a few leads."

Lori Townsend glanced at a delicate watch on her wrist. "Thank you for coming to see Roger off. I really must be going."

Emily watched the widow saunter to her Porsche, where she casually tossed her husband's remains into the passenger seat for one last drive. The sports car's engine rumbled, and Lori sped out of the parking area with tires chirping as she changed gears.

Mr. Stoneface finally broke his silence. "Is there anything else I can do for you?"

Emily didn't respond and headed to the Crown Vic with Javier. "Why the big rush to dispose of the body? That's got me bugged," she said.

"You told her we're following up on a couple of leads. Care to share those with your partner?"

"I wanted to see if she reacted to that—she didn't. And we don't have much to go on."

"If I know Sharon Pixley, she got everything she could from the body before she turned it over to the funeral home. Still, it'll be harder to prosecute without some overlooked evidence of a murder Sharon could have discovered with more time," Javier said.

Emily asked where Javier wanted her to drop him. She hoped he didn't say police headquarters, risking another confrontation with Chief Clark, who by now probably received another call from the grieving widow and her pal the Mayor. She ended up dropping him at his place in East Sacramento and agreed to pick him up in the morning.

Emily accelerated back to her place while she ruminated over the quick cremation of Townsend's body, the pressure put on Sharon Pixley, the man from the pawnshop, and the crazy tall white guy from Pelican Bay. None of it fit together—and Lori Townsend's sexual appetites thread through everything.

Emily crossed the threshold, forecasting the fears of what she'd face. The unknown always played a part in a cop's life. Entering a biker meth lab she could deal with, but this entry terrified her. Did her mom attack Lucinda—or barricade herself in the bathroom, driven to the edge by a frail and failing mind?

Always anticipate the worst, but Emily couldn't foresee Connie and Lucinda at the dining room table playing cards and laughing. They were engrossed in their game; the pair hadn't noticed Emily come inside.

"What are we playing?" Emily asked.

Connie turned, and her eyes were clearer than Emily had seen in months. And she was smiling, a small expression surfacing in fleeting moments over the last few years.

"Hello, dear, sit. We'll deal you in."

Emily pulled out a chair and listened to her mother explain the rules to the card game. Lucinda smiled at Emily and nodded. After an hour of playing some hybrid of Texas Hold'em and Go Fish, the game broke up, and Connie left for the kitchen to make a pot of tea.

"She had a good day," Lucinda said.

"Best I've seen in a long, long time. Thank you. I don't know what you did, but she seems back to her old self." Emily felt the pressure in her chest lighten.

"I'm guessing whoever you used as the caregiver service didn't interact with Connie often. People going through what she's dealing with need personal interaction and stimulation. It's important to keep the disease from progressing."

"The more I hear about the service I used, the more pissed-off I get."

"It's pretty common, based on what I heard from the families I worked with at my facility. If you can start them interacting with others, and get them on the right medication, the better the outcome."

Emily glanced in the kitchen, and her mother paused, a teapot in one hand, trying to remember why she went to the kitchen. Connie glanced around the room, and Emily saw the growing confusion until her mom remembered she needed cups to go with that pot of tea.

"She can't live on her own, and I'm not around enough to give her the interaction you're talking about. Above everything, I want her to be safe."

"I think you need to look at options for a supportive environment, the right live-in caregiver or a place with other people going through the same thing. I can give you some recommendations."

"Thanks, I appreciate anything you can tell me. This is new to me. Brian, the officer who came last night, is supposed to give me a list too. His mom went through this . . ."

"My Javier told me about this boy."

"He what? There is nothing to say—"

"I want you and your friend to come over for dinner this Sunday."

"I don't want to impose and—"

"Nonsense. You, Connie, and your new friend will come for dinner at seven on Sunday."

"We'll see."

Lucinda got up from the table and gave Emily a motherly hug. "Yes, we will see. I want to see what this new boy of yours has going for him."

"Javi and I need to talk," Emily said.

Lucinda slipped into the kitchen and said goodbye to Connie. "I'll be back in the morning, Emily."

"I can't ask you to do that."

"You're not asking, and I'm doing it."

After Lucinda left, Emily found her mother pouring tea for the two of them.

"Lucinda is so nice," Connie said.

"She is, isn't she? You know she's Javier's mom, right? You've heard me talk about him?"

"Your partner, of course."

A moment of silence passed between them. Emily wondered how to broach the subject of moving into a facility—an old folks home, as her mom called them. *Rip the Band-Aid off, Emily.*

"Mom, what would you think about moving into a place of your own. You know, easy to take care of . . ."

"I can take care of myself."

"But you wouldn't have to do it by yourself. We can find you a place where you can relax, and I'll know you're safe."

"I'm safe here. What are you trying to say? That I'm old and feeble-minded and need to be locked away?"

She sensed her mom's defenses coming up; she needed to approach the subject differently.

"No, not at all. What I'm saying is you deserve a nice place to retire, somewhere I know you'll be safe, where your meals are cooked for you, and you have help housekeeping."

Connie shrugged and sipped from her teacup.

Emily lifted her cup to take a sip of her tea and noticed her mother neglected to add tea to the water. A daughter's heart broke again.

Acting on Lucinda's advice about keeping her mother's mind busy, Emily put her hand on her mother's. "Mom, want to help me work a case?"

"I'm not dressed for it." Connie gestured at her housecoat.

"We can do it from the living room." Emily snagged her laptop from her office, logged in, and downloaded the emailed pawnshop video file.

She patted the seat next to her, and Connie Hunter waited while Emily loaded the file. She hit PLAY and paused for the camera feed to freeze on the frame where the hooded man faced the camera. Emily absently picked up a warm chocolate chip cookie and took a bite.

"Did Lucinda make these?"

"No dear, I did."

"When did you bake last?"

"I don't know. I guess I felt I wanted to today. Lucinda knew how to turn the gas back on and make sure I turned off the stove after we were done. I know I forget things sometimes, honey."

Emily made sure Lucinda had shut the gas off and came back to the computer. She found the frames where the man selling the watch came into the store and stopped the playback. She selected screenshots of a half dozen different images.

Connie leaned in and squinted at the screen, staring at the last image of the guy in a grey hooded sweatshirt.

"He's probably one of those losers who hang out in Fremont Park," she said.

"What do you mean?" Emily asked, glancing at her mother.

"You know . . . the boys who hang out in that park and cruise K Street looking for handouts, or a quick score."

She turned, surprised by what she heard from her septuagenarian mother. "How do you know about that?"

Her mother's face drew up with serious concern. "Sheila would take me out to the store, and every once in a while she'd park and leave me in the car. I saw all sorts of things."

"She left you? Alone?" Emily readied to tear Senior Care Solutions a new one.

"Sometimes. Sheila said she needed to take some of my prescriptions back to a pharmacy she knew. I think she sold them. Besides, I'm taking them now."

"Mom! Why didn't you say anything?"

"I didn't want to cause trouble. But one time, this group of men started banging on my window. I think they were having fun trying to spook an old woman. They ran off when Sheila came back. She made a fuss over how lucky I was that she came along. Those guys rob people at knifepoint in the park and in the mall."

Emily glanced back at the image of the pawnshop exchange. The guy in the grey hoodie would look at home with the thugs cruising the streets after dark. The pawnshop was only a few blocks away from Fremont Park.

"You're pretty smart, Mom."

"You say that as if it's a surprise," Connie said, followed by a yawn.

"Let's get you ready for bed."

Connie stood unsteadily. Emily hugged her mother. "I love you, Mom."

"Love you too, honey."

CHAPTER TWELVE

AT HALF-PAST SEVEN, Emily cruised by Fremont Park on her way to Javier's place. Park benches, doorways, and alleys in the surrounding area held homeless souls, covered with thin newspaper or dampened cardboard. A few lucky street dwellers clutched blankets or heavy coats donated by the local churches.

The hooded man's picture rested on the dashboard while Emily prowled through the neighborhood. She managed to print off a few before she left home. Few homeless gave her any attention, and those who did notice were only interested in the threat the woman in the car posed. One man with long dirty grey hair possessed an animalistic, wild quality that caught the detective's attention. She slowed the Crown Vic and the homeless man yelled about the devil, roughly grabbed his meager possessions, and stumbled away listening to the voices crying for attention in his broken mind.

Acting on an unseen cue, the homeless population in the park began to stir, almost in unison. Slowly, they carried or rolled their belongings toward the shelter a few blocks away where a hot meal waited. The timing of their migration had more to do with the morning drive-by of the big boxy blue police wagon than hunger pangs. The wagon stopped every so often and roused the park dwellers. The city's, on-again, off-again enforcements of urban camping regulations kept the homeless population on edge. The veterans of the street knew if you couldn't move on when the wagon showed up, you'd earn a ride to the high-rise downtown Sacramento County Jail, visible from the northwest corner of the park.

As the temperatures dropped below freezing, the officers on the wagon crew found homeless who died from exposure during the long dark nights. An ambulance scooped away any trace of the person's existence, and for the others on the street, life ebbed on.

Emily figured her park excursion was a bust and headed east on J Street late to pick up Javier. The crosstown morning commute traffic, always miserable with bleary-eyed downtown workers, coffees in one hand and cell phones in the other, crept toward their destinations.

Javier waited at the curb wearing a navy blue pea coat buttoned up, with the collar turned up against the light morning breeze.

He tugged open the car door before Emily pulled to a stop. Javier's face was pink from the cold, and he reached over and turned up the heater.

"Sorry, I got caught up in traffic," Emily apologized. She checked the digital clock on the dashboard, and it read 7:58.

With a shiver, Javier replied, "I couldn't sleep much last night, so I got up early and needed a walk."

"I cruised the area around Fremont Park, looking for our boy there." She pointed to the photo of the hooded man on the dash.

She noticed the question in Javier's face, and she explained her mom's observations about the park and the men who came up to the car while she waited for Sheila.

"I needed to give it a try, but these people are transient. Pinning them down is tough."

Javier found the folder with copies of the pawnshop photos stuffed between the seats. "What do you say we start with the area around the pawnshop and show the picture around?"

Emily nodded and in a few minutes found a broken parking meter with a canvas hood locked to the thick metal pole. She tossed an Official Police Business placard in the window and grabbed the photographs of the man from the pawnshop. The bitter smell of leftover diesel exhaust from the abandoned Greyhound Bus depot clung to the concrete from a block away. Emily felt her thin tweed jacket absorb the odor as she plodded up to K Street.

The K Street Mall served as one of Sacramento's first experiences with urban renewal. The term "mall" was a bit of a stretch, so the city poohbahs began calling it "The Kay." The area was renamed as "Do-Co" for Downtown Commons, after another urban makeover. It remained little more than a section of street where car traffic was diverted to make way for light rail train service. There were city hall shelves packed with plans for redevelopment and gentrification of the downtown strip, but after nearly a decade, most of the small businesses folded and at least a third of the storefronts went vacant. At one end of the mall, a decent upscale shopping center once anchored the project, but local patrons didn't dare shop there after dark. It faded after a few costly years. Now a sports arena complex dominated the space, a flattened chrome football bringing ticket scalpers and pickpockets.

A few remaining single room occupancy hotels dumped their boarders out into the mall every morning where they lounged on light rail transit benches or squatted under storefront canopies. These residential buildings were slated for gentrification, but what happened to those who lived in them became someone else's problem.

Emily chose one side of the street, and Javier canvassed the opposite, showing the photo to street dwellers and businesspeople out on the mall. No one coughed up any information about the man in the pawnshop video. The people who slept in the street and parks weren't excited to cooperate with the police against someone who could be a member of their own community. An executive in his tailored three-piece suit held his distance from Emily, mistaking her for a religious peddler.

Another block down, Javier pointed to a spot ahead. Emily tensed and scanned the area for their hooded target. Instead, she spotted Buster, the junkie from the pawnshop, nodding off in front of a boarded-up restaurant. Javier cut across the pedestrian traffic and met Emily, who tapped Buster's leg with her boot.

"Hey . . . hey . . . hey, you don't gotta be up in my business. Social distance, dude." Buster's eyes couldn't focus, but a smile grew on his unshaven face after his eyes settled on Emily.

"Hey, baby, I knew you'd come to your senses and get wit 'ol Buster." He wriggled and leaned heavily on the window behind him, and noticed Javier. "I aint's into that . . . jus' you and me, baby."

Emily said, "Don't worry, I'm not into bestiality."

"Beasty-whaty?" Buster asked from behind confused eyes.

Emily tapped his leg again and got his attention back. "Buster, you seen this guy around here?"

She handed him a photograph, and he kept moving it until it came into focus.

"Could be. Why?"

"Tell me if you've seen him," Emily said.

Buster sensed the detective needed something from him and said, "What's in it for me, baby?"

"Maybe a nice romantic dinner," Javier said.

Emily backhanded her partner's shoulder and said, "I'll give you ten bucks if you tell me where I can find him."

Buster pointed over at Javier. "I want what he said."

Emily pulled a ten-dollar bill from a pocket of her jeans and held it in front of Buster's face. "Where is he?"

He snatched the bill quickly, and in a low voice said, "Dude lives down the hall from me at the Marshall. Third floor . . . 306, 307, somethin' around there."

"Dude have a name?" she asked.

Buster figured he wasn't going to get more. "He goes by 'Patches,' 'cause of the scars where he tried to burn off his old tats."

"Thanks, Buster," Emily responded and nodded to her partner to move off.

Javier made a few tentative steps away from Emily as she squatted in front of the junkie. She talked to him seriously, and he listened. She handed Buster another ten bucks and joined her partner.

While they headed toward the Marshall Hotel, Javier asked, "You mind telling me what that was about?"

Emily made it a few steps, shoved her hands in the pocket of her coat, said, "I asked if he wanted me to take him to detox. He's gonna die if he keeps up this life."

"He's not the only one, that's for certain. Let me guess? He turned you down?"

"He said he'd think about it." She grew silent.

"Well, I hope he does . . . Officer Booty Bandit needs a little competition."

"Asshole," Emily muttered.

The Marshall Hotel sat across the street from the old bus station. To call the single room occupancy hotel a fleabag carried an insult to fleas everywhere. The City announced plans to demolish the building to make way for high-end loft housing, but those plans bogged down in the city bureaucracy. The hotel's neon tubes were long lost, but the blue and white sign out front attracted the wretched refuse of downtown: the mentally ill, the sex offenders, and the junkies who burned their families for the last time.

Emily never knew if the dark paneling in the lobby was originally a burnt chocolate color, or if the tint came with years of grime, filth, and phlegm.

An old man in his seventies waited in a torn upholstered chair watching the people walk by outside. He didn't focus on life on the sidewalk; he was lost in a world of his own. Wherever his mind let him escape to, Emily knew it was better than the real world of the Marshall Hotel.

Emily and Javier approached the desk where a middle-aged man, in a yellowed, stained tank top read, or rather viewed, a skin magazine. His greasy hair parted in the middle and dripped off each side. He glanced up, slid his feet down from the counter, and rubbed his sweaty palm on the belly of his shirt. He eyed the detectives with suspicion and said, "What do you want?"

"The Honeymoon suite is probably already booked, so could you tell me if this guy is in?" Emily said.

Emily slid a copy of the photo through the grime on the counter. The man's eyes betrayed him before he even picked up the picture.

"I don't know. I'm not paid to watch folks coming and going."

"Cut the crap. What room is he in?" Emily said and slapped her badge on the counter.

After a pause, the deskman figured it wasn't worth his effort and handed her a key. "Room 308." The greasy man returned to his skin magazine, and peeked over it, leering at Emily as she walked away.

The detectives punched the UP button on the sketchy-looking elevator when the light in the lobby suddenly brightened. Someone opened the front door, and Emily caught it first. Bracketed by the light from the open front door, the man in the photo entered the hotel lobby.

The man froze at the sight of the two detectives with his picture in their hands. His eyes darted from their faces to the photo and back again. Their prey bounded back out into the street and dropped a plastic bag of grocery items on the sidewalk.

Emily hit the door seconds later and caught a glimpse of the man to the left, up the slight incline toward the remnants of the vacant Hard Rock Café on the K Street Mall. The man's legs pumped furiously, and he pulled away from his pursuers. He suddenly darted right and crossed in front of a light-rail train turning the corner. He missed the crushing steel wheels by inches but separated himself from Emily by the blue and white train cars. The train's operator sounded the horn, but the train continued forward.

From where the detectives stood, they couldn't see through the train cars, packed with morning commuters. Their suspect gained ground while they waited for the multiple train cars to pass. Emily gestured for Javier to take the downhill side to the right, and she ran toward the front of the moving train.

Seconds later, the train slowed for the next stop. Emily passed the lead car of the train and crossed the tracks. The train doors opened and dumped dozens of people out onto the sidewalk, obscuring her view. She stood on her toes and peered over the heads of the crowd for the man. Emily gripped the rails of an elevated wheelchair ramp and pulled herself up to the platform watching the crowd get on and off the train. She scanned the faces on the sidewalk and caught a person under a grey hoodie waiting to board. She wasn't sure until the man's eyes peered out from under the hood and locked with hers.

He pushed his way out of the crowd and raced away in front of the train. Emily jumped from the wheelchair ramp and followed, but lost sight of him as he shot down an alley to the right. Emily reached the alley and found nothing but a line of dumpsters and wet pavement. She keyed her small radio and relayed her position to Javier. Seconds later, her partner appeared two blocks down at the far end of the same alley. In spite of the noise from the morning traffic, Emily heard her steps reverberate off the alley walls.

She felt his presence, hidden among the dozen dumpsters or doorways in the dark alleyway. Emily pulled her Glock from her hip holster and crept up the alley.

From her left, a door flew open. Emily wheeled around and covered the doorway with her weapon. An older woman screamed, startled to find a woman pointing a gun at her. She dropped her bag of garbage, spilling the contents around her thick ankles.

"Police," Emily yelled to the frightened woman.

The woman screamed again, and her eyes grew large. Emily spun to her right, but not fast enough. The man came out from behind a dumpster, rammed his shoulder into Emily's back, and sent her sprawling face-first to the pavement; her gun skidded out in front of her.

Javier ran toward her from the other end of the alley. The hooded man paused over Emily and reached for her gun. Javier pulled his weapon and yelled, "Don't do it!"

The man jerked his head up as Javier barreled toward him. Emily rolled on her right side, kicked out with the heel of her left boot, and caught the man on the side of his knee.

He howled in pain and dove toward the door where the old woman stood transfixed by the action behind her clothing shop. The man seized the woman and pushed her inside.

Emily jumped back on her feet and retrieved her weapon before Javier reached her. She threw open the alley door and heard the loud crash of breaking glass from the front of the store.

Javier entered first and cleared the small cramped storage room. Then Emily pushed past and opened the curtain to the front of the store. On the floor, leaning against the counter, the old woman cried into her hands. The plate glass window facing the K Street Mall lay in shards after being shattered by a mannequin clad only in a midnight blue negligee. Emily stuck her head out the window frame and clocked their suspect limping away.

"We'll be right back," Emily told the old woman. She noticed another employee hiding behind the clothing racks and told her, "Call 911 and stay with her."

The detectives dashed out the window and ran after their prey. The runner pulled the grey sweatshirt over his head and tossed it to the ground. Emily noticed bloodstains on the garment—the man had cut himself going through the window.

They gained on him. Desperate and scared, he glanced over his shoulder at the two detectives. His eyes grew wide and he tried to pick up speed as he crossed a busy intersection. Horns blared, cars skidded to avoid hitting him.

Concerned over his pursuers, he failed to notice the huge Regional Transit bus parked on the far side of the intersection. Looking over his shoulder, he ran into the side of the bus at full limping speed. The sudden stop knocked him backward, flat on his back. A small gash on the side of his head bled where it connected with the bus. A hunk of his hair hung from the bus window frame.

Not unconscious, but stunned, the man groaned and writhed in pain. The first thing he registered when his eyes focused was the dark barrel of Emily's Glock. His eyes crossed, focusing on the far end of the barrel. He gave up and fell limp, while Javier pulled his hands behind his back and put him in handcuffs.

A half a block away, a biker, clad in black leather chaps and a long black shirt under a leather vest, watched the activity through his dark sunglasses. He tossed his half-full Styrofoam coffee in the gutter and pulled a cell phone from a vest pocket. He quickly dialed a number and waited. After a voice sounded on the other end, the biker said, "Hey, brother, I think you have a problem."

"How so?" the voice replied.

"You know that Peckerwood you used on that job a few days ago?"

"Patches? Yeah."

"Well, he got himself picked up by the cops."

"What did he get himself into?" the voice asked.

"Two plain-clothed cops and they have him prone out in the street." The biker laughed slightly. "Your dude ran into a city bus and bounced off it. He's not very smooth." The biker got more serious and asked, "Is this going to be a problem for the Boys?"

"It could be. The kid knows enough to make the Federal Prosecutors rub their hands together, again. I'm not sure he can hold his mud."

"That's all I need to hear, brother. I'll handle it. Give my best to the Boys at Pelican Bay."

The biker put the cell phone away in his vest and stood on the starter of the Harley-Davidson chopper. The engine kicked over, and the low rumble echoed off the buildings around him. He pulled back on the throttle a couple of times, letting the engine roar through the twin chrome pipes. He donned a black bike helmet, styled after the World War II German Army headgear, over his long dark hair and pulled out into the traffic. He passed the handcuffed man, taking his left hand, made a gesture resembling a gun, and pulled an imaginary trigger. The biker sped up and away from the man as the police lifted the injured man to his feet; the suspect's eyes followed the biker down the street until he disappeared around a corner.

Javier caught the biker's hand gesture and commented, "Emily, I don't think he likes you."

"No, that was meant for me," their suspect said. Without another word, the man ducked his head as a uniformed officer put him in the rear seat of a patrol car.

CHAPTER THIRTEEN

THE TWO DETECTIVES returned to the Hotel Marshall where the sleazy desk clerk remained in deep reflection with his skin magazine. He lifted his head as Emily and Javier passed his desk, then reaffixed his eyes on the curves of a redhead featured in this month's issue.

Emily called out, "We're heading up to 308."

A raised hand was the sole response from the desk man.

"I guess the articles are very intriguing this month," Javier said as they trudged up the first staircase. The elevator didn't look safe after closer inspection.

"Thanks."

"For what?"

She stopped on the first landing, faced Javier, and clutched him by the lapels on his jacket. "Back there in the alley. I can't believe I let that dirtbag get the jump on me. I mean, if you hadn't yelled and distracted him—he wanted my gun."

Emily tried to shake off the alley encounter. They'd been through a score of tough situations before, and most of the time she rolled with the punches. This last one stuck with her and bothered her.

"Emily, listen, you'd do the same thing. Hell, you have covered my ass before. Besides, when I have kids, I'll need you to babysit now and again."

"First, you need to pick out a mail order bride."

"They're expensive. I'm cheap. I'm gonna need to do it the old-fashion way."

"What's that? Back to the online dating world?"

"Never again. Talk about false advertising. Mom set me up with the daughter of a friend-of-a-friend."

"Oh, what could possibly go wrong?"

"No kidding. I can alienate and embarrass two Mexican American families at once. It's a challenge. Speaking of challenges—what's got you distracted, partner?"

"I honestly didn't think I was. I never let a creep get the upper hand. I lost focus. Maybe it's Mom's whole deal. It's keeping me up at night, I know that."

"Her memory issues?"

"Yeah, they're getting worse. Your mom is a godsend. A day with her and Mom's already showing some improvement. I know she's never going to be able to live without supervision."

"Damn. I'm sorry to hear that. Scary."

"It is. Now I need to look at maybe moving her into a facility. I thought having her live with me would be enough. God, I don't want to toss her in one of those places."

"Have you checked any of them out yet?"

"Your mom and Brian are giving me places to go look at. Speaking of which, you blabbed to your mom about Brian?"

"I may have mentioned your boy toy."

"Well, she's invited, I should say ordered, Brian and me to come for dinner this Sunday. We haven't even gone out on a proper date yet."

"Shit. That means she's going to expect me to show up with a date. Come on, you got to bring him with you to take the heat off me."

On the third-floor landing, the hallways spread out in both directions, all but three lights burnt out or broken. It left the hallways dim and shadowy. The room they wanted was at the end of the hall on the right. They passed darkened doors, where radios dueled rap and hard rock at impressive volume, a numbing curtain of anxiety-inducing noise.

Emily tried the knob on Room 308 and found it locked, so she inserted the key, unlatched the door, and pushed it open with her foot.

The single room unit boasted its own bathroom facilities, which made it one of the hotel's deluxe accommodations. A chipped china sink and toilet hung along one wall. A thin particle-board barrier separated the rudimentary facilities from the rest of the room. The coiled iron bed frame held a thin, soiled mattress off the floor and took up most of the room. A battered green bureau and small metal desk completed the décor.

"I think this room was on one of the websites when I booked my last vacation," Emily said.

A cockroach skittered near the base of the sink. "And look, they're pet friendly," Javier said.

Emily examined the bureau top and found most of the clutter on the surface layer was garbage: food wrappers, used Kleenex, and trash. She poked around the mess with the tip of a pencil and found two White Supremacy leaflets. A small poorly printed newspaper under the trash pile proclaimed White Power and outlined recent activities of some of its followers.

Opening one of the three drawers of the bureau, Javier found sweat- and urine-stained underwear. He pulled the drawer out and dumped the contents on the floor. He repeated the process with the second drawer containing a well-used *Hustler* magazine, two pairs of socks, and two instant soup packages. The third drawer hadn't been used, and he almost disregarded it, but Javier pulled it away from the dresser. Taped to the back of the drawer, he found a syringe, a crack pipe, and three small bindles of an off-white crystalline substance.

"I wonder if we can tie this to the powder we found in the safe at the Townsend residence." Javier pointed to the bindles. "Look like the tape job in Corona's place where we found the pistol?"

Emily nodded, bent over an oddly lumped pair of socks. She unrolled them and exposed a shiny Vacheron Constantin Malte watch. The interior workings of the watch clicked away, unaffected by the dank hotel room.

"I know we can tie this to the murder scene. It's one of the watches on the list Lori Townsend provided," she said.

Javier bumped the empty bureau with his hip to move it to the wall, and it wouldn't move flush to the wall on one end. He pulled the bureau away from the wall and found another taped bundle— this one long and wrapped in thick layers of duct tape.

"Emily, take a look. Could we be lucky enough to find the murder weapon?"

The faint outline of a knife showed through the duct tape pressed to the back of the bureau.

"Let's call the crime techs to photograph and document everything," Emily said.

She called a request for techs to respond, collect, and tag the evidence the room held. They were in luck as a team had just finished working an attempted strong-armed robbery across the street at the old Greyhound Bus terminal. They were only minutes out.

Emily put her phone away and tried to open the window to let some of the musty, dank smell out of the small room. It wouldn't budge from layer upon layer of thick paint over the window frame. She tried again, and the window refused to move, but the floorboards at her feet buckled.

"Hey, Javi, give me a hand here, would ya?"

The detectives lifted a section of unattached floorboards and set them aside, exposing a two-foot-by-two-foot opening in the floor. Inside the cavity, along with inches of rodent droppings, sat three canvas bags. The bags were well worn, but not covered with dust from neglect.

"Detectives—what do you have for me?" The question came from Lillian Cole, a crime scene technician, dressed in a set of dark blue coveralls. She dropped two heavy equipment bags on the floor with a thud and pulled a large digital camera from one of them.

Emily got up from the floor, surprised she'd grown stiff from her fall in the alley.

"Let's start over here with a few shots of the floor," Emily said.

Lillian got into position above the open floorboards and sighted in several shots, the strobe light, illuminated the darkest corners of the hole. "Yuck," she said as she moved closer for another shot.

"That's strange from someone who takes pictures of dead people for a living," Javier said.

"Spiders—there's a bunch of them down there," she explained.

Javier moved his hands back slightly from the opening because he wasn't fond of the little critters either, especially the kind that hopped about.

Emily sighed at both of them, said, "Oh, please," and reached in and pulled the first bag onto the floor next to them. A dozen rat pellets fell from the sides of the bag as it hit the floor.

Lillian clicked off photographs as Emily pulled on the bag's heavy gauge zipper. Four MAC-10 machine pistols, with suppressors, along with a dozen high capacity magazines, filled the canvas satchel. An oil coating on the black .45 caliber weapons with their folding metal stocks gleamed in the flash of the strobe.

Emily pulled the next bag to the opening and needed two hands to pull the heavy leather-bottomed canvas bag from beneath the floor. A metallic clank sounded from within the bag as it touched down on the floor. She unzipped the bag and expected to find more automatic weapons. Instead, she found five long bayonets, the kind attached to vintage World War II military rifles. The markings and lettering appeared German—the swastika engraved on the hilt of one of them confirmed as much. Under the old bayonets, Emily reached in and pulled out brick after brick of cash wrapped in layers of clear plastic. Paper bands around each brick identified the denomination and total amount of currency in each bundle. If the numbers were accurate, two hundred and fifty thousand dollars lay on the floor, a very expensive set of children's building blocks.

"What was our boy into?" Emily wondered aloud.

She pulled up the last bag from its floorboard hidey-hole, and it weighed half as much as the previous two. Emily turned the bag over, and forty-seven bindles of white crystal poured onto the floor.

"These are packaged like the stuff we found on the back of the dresser," Javier said.

Littered among the plastic-wrapped bindles were three syringes, two of them used, and two small baggies of marijuana. But Emily's attention went to a black USB thumb drive. She picked it up, turned it in her gloved hand, and found no markings hinting at the drive's content.

A curled sliver of paper lay partially under the marijuana. Emily carefully unrolled the scrap of paper. The label from the USB drive lost its adhesive and fell to the bottom of the bag. In block letters, "Townsend," was printed neatly.

Emily raised her arm for her partner to help her up from the floor. She moaned slightly as he pulled her to her feet.

"You want to drop by the hospital to get checked out? You took a pretty hard fall."

"No, I'm fine. I'm pissed, that's all. And I want to take this back and see what's on it."

The crime scene tech spent two hours combing through the small hotel room for fibers, prints, and stains. It was debatable if the ratty bedsheets had made it to a washing machine since the day they landed on a mattress. Sweat stains, urine streaks, and other yet unidentified bodily fluids made a tie-dye art project out of the frayed bed linen.

The hotel deskman made an appearance up in the room. He must've finished his heavy reading downstairs. He stood at the open doorway, said, "Who's gonna pay to fix that?" pointing at the hole in the floor.

"Why don't you ask your tenant?" Emily said.

"It don't look like he'll be back, does it?" The deskman wiped a gleam of sweat from his forehead and noticed they bagged up the sheets and towels.

"Hey, you can't take those! What am I supposed to do?"

"I left you a receipt on the sink for the stuff we confiscated." Javier pulled off his latex gloves, tossed them in a trash bag, and dug deep in his pocket. He flipped a quarter at the deskman and said, "This should buy you a whole new set. Keep the change." Javier pushed his way past the man and started down the hall.

Emily followed, not bothering to glance at the sleazy deskman. She called back, "You may want to send housekeeping to freshen up the room a bit."

CHAPTER FOURTEEN

BY THE TIME the detectives logged and tagged the evidence, the man in the hoodie was cleared for processing from the hospital with a broken nose, strained neck, and fractured wrist. At booking, he refused to give his name to the officers. That worked briefly until one of the jail officers recognized him as a frequent guest of the county correctional facility. John Parkes, or "Johnny P." as he was known locally, was printed, photographed, and processed into the Sacramento County Jail. Showered and clothed in an orange jumpsuit, he waited in an interrogation room.

Thirty minutes later, Johnny P's headache worsened, and his anxiety made him twitch. He'd given up the thinly padded metal chair and paced back and forth, the legs of the orange jumpsuit hanging over his plastic shower shoes.

He wasn't surprised to see the two detectives, especially the woman he knocked down and who chased him into the side of the bus. There was no way to tell his story and retain any thread of street cred.

"Sit down, Parkes," Javier said and pointed to the metal chair.

The man tried to puff up his chest, but the folds of the large jumpsuit prevented his attempt to "man-up." Parkes narrowed his eyes, trying for the stoic appearance of a hardened convict, jaw tight, head up and slightly back, looking down his nose at Emily.

"Why'd you run, Parkes?"

"I got nothin' to say to you."

"Well, what do you have to say about this?" Javier slid the photograph of Parkes in the pawnshop on the table.

Parkes didn't touch the photo and barely glanced at it. "That ain't me."

"Huh—really?" He reached into his pocket and withdrew a small plastic bag with the word EVIDENCE labeled at the top. "Tell me about this watch we found in your room."

Parkes' eyes widened slightly as the bright stainless-steel trim on the Vacheron Constantin flashed on the tabletop. "I got it from a guy."

"I'm sure you did. You steal it from Roger Townsend?" Emily asked calmly.

"I don't know no Roger Town-whatever." Parkes fidgeted in the chair.

Emily put both of her hands flat on the table. "I think you do. How else can you explain having his watch?"

"Listen, I told you I don't know the dude. I got this watch from a guy who owed me some cash." His voice started to rise, and a small bead of sweat formed on his forehead.

"Okay, okay. Let's try this instead." Javier opened a file and sorted through the photos from the motel room. "Explain this." He shuffled to the photo of the MAC-10 machine pistols taken from under the floorboards in his room and smacked it down in front of Parkes.

The orange-clad prisoner said nothing, but he couldn't take his eyes from the photo.

"How about this?" Another photo slammed down on the table, this one of the plastic-wrapped money and the bayonets.

"Or this?" Javier hit the table with the palm of his hand, making Parkes jump. Under his hand, a photo of the last canvas bag containing the individual bindles of methamphetamine and the USB drive.

"Oh dude—you have no idea what you've done," Parkes complained as he leaned back in the chair.

Emily leaned and stepped toward Parkes. "Then why don't you tell us about it, you little weasel," she said.

Parkes opened his mouth to respond, but he gave up and put his head down and slumped in his chair. The hardened convict veneer slipped away.

Javier gathered the photos into a disorganized pile. He put his hand on top of them and said, "All this ties you to the murder of Roger Townsend."

Parkes' head snapped up. "I didn't do it!"

Javier continued in a deliberately slow manner. "I'm sure the D.A. is gonna file special circumstances—that means you'll get the death penalty, Parkes. You ever see someone get the needle? I have. Some people say you feel everything and scream in agonizing pain, but you can't open your mouth to let the screams out. I'll be there to watch it."

"You gotta believe me. Yeah, I mighta been there when it happened, but I didn't do it, you hear me?"

"Oh yeah, sure, I'm supposed to take your word for it?" Javier crossed his arms over his chest.

"Dude, I ain't no snitch." Parkes tried to regain some strength.

Emily patted the photographs piled on the tabletop and replied, "My partner made it crystal—Dude—you participated in this crime. The stolen watches were in your possession. Roger Townsend died in the commission of a robbery. That's the Felony Murder Rule. Doesn't matter if you shot him, or cut his throat, you're gonna burn for this."

"Well, I'm done talking to you then. Unless you give me a deal, I'll take my chances with a jury." He sighed, hung his head again, and said, barely above a whisper, "It don't matter anyway."

Javier brought up the bags and weapons found in the hotel room once more. "You hid enough firepower in your room to take over a third-world country. What were you going to do with that?"

After a pause, Parkes responded by shaking his head, and softly commented, "They didn't belong to me. Once they find out I let the cops get their hands on their stuff, I'm dead anyway. Either the State's gonna put me down, or the Brand will."

"The A.B.?" Emily asked.

Parkes refused to respond, resigned to his fate, taking the hit on the Townsend murder to stay in good standing with the Aryan Brotherhood prison gang.

Emily signaled a Sheriff's Deputy they'd finished with Parkes. The deputy pulled the handcuffed prisoner from the chair.

"Oh man, what'd you do?" the deputy asked. Parkes had urinated on the chair and soaked his jumpsuit. "Well, you ain't getting a new one right now."

The deputy pushed Parkes out of the room by the elbow and the collar of his jumpsuit, holding him at a distance as if he were toxic waste.

A Sheriff's Sergeant stepped inside and asked if the detectives needed another prisoner for an interview. Emily let him know they didn't, but she raised concerns about Parkes and possible threats from the Aryan Brotherhood. The Sergeant said they'd assigned Parkes to a single cell, meaning he'd be the only prisoner in his cell, and the safety concerns would be passed on to the housing unit officers.

As the detectives left the jail, they showed their identification and picked up their weapons at the sally port. The addition of the Aryan Brotherhood in the case disturbed Emily.

The prison gang spawned out of San Quentin State Prison in the late 1960s to organize and protect White inmates against the strong influences of Black and Hispanic gangs. In the decades after, the A.B. established a network of intimidation, protection, drug trafficking, and murder. Although the members of the Brand, a term used by gang insiders, made up less than one-tenth of the prison population, FBI estimated they were responsible for over twenty-four percent of in-prison homicides.

Emily knew the California Department of Corrections segregated the known members and heavy associates of the A.B. in Pelican Bay State Prison in the late 1980s. Despite the geographical separation, the gang leaders communicated with their sympathizers throughout the state, using arranged court appearances where other subpoenaed members met, or with messages sent out of the prison with invisible ink made from their own urine.

Once released on parole, the A.B. members adhered to a code to support their brothers behind prison walls and Emily couldn't determine how the murders of Roger Townsend and his attorney, Wayne Corona, fit together with the Brand and their particular type of homegrown terrorism.

"You did a good job in there. This puts a whole new spin on this case. Why would the Aryan Brotherhood be interested in Townsend?" Emily asked Javier as they returned to her Crown Victoria.

"You think Parkes and his A.B. contacts took him out? They wouldn't do him if it didn't further their White Supremacy ends. I don't know what they could gain from killing him," Javier said.

"I could see keeping him alive and using his contacts to funnel and launder some of their drug money, then Townsend grew a spine and threw the arrangement off. The white boys turned on him for a reason."

"Parkes is weak. We can squeeze him for more. I bet we can make him give up his role in the murder and who else played a part. He knows," Javier said.

"I believe he was there and stole the watches from the place. Look at the guy—he's a meth-head. I don't think he'd be strong enough to beat Townsend down. Let alone slice through his neck."

"He could be the shooter. But Parkes doesn't fit with the description that Corona's guy, Tooker, gave us either," Javier added.

"We need some leverage on Parkes to force him to give us the other guy in the house. We can see if the D.A. is willing to give him some kind of deal to loosen his tongue. Maybe we'll find the leverage we need on the USB thumb drive we found hidden under the floorboards."

"You're forever the optimist. I'll bring the popcorn." Javier paused and wrinkled his nose. "On second thought, if it's a video of Lori Townsend, doing what she does, I think I'll pass."

Emily reached for the cell phone vibrating in her pocket. "Hunter here."

"Hi, Emily, it's Sandy in the Chief's office."

"What's up," Emily said warily.

"The Chief wants to see you. Emily, don't even think about it. He said if you're not here within thirty minutes, he'll have you suspended. I think he's serious."

"Thanks for the heads-up. We'll be there in thirty," she responded and tossed the phone on the seat.

"Another audience with his highness?"

"The Chief this time, but we have time for a cup of coffee," Emily said while turning into the crowded parking lot at a Starbucks, off Broadway.

After a wait in line listening to patrons call out their designer drink orders, with overcomplicated names like triple-decaf-non-fat-soy-low-foam-latte-extra-hot, Emily ordered, "Two medium-coffees-black-no-cream-no-sugar-extra-hot."

The high school–aged girl behind the counter frowned, tugged at her green apron nervously, and searched the keys on the register for medium-coffees-black-no-cream-no-sugar-extra-hot. Her face wrinkled, and she didn't know what to do next. She glanced behind Emily at the line, feeding her frustration even more.

Javier stepped in and rescued the girl. "Two grande drip coffees, please."

"Oh, okay." She turned and pulled two white and green paper cups and filled them with the day's selected brew. She capped them and placed them on the counter in front of Emily. "Here you go, ma'am."

Javier paid with a ten-dollar bill. "Keep the change," he offered.

The girl whispered, "Is she your wife?" The look on the girl's face betrayed her disbelief and revulsion.

Javier whispered back, "Oh God, no. She's on work release from jail, and it's my day to watch her."

The girl's eyes grew large. "No way."

"Way," Javier responded while handing a coffee to Emily and then leading her away by her arm.

"Work release?" Emily questioned.

"You didn't have to be mean to the girl. And yeah, if you stand up the Chief again, you may be on work release."

CHAPTER FIFTEEN

By the time they parked in the police department lot and made their way inside to the Chief's office, it was twenty-nine minutes after Sandy had summoned them. Emily plopped down on the sofa in the Chief's waiting room and waved at Sandy, occupied on the phone.

Javier waited next to his partner. "Please don't poke him with a stick." He pointed his jaw toward Chief Clark's office.

With her hands open, Emily asked, "What stick?"

"Take it easy, would you? For my sake?"

"He's getting pushed around by Mayor—"

Javier cut her off and pointed a finger in her face as if she were a disobedient child. "Emily, I mean it."

Sandy cleared her throat loudly and interrupted their bickering. "Please go in, Detectives. Chief Clark is waiting for you."

The Chief closed a use of force review file when they entered.

"Please take a seat."

"What's up, Chief?" Emily asked.

"Good work taking down Parkes."

"Thanks, but—"

"Let me tell you how it's gonna be," Chief Clark said while he leaned back in his chair. "I've already spoken with the Mayor and the D.A. They intend to charge Parkes with First Degree Murder, with Special Circumstances, Armed Robbery, Home Invasion, and Assault with a Deadly Weapon on Lori Townsend."

"Good," Emily replied.

"This closes out your interest in this case. You've got your suspect in custody; case closed. Now, go write up those reports and lock this thing down."

"Chief, we've got evidence of another suspect in the house with Parkes. I have a gut feeling he's the guy who actually killed Townsend and Corona."

"I'm not Dr. Phil, and you know I don't work on 'feelings.' As far as the Mayor, the city council, and the press are concerned, we have the killer in custody."

"Chief, I'm telling you, there is solid evidence the Aryan Brotherhood is—"

"The last thing the mayor wants to hear from us is a rumor of a criminal enterprise preying on upstanding citizens of the caliber of Roger Townsend. If we go out on a limb and hint one of the mayor's financial backers is involved in some criminal conspiracy, the mayor will personally saw that limb off. Officially, the Townsend case is closed."

"You want me to stop investigating the murder of Roger Townsend? Right? I mean, I want to be clear about which crimes the mayor wants me to ignore when the Grand Jury asks, Chief. I get it—no more work on Townsend." Emily put her hands in the air in mock surrender.

"Go work on some other cases," the Chief said.

"Any the mayor would prefer we work on?"

"I'm sure you can work a case other than the Roger Townsend homicide."

"Yeah—yeah, we have other cases." Emily's eyes locked with the Chief's and exchanged a moment of silence.

She stood and left the office, with Javier in tow.

Once outside, Javier caught his partner by the arm. "I can't believe you!"

"What now?"

"You practically threatened the Chief with going to the Grand Jury. What were you thinking?"

"I don't think that will be necessary. But you and I are not doing any further investigation on Roger Townsend's murder." Emily started walking away until he caught her elbow.

"But?"

"The Chief made it very clear about the Townsend investigation. That order doesn't stop us from investigating the Corona murder, or the weapons charges on Parkes for the stuff we found under his floor." Emily smiled.

Javier dropped her elbow. "You've got to be kidding. Do you have a death wish or what?"

"Listen, the Chief can't come out and say it. He wants to nail whoever killed Roger Townsend as much as we do, but he's handcuffed by the mayor and city council. We'll find another way into that mess—and the Corona murder is the way in."

Javier's jaw tensed. "If it blows up, we are the ones taking the fall, not the Chief."

"That's the way it works. Let's go check out that USB drive we found in Parkes' room."

Emily removed the thumb drive from the plastic evidence bag and shoved it into a slot in her computer. The storage device held a single untitled MP4 video file.

"Here we go," she said.

A few seconds of high-pitched electronic purr came from the computer before the screen brightened.

Javier perched in his chair with his feet up on his desk and offered Emily some of the microwave popcorn he nearly burned. The odor of smoky butter saturated the room, building the anticipation of the feature film.

They both expected the video to document another sexual encounter featuring the seemingly insatiable appetites of Lori Townsend. The video started to roll and sure enough, Lori featured in the frame, but instead of an anonymous hotel suite, the grainy surveillance tape focused on the trim blonde as she stood at the fountain in the center of Caesar Chavez Park. She waited for someone, pacing slowly back and forth, lugging an expensive silver briefcase.

"Check out the trees," Emily mentioned as she paused the tape.

"What?" Javier focused on Lori strutting back and forth.

"They're bare. The trees don't have any leaves. This took place in the winter—don't know how long ago," she replied, starting the tape once more. "Look—"

"There's no date stamp on the screen—" The sound from the video interrupted him. "She's wired," Javier said.

Car noise and bits of conversation peppered the background. Lori stopped pacing, stood on her toes, and waved to someone outside of the frame. Five seconds later, a man in a long black coat over a charcoal suit approached her.

"Shit," Emily said as she tensed in her chair. "That's Stephen Lawson, the Assistant United States Attorney. He's a heavyweight in organized crime prosecution."

The tape moved forward, Lori gave Stephen a friendly peck on the cheek and remained close, a hand resting on Lawson's chest.

"I have what you want," she whispered.

"Oh, she's subtle," Javier said while he tossed some popcorn in his mouth.

The man in the video fidgeted with his jacket, nervous, with a thin sheen of sweat on his brow. He kept checking over his shoulders at passersby on the street.

"Lori, why couldn't we meet somewhere private?"

"Haven't you ever heard of 'hiding in plain sight'? This is more exciting, don't you think?"

Lori handed him the silver briefcase and casually bent over to adjust a small strap on her shoe.

"Stephen, there is a hundred thousand in the briefcase, as you agreed with Roger."

"Why isn't Roger here?" Stephen moved a step back.

"Would you relax? Jesus, Stephen, you're gonna have a stroke. Roger thought it would be best if you and he weren't seen together."

"Seen?"

"Calm down. Do you have the files Roger wanted?"

"I don't feel right about this, Lori." His voice betrayed his anxiety and started to crack.

She reached to take the silver case back. "If you don't want the money . . ."

He grasped her hand and replied, "No—I need it. I've never done this before. I've never thrown a case before, and these guys are heavyweights."

"Sweetie, simply put this behind you and move on. Roger knows what to do with these RICO files, don't worry."

Slowly, Stephen put a bulky black briefcase down at his feet and gripped the silver case with his hundred thousand in cash. He paused and locked eyes with Lori. "You be careful with these guys—they'll kill you for looking at them the wrong way."

"Stephen, you worry too much. Now, Roger wanted me to ask you if these files are the only copies?"

"That's it."

"And the case against these guys goes away?"

"It's gone."

Lori pulled up an expandable handle from the boxy black brief-case and wheeled the case out of the frame, her heels sounding off the cement walkway.

The Assistant U.S. Attorney held the silver briefcase, and his expression went slack. In spite of the uneven contrast of the video, Lawson's face paled. He glanced around the park for a few seconds, then turned and left in the opposite direction. The video flickered twice and dissolved into blackness.

"What the hell happened?" Emily uttered. The popcorn bag flopped over on the table, oozing buttered-flavored oils onto the papers underneath.

"We witnessed a federal prosecutor take a payoff to dump a case. Did you hear Lori mention RICO?"

"Yeah, as in racketeering and organized crime. That's where the Aryan Brotherhood fits in."

Emily nodded. "We've come full circle—back to Lori Townsend."

CHAPTER SIXTEEN

THE PHONE MADE Emily jump, and she knocked the popcorn bag from the desk, spreading the oily, smoky-smelling, congealing mass onto the desktop. Javier slid his feet down from the desk, grabbed a nearby spare evidence bag, and swept the mess into the bag with the edge of a file folder from Emily's inbox. A thin sheet of slime marked the path of the popcorn's escape.

Emily clutched the phone so tight her knuckles turned white.

Javier whispered, "What?" as he wiped down the oil slick on the desk.

In response, Emily closed her eyes and interrupted the caller. "How did this happen?"

"Your mom okay?" Javier whispered.

Emily nodded.

Another moment of silence and Emily slammed the phone on the cradle. "Johnny Parkes is dead."

The news made Emily numb, and she felt a cold orb in her stomach. "How—how could that happen? They knew he had a target on his back . . ."

"The jail staff told us they'd assigned him to a single cell," Javier said.

"According to the Jail Commander, it didn't happen in his cell."

"Then how'd he die?"

"They assigned him to a protective custody housing unit, and he and a couple of other PC inmates were released for a med check by the jail doctors. He got rushed and stabbed up by two other White inmates, who were supposedly also legit protective custody cases."

"The guys who hit him were P.C. too? That's incredible," Javier said.

"The Jail Commander thinks they were 'sleepers' hiding out in the P.C. unit until ordered to take someone out. I understand that. But, how did the order to hit Parkes get to the jail so quickly? He'd only been there a few hours."

"There are only a few ways to send information into the jail: by visitors, either in person, by phone, mail, or with the help of jail staff," Javier said.

"We can rule out mail," Emily added. "Because this happened before you could lick a stamp and drop it at the post office."

"I take it the two hitters aren't talking?"

"Not a word. Both were pending trial on carjacking and assault charges. This ups the ante for them from a couple years to life."

"Let's say someone wanted Parkes out of the picture. Why? Because he let us confiscate the stuff in the hotel room?"

"Or because he knew what happened to Roger Townsend," Emily finished.

"Where does the video fit in? What would get a U.S. Attorney all twisted up in knots?" Javier used his hands to emphasize his point. He held the file folder with its large oil stain in his grasp.

Emily made a comment about his housekeeping skills, and he tossed the file folder at her. The folder contents spilled as it flew past. Three pages of a report, neatly scribed in block printing, lay in her lap. Emily picked it up and began reading, silently turning the first page.

Without taking her eyes off of the report, Emily said, "I asked for a uniform to interview the sleazy deskman at the hotel and find out more about Parkes renting the room." After the detective finished reading the concise report, she handed it to Javier. "It turns out Parkes never rented the place. The deskman told the officer he'd been paid for the room six months in advance."

"Did the guy give us a name?"

"The desk guy claims he didn't. His orders were to keep the room locked at all times and let anyone using a code word use the room, no questions asked."

Javier shrugged. "A code word? What the hell is this? A spy movie?" He moved his chair closer and picked up the report. "Shamrock? That's the code word? What kind of crap is that?"

"The shamrock is central to the Aryan Brotherhood. Members have shamrock tattoos, sometimes with the number 666 inside the leaf. The hotel room was an A.B. crash pad."

"Which means anyone could've stashed that stuff there." Javier turned to the last page of the report. The officer had provided a description of the man who instructed the desk clerk. A white man, six-foot-three to six-five, two hundred pounds, long hair mostly grey, but with dark streaks through it. The man had tattoos on both arms, in the form of prison walls, a smoking revolver, the words "White Pride" printed in an elaborate scroll, and a semi-nude Viking woman on each forearm.

"This is a good description. We should be able to get some traction with this," she said.

"I'll push copies over to the gang units and see what they can come up with."

"Ah . . . hem," the Chief cleared his throat.

The detectives turned in response.

"I assume by now you've heard John Parkes was killed over at the jail."

Emily silently nodded. She didn't have a good feeling about where this conversation was headed. The Chief had gotten his information too quickly for her comfort.

"I'm holding a press conference with Mayor Stone to announce the man responsible for the Townsend murder is dead, and no longer a threat to the community."

"But he's not—"

"Your investigation is over. This is closed. You hear me, Detective?"

Before Emily responded, Javier clicked the computer mouse and the video file started, with Lori Townsend's voice filling the room.

The Chief quickly turned to the screen. "What is this?"

"Watch, Chief. Someone shot this video a couple of months ago," Javier said.

The sound from the video echoed as Lori Townsend said, "Stephen, you worry too much. Now, Roger wanted me to ask you if these files are the only copies?"

"That's it," the man in the picture responded.

"And the case against these guys goes away?" Lori touched the other man in a very familiar way.

"It's gone," the man on the tape responded.

Javier froze the tape after Lori wheeled the case out of the frame.

The Chief didn't take his eyes off the screen even after the images disappeared. "What did he hand over to her in the case?" he asked in a low voice.

Emily responded, "We found this thumb drive in an Aryan Brotherhood crash pad. It ties Roger to some conspiracy to interfere with an investigation of the gang's activities."

"Why would he involve Lori in this kind of thing?" Chief Clark rubbed his forehead, trying to clear his thoughts. "Why would Roger put her in such a position?"

"Chief, do you recognize the man in the picture?" Emily asked her boss.

"It's Stephen Lawson—he's a federal prosecutor," he said.

"Exactly. I don't suppose he asked you not to pursue the Townsend case?"

"He told the Mayor he held deep concerns and was worried about Lori, and now I know why."

"We have enough to get obstruction, conspiracy, and I know there would be federal charges for turning over prosecution files and tanking an investigation," Javier said.

"We are going to bring Lori in and interview her," Emily said.

"You'll do no such thing. You don't hold a shred of any verifiable proof of what her briefcase actually held. Find me corroboration, then we can pull Lori in. We know she has His Honor the Mayor on speed dial. Follow her and maybe she'll lead you to who else was involved in this with her husband."

Emily snagged her jacket.

"You need an invitation? Let's start with a certain U.S. Attorney."

CHAPTER SEVENTEEN

THE WILLIAM JEFFERSON Clinton Federal Building in Sacramento was the oddest assortment of angles and shapes in a city with buildings named after Darth Vader and a stick of deodorant. The recently constructed federal building gave off an unfinished vibe with circular windows jutting out over an expansive glass lobby and arches sprouting from nowhere. The end result was an out-of-sync modern construction project glued onto a towering conservative rectangular box in the skyline. Architectural design by committee seemed the popular belief among city dwellers.

Emily found a parking spot on I Street, a block down from the building, and pulled the Crown Vic into the tight slot. She tossed an Official Police Business placard on the dash and met Javier on the sidewalk. From this distance, they could see a group of a dozen protesters near the entrance of the Federal Building. As they got closer, they read the signs carried by a diverse group, which ranged from conservative suit-wearing men to frizzy-haired women donning multicolored tie-dyed t-shirts. One of the signs read, "Medical Marijuana is Not a Crime." Another claimed, "Compassion, Not Shame."

The two detectives picked their way through the small knot of protesters and entered the federal building lobby. They held their police credentials for an older man with thinning hair who wore the red blazer of the security staff. Emily asked him, "Where can I find the U.S. Attorney's office?"

The balding security man swiveled in his chair and pointed to the elevators. "Take the elevator to the tenth floor. U.S. Attorney is in Suite 100." He stared out the window toward the protesters, and he muttered, "Damn hippies."

The elevators were to the right of the huge polished marble lobby. People squirted out of the elevators as the bronze doors spread apart. "I guess some of these offices shut down at four," Emily said, looking at her watch.

"You think Lawson is here?" Javier asked, surveying the tired faces of the workers who were leaving for the day.

Emily shrugged and held the elevator door open for her partner. "Only one way to find out," she said.

They rode in the car by themselves until it opened on the tenth floor where four women stepped into the car before they had a chance to exit. They wiggled their way past the women and stepped into the blue-carpeted hallway. Directly in front of them, a sign announced visitors to the U.S. Attorney's Offices were subject to search. An additional warning in smaller print cautioned weapons, explosives, and caustic chemicals were prohibited.

"Well, that makes me feel better. Al-Qaeda will turn and run at that warning," Emily said while she pulled open the large wooden door into Suite 100.

The comfortably furnished waiting room featured walls adorned with the usual photograph of the President, the U.S. Attorney General, and other functionaries.

Javier pointed to a photo on the bottom row. "There's our guy, Assistant U.S. Attorney Stephen Lawson."

"May I help you?" a woman's voice called out from behind a glass window. She didn't sound too friendly, and her harsh appearance did little to soften the effect. She was in her mid-forties, dark hair pulled back tightly into a knot. The slim dark business suit gave off a funereal vibe.

Emily replied, "We're here to see Stephen Lawson."

"And you are?" The woman's features were sharp, birdlike, and made her unapproachable.

"I'm Detective Hunter, this is Detective Medina, Sacramento P.D.—"

The raven cut her off. "Do you have an appointment? Mr. Lawson is a very busy man."

"Is he here, or not?"

The woman put her hands on her hips, which made her look more avian. "Can I at least tell him what this is about?"

"Tell him we're investigating a homicide."

The woman fluttered off and left them alone in the waiting room. Emily peered through the glass barrier and pointed out a magnetic in and out board with the names of the staff. Small magnetic dots marked their status and whereabouts. "Lawson's here, according to the board."

The bird woman returned and passed a harsh glance at Emily, close to the glass. "Mr. Lawson will be with you shortly. Please take a seat—over there," pointing to a sofa on the far wall.

"No thanks, I'm fine right here," Emily said, sensing the woman's discomfort.

"Humph . . ." The raven turned away and sorted some paperwork on her desk.

A second later, a metallic pop sounded, and the interior door opened. Stephen Lawson appeared, dressed in tan dress slacks, a starched white shirt, sleeves rolled up to his elbows and his pricey silk tie loosened around his neck. "Detectives? Stephen Lawson. What can I do for you?"

Emily responded carefully. "We need your help on an investigation."

"Come with me." Lawson held the door open for them and led them to his office. The office seemed gloomy and oddly dark, with the blinds drawn tight cutting off what would be a striking view from the tenth-floor corner office.

The only illumination in the room came from a task light on his desk, and the flare provided by a computer screen behind the man. "Excuse me," he said while he flipped on an overhead light.

He plopped into his chair behind the cluttered desk and sighed. "All right, what is this about. Cynthia said something about a homicide. That's really more the FBI's bailiwick."

Emily pulled a stack of files and documents from a chair and tossed them on the floor before she sat. "Detective Medina and I are investigating the murder of Roger Townsend."

Lawson made no outward reaction to the statement. "I'm not sure how I can help you, Detective."

"Did you know Roger Townsend?"

"Yes—of course. His death took me by surprise," Lawson replied in an emotionless tone.

"Murder," Emily corrected.

"What?"

"Mr. Townsend was murdered," Emily replied while she observed Lawson.

"He's dead either way, Detective. Now, I'm quite busy. Can you get to the point?" Annoyance surfaced in Lawson's voice.

"Do you know Lori Townsend?"

"Yes." Lawson's response came out more cautious this time.

"How about John Parkes?"

"No, that one doesn't ring a bell."

"Back to Lori Townsend for a second. How well do you know her?" Emily leaned back in the chair and casually stretched her legs out in front of her.

"I'm not sure if I know what you mean, Detective?"

"Sure you do, are you banging her or what?"

Lawson reacted as if hit by lightning. He put both hands flat on the desk and leaned forward. His face reddened, as he said, "You've got no right to ask that kind of question, Detective."

"Are you gonna answer?"

"No, I'm not going to dignify it with a response," Lawson said.

"Javier, that means he was," Emily said in a side comment to her partner.

Emily shook her head in mock disgust. "Let's forget about your sexual encounters with the widow. Tell me when you decided to leak investigation material to Roger?"

"What are you talking about? What investigation? The only thing I've provided to Roger Townsend was a list of high-level federal employees who may be willing to donate to one of Roger's various causes."

"See how they do it, Javi? Lawyers always pretend to answer your question, but they muddy it up. Notice he said he never gave anything to Roger. He didn't say he never gave anything to Lori." Emily stared at Lawson and then slowly spoke. "We know about the meeting in the park. We have the exchange on video."

Lawson stood up and shouted, "That's crap. I kept a copy of the list of employees I gave her. I'll show you." He got up and called for Cynthia. He turned at Emily and pleaded, "I'll get you a copy of what I gave her—I'll show you. It's in the files out here."

Lawson banged metal drawers open and shut, echoing in the outer office, feet from where the detectives waited. One second of silence grew to five, and Emily jumped up and darted into the hall. File drawers were askew, but Lawson disappeared, nowhere to be seen. The entry door banged closed.

"He's running!" Emily sprinted down the hallway, dodging the partially open file drawers.

Outside the outer door to Suite 100, the detectives heard the soft *dong* of the elevator. They ran toward the closing doors, and Emily tried to shove her hand into the crack a half-second late, and the elevator car descended to the lobby.

"Over here," Javier yelled and ran through the stairwell door around the corner from the elevators.

They bounded down the metal staircase, taking two and three steps at a time. The sound of their footfalls echoed off of the cement walls as they ran downward toward the first-floor landing. Emily hit the bar on the back side of the door, and it flew open abruptly into the busy lobby. A few employees sought out the source of the commotion, but leaving the building after the end of their workday remained more important.

The detectives scanned the faces, and they couldn't spot Lawson hiding among them. Emily ran to the aging security man and startled him, gripping him by the arm.

"Did you see Stephen Lawson?"

The man's eyes were wide in shock from the detective's sudden appearance. He opened his mouth and tried to form the words, but he nodded and pointed to the exit doors.

Javier spotted him first. "There he is! He's outside!"

They ran through the exiting employees, made it to the doors, and threw them open. Twenty feet away, Lawson broke into a run, pushing his way through the crowd in the courtyard, knocking a frail old woman to the ground.

Emily and Javier sprinted to the edge of the courtyard where the medical marijuana protesters blocked their view of Lawson. They waded into the gathering and smelled a few of the protesters expressing their opinion by lighting up a couple of fatties in front of the Federal building.

A sudden blur caught their attention. Lawson tripped and grabbed onto one of the protesters to break his fall. Both men fell to the pavement, followed by a panicked scream from a nearby tie-dyed protester. Lawson rolled onto his back and shielded his face from a woman who pummeled him with a compassion protest sign.

Emily grabbed Lawson by his feet and pulled him from under the group gathered around him. She quickly rolled the Assistant U.S. Attorney over on his stomach and placed him in handcuffs.

The potheads cheered as Javier helped Emily pull Lawson to his feet. The crowd believed the attorney attacked them, and she arrested him for interfering with their right to gather peacefully. Emily figured the protesters wouldn't be much trouble as soon as the munchies hit and drove them off in search of onion rings or corn nuts.

Lawson didn't utter a word while Emily pulled him away from the mob by his arm. A small line of blood trickled down the attorney's cheek where the protest sign had cut his face. A crimson knot above his eye began to swell.

They escorted Lawson to the Crown Vic and tossed him in the back seat. Javier spoke across the roof of the car. "He's got more going on than giving up some investigation material. You think he could be involved in Townsend's murder? Was Townsend black-mailing him?"

"He started getting squirrelly after we made the connection between Roger Townsend and the investigation," Emily said. "That's the angle we use. You don't run like that unless you're hiding something. I'll bet you dinner he'll cave."

Javier opened the car door and got in as he said, "You're on. But if I win, you come and have dinner with my family on Sunday."

CHAPTER EIGHTEEN

LEFT TO STEW for an hour and a half in a dimly lit interrogation room, Lawson hadn't said a word since being placed in cuffs at the Federal Building. The attorney waited in a hard metal chair and kept looking at the mirrored panel he recognized as an observation point for the detectives. He'd been in the room before, but never the one in restraints.

His expression turned quizzical after Emily entered with a laptop under her arm. When it registered with him, Lawson's face turned pale, and his shoulders fell slightly limp.

"I thought you might enjoy a little independent film while you wait," Emily suggested as she plugged the USB drive into the laptop.

Javier trailed with three cups of coffee on a brown cardboard tray. He set the tray down in the center of the table, removed one of the cups, and peeled back the white plastic cover. The liquid steamed as he held it up to his lips. He drew a tentative sip and put the cup on the table.

"Can I offer you a coffee, Stephen?" Emily asked.

Lawson nodded his head and whispered, "Yes, that would be nice."

Emily released Lawson from his handcuffs while Javier placed one of the cups in front of the attorney. He rubbed his wrists where they chaffed from the metal edges of the cuffs.

Emily hit the play button on the laptop, and an image of Lori Townsend waiting by the fountain in the park filled the small screen. Emily froze the image on the screen and said, "You may want to take that coffee now—this is captivating cinematography."

The attorney picked up the cup, pulled back the cover, and sipped. He held it in both hands and shrugged his shoulders in a gesture pretending to be bored. His eyes betrayed his thin veneer— they grew intent and narrow, focused on the laptop screen.

The tape rolled, and Lori paced back and forth, waiting.

"Oh, did I mention there's sound too?" and Emily turned up the volume until the background sounds of the park came to life.

Within seconds, Stephen Lawson caught himself on the screen. His bravado visibly melted as the first bits of conversation were heard. The U.S. Attorney's head slumped forward. Almost inaudibly, he said, "You have no idea what you've done."

Emily let the tape play, and she responded, "What *we've* done? This is all about you. You handed over prosecution files and jeopardized an investigation." Emily let it soak in for a second and pointed to the screen. "Here's my favorite part."

Lori's voice condemning him, "Stephen, you worry too much. Now, Roger wanted me to ask you if these files are the only copies?"

"That's it."

"And the case against these guys goes away?"

"It's gone."

Emily stopped the tape. "What investigation files are we talking about here anyway?"

Lawson remained silent. He'd given up hope of explaining the illicit exchange away.

"What did you receive from Lori in that briefcase anyway?"

A sigh from Lawson's lips. "Nothing but pain."

Emily put a hand on his arm and suggested, "Why don't we start at the beginning. How'd Roger Townsend convince you to give up your files?"

"It wasn't him. It was me. I approached Roger. I got in trouble and needed money. Roger helped bail me out the last time my gambling got out of control."

"How much were you down?" Javier asked.

"Forty-seven thousand."

"How'd you get there? What were you betting on?"

"No, it wasn't like I owed a bookie. I like playing cards. I found some underground poker club out in South Sacramento. I went up big and next thing I know I'm getting tossed out, nearly fifty thousand down."

Emily asked, "Who did you owe?"

"I didn't know who ran the place. I heard about it by word of mouth—you know, a private, no-limit card room for serious players." He cleared his throat. "I found out later some bikers ran the collections part of the business. They knew who I was all along. They also let me know they were watching what I did with the RICO investigation into the Aryan Brotherhood."

"When did you call Roger Townsend?" Emily asked.

"The very next day after the biker who runs their collections threatened to kill me in front of my family. I had to pay them off. It was about a year ago."

"Know who this biker is?" Emily asked.

He shook his head. "I never heard a name. He's a big guy, tatted up, and could pass himself off as a skinhead."

"How'd you go from a gambling debt to giving up prosecution files?"

"Roger did what he does best: negotiate. He actually met with these assholes and found they were interested in a case I had taken on. Like I said, how they found out about the A.B. RICO investigation, I have no idea. They must have someone on the inside who told them about our work to obtain a RICO indictment. But Roger came back with a settlement; if my case files disappeared, then so would my debt. In fact, he got them to throw in fifty grand for my trouble." Lawson shook his head in amazement.

"Who was the target of your investigation into the Aryan Brotherhood?"

"There were two primary targets, actually. Dean Sands, and Artie Miller, both validated A.B. members. We'd been trying to wrap up these guys with the RICO statutes, but they were very careful about how they conducted their business; always isolating themselves from the dirty work and there was a lot of it."

Javier took another sip of his cooling coffee, then asked, "How close were you to having enough to prosecute?"

"I'd gotten the last piece I needed to go to the Grand Jury for an indictment. Miller got greedy and participated in a bank robbery last summer. We gathered surveillance video, and it's pretty clear it's him."

Javier continued, "What happened after you turned the files over to Roger and Lori?"

Lawson shook his head and stated, "That's when the wheels fell off. Roger was supposed to hand over the files to the bikers at the card club." He drew a deep breath. "But he didn't. He claimed they disappeared. A week later, I got a letter in the mail with photos of me in the park with her fricken briefcase." He pointed to the laptop screen. "The letter said I needed to send ten grand a month to a post office box, or these pictures would go to the U.S. Attorney for the Eastern District."

Emily lowered heavily in her chair. "You were being blackmailed?"

Lawson nodded. "I paid. Then I got another note and another. They wanted their fifty grand back and I paid until last month."

"What happened then?" Emily urged him to continue.

"I got tired—and fed up. I told Lori about it, and she said it wasn't her problem. I couldn't sleep anymore and kept looking over my shoulder. Then last month I sent a note back to the post office box telling them to fuck off."

"And then?"

"Roger got killed."

"Who got to him?" Emily asked.

"I was in San Diego on another case—you can check it out. I got back in town last night. I think Sands, Miller, and their crew got to Roger."

Emily felt the link was missing from the story, and then an idea hit her. "When was the last time you heard from Lori Townsend?"

"This morning. She invited me to attend Roger's funeral service."

"And before that?"

Lawson paused and swallowed. "Lori called me two days before Roger was killed, urging me to pay an additional ten grand."

"She knew about it? Did you tell her?"

"She knew, but I never told anyone. She said Roger got hit for monthly payments also."

Javier shared a glance with his partner. "She neglected to mention that little detail."

"Stephen, you're in a heap of shit. How'd you think you were gonna get out of this mess?" Emily asked.

He shook his head slowly, looking at his expensive Italian leather loafers, which were now scarred and deeply scratched from his fall to the pavement. "I knew at some time or another, they'd come to collect." He tried to smile, but it made him look even more pathetic. "I thought that's what you came to my office for."

"Lucky for you—" A knock on the interrogation room door interrupted Emily.

Javier pushed back from the table and cracked open the door. Detective Josh Potter motioned him out into the hall.

Potter's assignment on the department's anti-gang task force put him in the middle of the seedy underbelly of organized street crime. He handed him an envelope.

"What's this?"

"I've been watching from the observation room behind the glass. After he started talking about the Aryan Brotherhood, I used these in a photo lineup we did a few weeks back. The photos include the known A.B. leadership in the Sacramento area," Potter said.

Javier opened the envelope and slid out four eight-by-ten cards with DMV photographs laid out in two rows of three on each card. Officers called them "six-packs." Javier thumbed through them quickly sorting the cards. He abruptly stopped at one photo and pointed. "John Parkes? He wasn't an Aryan Brotherhood member, was he?"

Josh tapped the photo and responded, "Oh, hell no. A sympathizer for sure, but he wasn't bright enough to make the cut. They'd use Johnny P. for lightweight work, drug pickups, that sort of thing."

Another photo caught his eye. "Anything you need to tell me, Josh," he said with a smirk. Javier held up a "six-pack" with Josh's photo up in the upper left corner.

The picture displayed his shaved head, lightning bolt tattoos on his neck, and a long walrus-like mustache down the edge of his jawline.

Josh laughed. "I forgot about that one. We have to be fair about it. God, my mustache itched, and it took a week to wash off the fake tattoo ink. My partner thought it would be funny to use a permanent marker." He reached to take the card back.

Javier held onto it and stuffed the photo cards back into the envelope.

"Thanks, Josh. I'll let you know if Lawson ID's any of these guys." They were fortunate Potter had overheard part of the conversation.

"See if he can tell you where those RICO files are. The information in there would put a number of these guys away for decades."

Javier nodded and ducked back inside where Lawson repeated the story of the exchange of files for the money in the park.

He waved the envelope at Emily and exposed the edge of one of the "six-packs." Emily understood and nodded in agreement.

"Mr. Lawson, I'm going to show you a number of photos. You tell me who you know." Javier proceeded to place the four cards side by side across the table in front of the attorney. Twenty-four angry white men stared back from the paper. The dim fluorescent lighting gave each photo a sinister grey pallor.

The attorney grew increasingly uncomfortable in this arrangement. He'd always been on the other side of the table, coercing someone else to make an identification of a suspect. After he got their testimony and put away the bad guy, the witnesses never posed a concern for him. Now, it looked like he pondered the consequences to himself and his family if he cooperated further.

Emily sensed his growing reluctance. "Which one is the man you know as Sands?"

Resembling a slow-moving Ouija board pointer, Lawson's finger centered over the third card and paused. Then suddenly he dropped his hand and tapped his finger on a face. "This one— that's Sands," he sighed.

The photo of a medium-build man with a shaved head and long dark mustache glowered back at Lawson. An old scar on the man's right cheek gave him the appearance of a permanent sneer.

"And Miller?"

More quickly this time, but reluctantly, Lawson identified Michael Miller on the first photo "six-pack."

Miller had long, greying dark hair and a thick muscular neck. The man's eyes were so light blue they were almost transparent— they appeared soulless. Beneath a white wifebeater T-shirt, the tops of his shoulders were visible in the photo, covered in various jailhouse tattoos, the detail of which couldn't be deciphered.

Javier scooped up the "six-packs" and shoved them back into the envelope. He smirked at his partner and said, "Guess who's coming to dinner?"

Leaving the broken attorney in the room to await federal authorities, the detectives returned to their desks.

Emily stopped. "Why don't you come by my place, and I'll cook."

In mock disappointment, Javier responded, "But I won the bet. I shouldn't have to eat that."

"Come on."

"A deal's a deal. You know my mom wanted to have you over for dinner. Tonight's the night, remember? So suck it up and do it."

She dropped the photo envelope on her desk, leaned back, and stretched her sore back. "Where do we go next?"

Emily rooted through her phone message slips and said, "I want to run the photos past Benjamin Tooker at Corona's office and see if either Sands or Miller is the guy who ransacked the place." She picked up a pink phone message slip and observed. "Tooker wanted to talk to us too. He's probably gone for the day, and I'm beat. Let's run past his place tomorrow morning."

Javier brushed a hand through his hair and nodded. "Besides, you're coming to our place and help Mom cook up a gourmet meal. That's her idea of getting to know you better. She expects to see you with Brian. Is six thirty all right?"

"Tonight? That only gives me about an hour and a half," Emily said.

"You're not getting ready for the prom, but shower—please—and get presentable."

Emily flipped him off.

CHAPTER NINETEEN

An hour later, the Medina kitchen hummed along in full swing. Lucinda waved Emily over to the cutting board and put her to work, preparing a yellow summer squash casserole. Emily took the task short on the details, but she started cutting up the vegetables while Lucinda seasoned and marinated the steaks. Emily brought her mom, and Connie worked prepping a mixed green salad.

"Honey, I forgot to ask, how was your day?" Connie said.

"The usual crazy."

"Don't forget to do your homework."

Emily's heart sunk again and she flicked her eyes at Lucinda who carried a casserole dish to the cutting board. In a whisper, Lucinda explained Connie had been confused all afternoon. The dementia was more pronounced than the day before.

"What am I going to do for her?" Emily said.

Lucinda slid a small slip of paper from a pocket in her apron and handed it to Emily. Emily unfolded it, revealing the names of three residential care facilities.

"I know all three places—they are safe and have good people working there."

Emily shook her head. "I guess I'm kidding myself—that she might improve."

"Dementia isn't the flu. You don't get over it. It's part of her now, and we need to help her cope with everything that comes with it—the lapses in memory, confusion, and agitation. It's not coming from her, it's coming from this condition that has her."

"You're right. My mind knows you're right, but my heart—God, this is so unfair."

The front door opened and Javier entered, and he wasn't alone. A petite woman with olive skin, jet black long hair, and the darkest eyes Emily had ever seen came inside with him. Emily bit her lip.

Javier caught Emily's reaction. "Emily, this is Theresa."

Emily wiped her hands on a towel and greeted them. Theresa seemed comfortable with Javier, leaning on him, then taking his jacket before stepping away to hang it up. She'd been here before.

"She is so out of your league," Emily whispered.

"Tell me about it," he responded.

"Theresa, where did you meet Javier?"

Theresa unfolded an apron from a drawer and needed to wrap the ties around twice to secure it around her slim waist.

"So out of your league," Emily repeated.

Theresa didn't hear the comment. "Javi and I met at the station."

"Station?"

"Theresa is a broadcast journalist down at Channel 8. Remember the interview for the department's recruitment? Theresa interviewed me."

"That was six months ago."

"Yeah . . ."

"How did you, of all people, keep this a secret for six fricken months?"

Lucinda intervened. "Javier, please start the grill."

He wasted no time in slipping out the door.

"He talks a lot about you, Emily. He says you do the job while everyone else stands around with an opinion about how to start."

"I'm usually more of a cautionary tale."

"He says you're smart and can think your way around obstacles."

"I'll have to remind him."

Theresa turned to tend a pot on the stove, a task Lucinda didn't relegate to Emily.

"I'm gonna check on Javier and make sure he doesn't burn the place down," Emily said. She pulled two bottles of a local micro-brew beer from the refrigerator and stepped out to the patio where Javi tended to the charcoal. She handed a cold bottle over.

"Thanks," Javier said.

"I see you're drinking your hipster beer."

"It's not hipster."

"It couldn't be any more hipster if it had kale in it."

"Whatever. I prefer it."

"It reeks of patchouli and pretense." She sipped the bottle, winced and paused. "Theresa seems nice. So, six months?"

"I'm about to throw the steaks on. How do you want yours?"

"I'm guessing by the way you are avoiding the subject, you feel guilty about keeping secrets from your partner."

Javier held his hand over the white-hot coals. "Maybe a little. It's—"

"You're afraid Theresa is jealous of me?" Emily couldn't keep from laughing.

"I don't want to ruin this. I mean, if I talk too much about it, or show her too much of what it is we do, she'll run off."

"Give her some credit, Javi. She's a bright girl."

"That's what's got me worried. She might be too bright, and she doesn't need the 'stuff' we bring home every night."

"You need to compartmentalize. Leave work at work."

"How does that work out for you?"

"It doesn't. But that's what the experts tell you to do." Emily pulled another swig from her bottle.

"Let me put the steaks on."

Javier opened the back door and returned with a platter of marinated New York strips. Each steak sizzled as it hit the hot grill.

"The backyard's nice. The barbecue island is new, right?" Emily said.

"About four months. I saw what you did, and I convinced Mom to put one in here. I live in my little condo, and there's no room for an upscale outdoor kitchen."

"I've got to think about how to babyproof my yard if Mom stays with me. I can't have her hurting herself with the grill or the wrought-iron garden fencing. I need to make sure she can't escape either."

"Having her living with you has been a big adjustment for both of you."

"Yeah, no—I don't know what to do about her. Your mom gave me a few references for facilities I can look at, but it seems to me I'm throwing her away—know what I mean?"

"I get that, I do. Can you give your mom what she needs twenty-four seven? That's when a place for people with memory care issues starts to look better," Javier said.

"I need to think about it, and figure out how I can afford a place for her on my salary."

Javier turned the steaks on the grill, and a fresh wave of sizzle drew Theresa outside.

"Almost ready?" She tucked her dark hair behind her ear. She pointed at the bottle in Emily's hand. "You drink those?"

"Usually? God no, but it's all he had."

"I keep telling him he doesn't need to drink skunk beer to be one of the cool kids."

"See, Javi, I told you she was a bright one."

Javier blushed and started taking the steaks off the grill.

Emily had changed from her nondescript business attire to a pair of tight fitting jeans, a flattering light blue sweater, and her hair was down.

"You look like this more often, and you could get a date with Officer Booty Bandit. Wasn't he supposed to come tonight?"

"Officer what?" Theresa said.

She pointed the barbecue fork at him. "I don't need your dating advice. Not that it's any of your business, I'm meeting Brian later tonight for a drink. I don't know if I'm gonna go through with it." She set her beer bottle on the barbecue island.

"Now I'm hurt," Javier replied and hefted the plate of steaks hot from the grill. "Here I thought you got dolled up for us."

Beer spit from Emily's mouth and nose. She coughed until she could breathe again.

"Did you borrow those clothes from Lori Townsend? I didn't know you owned anything that said, 'come hither.'"

"Ass. But speaking of the widow—I picked up the paper and found a funeral announcement for Roger's service tomorrow."

"Lori didn't waste too much time, did she?"

"No kidding. The guy's ashes haven't even cooled off yet."

"What time is the service?" he said as he carried the platter of steaks inside.

"It's at one, at East Lawn Memorial Cemetery, off of Folsom Boulevard and 46th Street."

"Let's say we follow her tomorrow after the service and see where she takes us," he suggested.

They devoured the meal quickly, and Emily begged off, letting Javier and Theresa enjoy some time together. Javier said she should go home and "get pretty," as he called it.

Emily drove Connie home and considered canceling her date, but her mom insisted she go out. Connie said she'd be in bed anyway.

She changed twice, checking out the wardrobe in the mirror, and ended up back in the jeans and blue sweater. As she opened the front door, her cell phone chimed. She smiled as she pulled up the text from Brian, Officer Booty Bandit. The smile evaporated with the message. He'd been held over on mandatory overtime and had to cancel their date.

She closed the door and leaned against the doorframe while she typed a response with her thumbs.

"Rain check?"

"Definitely! And I'm sorry I needed to cancel," he answered.

"It comes with the job."

Emily slogged up to her room and changed into comfy pants and a sweatshirt. She opened a bottle of the same brand of Javier's hipster beer from her refrigerator, positioned herself at the computer in her office, and put her feet up on the nearby two-drawer filing cabinet.

She'd never admit to Javier, but the microbrew wasn't half bad.

Within seconds, the cat that wasn't her cat hopped up and started purring.

"Where did you come from? Did Mom let you in?"

The cat ignored her and curled up in her lap while she booted up the PC. Emily connected to the internet and typed in the web address for a local paper. Within a minute, she found another obituary for Roger Townsend.

The abbreviated mention reported that Lori Townsend requested donations go in Roger's name to the Townsend Memorial Cancer Research Fund. Ever the upwardly mobile socialite, Lori Townsend featured in the printed piece more often than the dead man himself. Lori was his third wife, and twenty years his junior, if she gave the reporter an accurate date of birth.

Surfing to an internet search engine, Emily typed in Lori Townsend's name and hit the enter key. Seven pages of hits came back, the first three lines referring to an Alaskan Iditarod champion. She narrowed the search and typed in Sacramento in the search text along with the woman's name.

The first hit came from the local newspaper's account of the home invasion and death of prominent philanthropist Roger Townsend. The article closed with a mention of Lori Townsend, the victim's wife, suffering a brutal beating, then was bound, but managed to survive the vicious attack.

Another covered a social event approximately a year earlier—Roger and Lori caught in a photograph together with glasses of champagne. The caption read, *Roger Townsend donates fifty thousand dollars to local children's charity*. No mention of Lori.

The next five websites covered events more than six months ago. They were the same, featuring Roger Townsend. Lori, if mentioned, seemed to be arm candy for the venture capitalist and community advocate. Emily felt the emergence of a pattern much deeper than the photo opportunities. Lori depended on her husband for everything—the social status, the access to those in power, even her string of sexual encounters tied back to Roger. Without him, what would she have? There was a change six months ago.

Emily made a mental note to review Lori Townsend's bank records in the morning. She requested the account information on the husband the day following the murder but hadn't received them yet. Anderson provided the documents from Roger's firm, and pointed out a number of recent transactions within the last six months. Where was the four million dollars now?

The final website she checked surprised her, and she was happy her mom had gone to her room. The site contained venomous hate and anger directed at none other than Lori Townsend. The title of the page glared off the screen, "Lori is a Slut," in dripping red print. A two-paragraph essay in the center of the page described vividly how the writer found her husband sleeping with, as she described, "that two-bit whore, Lori." Arranged around the web page were photos of Lori with another man, presumably the woman's husband, in various states of undress. The offended woman placed black bars over her husband's face and sensitive areas to camouflage his appearance. Lori, on the other hand, was displayed bare, in all her glory.

Emily hit the print button on her computer, and a black-and-white version slowly rolled out of the printer. The woman's web page did not contain any contact information or her name. The computer guys at work would pull the IP address from the website and, hopefully, trace it back to the person who put this on the web.

She didn't realize she'd been at the computer for nearly three hours. She reached for a pull off the beer and found it musty and warm. Hipster beer needed to come with a serve-when-cold warning label. She shut down the computer and dumped the skunky beer down the sink, followed by a liberal dose of dish soap to cut the hipster aroma.

She let the cat out and locked the door. The yellow eyes glared at her in betrayal.

"What? Go home."

The cat turned her back to Emily and sat on the back porch.

"Whatever."

Emily turned out the kitchen light and headed upstairs, checking in on her mother on the way. Connie was sound asleep in her room. Emily couldn't settle and ended up dozing on the sofa in between thoughts of Lori Townsend's rise into prominence and the gang ties to her husband's murder. The gang hits on Roger, and Wayne Corona, were centered on getting what they needed from the victims. They were both beaten before they were killed, and their offices were ransacked. If they hadn't found what they searched for, it meant the killers would keep pressing until they did. Lori Townsend was next in line.

CHAPTER TWENTY

JAVIER JOINED HIS partner in the detective bureau at seven. He hung his jacket on the back of his chair and noticed Emily had stopped off at Starbucks on her way in. A large white and green paper cup with steam venting from the lid rested in the center of his desk. He picked it up and blew on the scalding surface. "You're an angel."

"So I keep hearing."

Javier raised an eyebrow. "Officer Booty?"

"We had to cancel," Emily said while looking through a thick document.

"Because?"

"Timing, Javi. It's always timing." She ended the line of conversation and picked up a document on her desk. "This is a report from the lab folks on the money and MAC-10s we found at the Marshall Hotel."

Javier carried his coffee and read the report over Emily's shoulder. The bulk of the document consisted of page after page of photocopies documenting each scrap of currency recovered. Without Emily pointing it out, he noticed the currency displayed in sequential serial number order.

"Now where'd they get this, some White Supremacy ATM?" Javier said.

Emily turned in her chair. "Actually I don't think you're too far off. The bills are twenties, exactly what you'd expect from an ATM."

She turned back around, picked up another report, this one much thinner than the first. "This is a list of bank robberies and ATM thefts in the last year within a fifty mile radius." The list contained four armed robberies and a dozen attempted and actual thefts from local ATMs.

Javier nodded. "Why only the last year? The cash bag could've lived with the spiders under the hotel floorboards for years."

Emily smiled and pointed to the photocopy image of one of the twenties. "See there next to Jackson's shoulder to the right? The year. This is a new bill."

"Huh—you traced the bills with the FBI to a specific bank yet?"

"I left a message with the Feds, but I don't think we need it." She turned the page on the robbery list. "There are only two with multiple white male suspects, and in both robberies, automatic weapons were fired into the ceiling to get everyone's attention."

She handed Javier the report, which identified the shell casings left at the robberies as .45 caliber. "They could have come from the MAC-10s."

"David Black down in the crime lab thought that too. He got the ATF to share the NIBIN data on the robberies."

Javier knew the Bureau of Alcohol, Tobacco, Firearms, and Explosives operated the National Integrated Ballistic Information Network with over three million pieces of ballistic evidence and worked with local law enforcement to secure arrests and convictions for gun crime. "They were in the database?"

"Sort of—Black compared the slugs and brass from the robberies, and NIBIN data against test-fired slugs from the weapons we recovered. The shell casings held similar scratches from the ejector ports of the MACs, but the slugs didn't match up."

"Similar ejection port marks? Must be another MAC-10; one we didn't recover at the Marshall."

"Exactly. But the good news is a partial print on a shell from the first robbery lines up with a print our folks got off the plastic wrap on the currency bundles. Michael Artie Miller, one of the guys Lawson identified for us yesterday."

"Must've been the dream of another chance at Officer Booty Bandit got your neurons fired up this morning."

"Oh, shut up," she said.

Emily pulled the envelope containing the photo "six-packs" from the desk and tapped it in her palm. "Let's run by Corona's law office and see if Benjamin Tooker can make out any of these guys as the one who ransacked the law office. He wanted me to call him yesterday, so let's drop by."

They pulled equipment together for a day of following Lori Townsend to the funeral service where they planned to observe the grieving widow in her glory. Digital cameras with telephoto lenses, radio equipment, and a slightly illegal magnetically mounted GPS unit were stashed in a zippered black nylon bag.

On their way out to the parking lot, a wheezing and puffing Captain Howard approached them with his hand held out in front of him. Someone had parked in the Captain's designated spot, and this time it wasn't Emily. After the Captain lifted the door handle on the trespassing sedan, he came away with a handful of soft dog poo, carefully tucked away under the handle, waiting.

"If you were involved with this, Hunter, I swear you'll be on parking enforcement before nightfall."

"Not me, Captain. I'm parked right over there. That's a motor pool car."

For months, someone had left dog droppings on the Captain's car. Emily wanted to express her thanks to the person and shake his hand; well, maybe a simple thank you would do.

The two detectives got into the Crown Vic and left Howard with one hand holding his utility belt up around his belly, and the other held out as if he'd touched a leper.

*   *   *

Corona's downtown law offices were minutes away. Finding a parking spot proved more of a challenge. Every metered spot within three blocks held a car displaying a disabled placard. Emily didn't mind those who needed the assistance using the handicapped spaces, but based upon the scores of blue parking placards hanging from rearview mirrors, Sacramento should be awash in wheelchairs, crutches, and guide dogs.

Finally, she pulled the sedan into a spot behind a fiery red Mazda Miata. An overweight woman climbed from the Mazda, clad in some odd purple-colored t-shirt with a message of support for a labor rally at the Capitol steps. She pulled a briefcase strap over one arm and toted a plastic blue and white lunch box, large enough to feed a small family, in the other. Seconds before she closed the car door, the woman hooked a disabled placard to the rearview mirror.

Emily watched her waddle across the traffic lanes, fully expecting the oncoming cars to stop for her. They did, with horns blaring.

The detectives traveled in the opposite direction, four blocks, until they were at the Corona law office storefront. Benjamin Tooker unlocked the front door as they arrived.

He looked flustered. Tooker clearly wasn't expecting them at the law office. "I thought you'd call. I left you a message yesterday. I think I found what the dude came looking for."

Tooker leaned a stack of folded empty cardboard boxes against the wall while he pocketed the keys and pulled on the door. As the detectives eyed the boxes, he explained, "With Wayne gone, we gotta close up. I'm packing up what I can and getting the stuff to storage. He's got family coming in from the East Coast to go through his things, but the landlord wants the office empty by the first."

Emily and Javier followed Tooker into the lobby area of the office where most of the books and office equipment rested in boxes, ready for the movers. Tooker dropped the stack of empty boxes on a vacant desktop.

"Where's everyone else?" Emily asked as she studied the vacant office space.

"Gone."

"Who's paying you to do this?"

"Nobody—I owe it to Mr. Corona. He gave me a chance when no one else did; me being an ex-con and all."

Javier asked, "What are you gonna do now?"

He shrugged. "Don't know. Not much of a calling for an ex-con with firearms priors."

"You could call some of Corona's lawyer friends and see if they need any help."

"I did make a couple of calls, but some of 'em are pretty shady."

Emily responded, "Of course they are, they're attorneys."

Tooker smiled and said, "Thanks. You didn't come here to see to my employment concerns, Detective." He reached back on the desk he sat on, picked up a file folder, and handed it over to Emily.

"What's this?" she asked while she opened the folder.

"I found it stuck behind the fax machine. Divorce papers. Roger Townsend was filing for divorce."

Tooker stepped over and turned a couple of pages in the file. "The papers say if Roger died, his estate would go to Lori. But if he divorced her, the prenuptial agreement would kick in."

Emily read the fax document. "Why bother with a divorce if he knew he was going to die soon?" she said.

"Have you met the missus?" Tooker responded. "From what Corona let leak, Roger Townsend didn't want her to cash in on his estate and didn't want Lori to get a dime after the divorce. He claims irreconcilable differences and adultery."

"No big shock there," Emily added. Then she asked, "Do you know when this was faxed?"

Tooker ruffled through the pages and pulled the printed confirmation from the bottom of the pile. "Three weeks ago. Here's the phone number." He pointed with a thick, scarred finger.

"Recognize the number?"

Tooker shook his head. "No. It doesn't register with me."

Emily asked, "Do you think this is what the guy broke in for?"

"Maybe—he stole all the Townsend files he could find. These papers weren't in the file at the time. But this wouldn't be worth getting Wayne killed."

Emily pulled the photo "six-packs" from their envelope and handed them to Tooker. "See anyone familiar?"

"I'm not used to being on this side of the lineup." He scanned the first photo card and pointed to the image of one of the men who had beaten and threatened the law office staff.

"This is one of the guys."

It wasn't Michael "Artie" Miller or Dean Sands; it was Detective Josh Potter.

CHAPTER TWENTY-ONE

"POTTER?" EMILY SAID. She rolled her eyes at the accusation. On the sidewalk outside the offices, she turned to her partner. "Tooker's lying. Josh and I were in the same academy class, and he's always been by the book."

After Benjamin Tooker identified the detective in the lineup, he identified Mike "Artie" Miller as the other man in the law office. Miller was the man Tooker remembered from Pelican Bay State Prison.

"That's one crazy dude. He'd fight the cops for the thrill. The man would get beat down every time, but he kept provoking 'em," Tooker said.

"How did Potter end up in the middle of this?" Javier said.

"He didn't. Tooker's an ex-con tryin' to save his own ass," Emily said.

"Why would he tell us Potter was involved?" Javier thought aloud. They turned to the street and watched the morning traffic strangle the intersections.

"He's hiding something. Tooker knows more than he told us and he's holding back 'cause he's afraid, or could be Tooker's somehow involved in taking out Wayne Corona," Emily said.

"Let's say Tooker is telling us the truth," Javier said.

"He isn't," Emily shot back.

"Then why would he identify Potter and Miller as the two guys who ransacked the law office?"

Emily grew silent, the way she did when she tried to piece a puzzle together. "To hide who was really at the office, looking for these documents." Emily held up the file folder.

Javier prodded her on. "What possible connection could tie Potter to Miller, Dean Sands, or Lori Townsend?"

She wrinkled her forehead and said, "Potter works the gang unit; Miller and Sands are gangsters, and Lori Townsend is, well . . ."

"Outgoing?" Javier offered.

"That's one way to put it."

"You think Potter and Lori Townsend have something going on?"

Emily shrugged. "I wouldn't think so, but if Potter is in this, that's the most logical angle."

The thought of Josh Potter doing Lori Townsend made Emily nauseous. A few weeks out of the academy, Emily acted so uncharacteristically it scared her. She met Josh at a bar and drank enough to lower her inhibitions, not intoxicated, but sufficiently tipsy to hit on Potter and his damned dark brown eyes. Not subtly either. She told him she wanted him to take her home and let nature take its course.

Josh did, and nature did, repeatedly for two months. Then abruptly, Josh called it off, without any reason Emily could understand. He mentioned department policy frowned on their kind of relationship. She wondered what that meant, and what kind of relationship was that? It was so Josh—by the book. What happened to the Josh she remembered, and where was the rule book now if he had a relationship going with a married Lori Townsend?

Javier jarred Emily back to the present when he said, "Could Tooker be right about the prenup? What would it leave Lori with after Roger filed for a divorce?"

"According to the agreement, she'd end up with one of the homes and about a hundred grand," Emily summarized from the document.

"That's not bad. She wasn't going to be destitute," Javier said.

"But it's a small fraction of what Roger and his company were worth. Assuming he died and no other will or trust contradicted it, she'd acquire all of his assets. The estate is worth millions."

At that moment, Benjamin Tooker came outside with a large box, surprised to see the detectives waiting in front of the office.

"Can I help you with anything else?" he responded awkwardly.

"What's in the box, Benjamin? I thought the movers were gonna take the stuff." Emily nodded to the large cardboard moving box.

He dropped the box to the sidewalk, and it hit with a thump. "Some personal files of Mr. Corona's and some of my things."

Emily pulled open a folded cardboard flap. A laptop computer, two cell phones, and a digital camera lay on top of a stack of plain manila file folders.

"Enough to start a new business here, huh, Benjamin?"

"Man, Mr. Corona would want me to keep them."

"You could sell and trade for the information on his computer?"

"It ain't like that," Tooker demanded.

"I'll tell you what," Emily said as she hit the remote trunk release on the Crown Vic. The trunk lid popped up down the block. "We're gonna take this as evidence, and if we feel warm and fuzzy about it, you'll get it back." Emily motioned Tooker to take the box to the car.

Javier went ahead and kept the street people from rummaging through the trunk while Emily escorted Tooker to the vehicle. The box ate up most of the available space after Javier pushed aside bulky first aid kits, blankets, raid jackets, and ballistic vests to make room. Emily handed Tooker a slip of paper as a receipt for the box and a quick inventory of the contents.

"This ain't right, Detective," Tooker complained. "I did what you asked. I called when I found them papers. And then you treat me this way?"

"If it checks out, I'll release it to you. Quit whining." Emily paused. "You're sure about the two men you saw in the office? The ones you ID'd from the pictures?"

"Yeah, man, I already told you. The big hairy guy is the crazy dude from Pelican Bay. The younger guy who came with him, I never seen before then. But young dude came off as one crazy white boy when he turned the place over for them files."

Emily listened as a pickup truck with large dual rear wheels roared into the intersection. The truck's high sheen paint and polished side panels told it never touched a country road. An impractically large vehicle attempted to make up for the driver's other shortcomings.

The back of the detective's brain began to fire, but she couldn't put her finger on it. Emily watched the truck inch forward, up onto the curb into the left turn lane, clearing the signal light pole by less than a foot before it bounced down into the traffic lane. The damn thing didn't belong on these streets.

"What?" Javier asked.

"It doesn't fit," she responded quietly.

"Of course not. He doesn't know what he's driving."

Emily's eyes sharpened. "Roger Townsend wasn't killed as part of some extortion plan. He didn't know what he was driving."

"What do you mean?"

"Why would these guys whack their money man? He had something else they wanted, really bad."

"The RICO files," Javier said matter-of-factly.

"Which means our grieving widow lied about the whole home invasion routine? She knew why they came for him."

"And with her husband's death, the divorce never got filed, and she inherits everything," Javier filled in the blanks.

Emily glanced at her watch and tapped her palm on the roof of the car. "Maybe we follow through with our plan to tail Lori today, to and from her husband's funeral service, with one little change."

"What's that?" Javier asked.

"We make sure she knows we're following her. It's time to turn up the heat."

CHAPTER TWENTY-TWO

LORI TOWNSEND'S BLOND ponytail bounced out of the back of her white baseball cap as she trotted down the imported stone tile walkway of her Granite Bay home. A white clingy low-cut crop top over a slim pair of low-rise khaki pants gave off a curated care-free vibe.

From the front seat of the Crown Vic, Javier held the telephoto lens of the camera at the front door as Lori popped out. There wasn't a hundred-dollar gym bag slung over her shoulder, so no aerobics class this morning. The camera made a slight electronic click when he hit the shutter button.

"I guess funerals are more casual these days," Javier said, looking through the viewfinder.

Lori hopped into the Porsche, accelerated out of the drive and away from the plush neighborhood. Emily pulled onto the street and followed within a hundred feet of Lori's car.

She drove north on Auburn-Folsom Road until she turned a quick left against a light at Douglas and parked in an upscale strip mall, in front of a coffee shop. Emily waited for a break in the traffic and ran the light also. She pulled in about four spots over from the Porsche and got out of the car.

"What are you doing?" Javier whispered.

"I've got a sudden urge for coffee. You?"

Javier tucked the camera under the front seat, got out of the car, and joined Emily at the front door of the busy coffee bistro.

Emily held the door for Javier, and the smell of roasted coffee beans, burnt espresso, and hot milk hit them. A menu scrawled in elaborate script on a blackboard above the counter listed no coffee beverage less than four and a half bucks.

Emily nodded to the head of the line where Lori Townsend placed her order. They couldn't hear exactly what she wanted, but it included non-fat and low foam.

Lori scooted to the other side of the curved wooden bar and waited while a twenty-year-old girl steamed up her beverage. She watched the girl's every move. To Emily, it looked like Lori waited for an opportunity to put the younger girl, a slight wisp of a thing with a naturally beautiful complexion, in her place. There was a slight air of jealousy turned loathing as the cute girl handed Lori the drink with a pert, "Thank you, ma'am."

Emily watched Lori while Javier ordered two black coffees. The cashier acted as if he'd asked her to change the oil in his car. She shrugged and poured two cups from a large metal tub behind her. He paid eight-fifty for the two black coffees and turned to Emily. Lori either didn't notice the two detectives or pretended indifference.

She motioned to a table outside, under a canopy, and Javier opened the door with his hip. The immediate relief from the humidity inside made it easier to breathe, not only for the two detectives but for Lori and three other women clustered around a table checking their makeup for heat damage. The opening and closing of small makeup kits made the sound of a herd of crickets— really big, mean, self-absorbed crickets.

Javier hovered at a table on the opposite side of the patio from Lori and her coven. Emily caught his eye and motioned him over. Javier knew what his partner wanted and gave her a serious look as he approached a table directly behind Lori.

Emily pulled a chair out, and the metal legs screamed across the flagstone patio. She got a few looks from those around her, but nothing from Lori and her companions.

Javier handed Emily a cup. They didn't need to wait long for a reaction. It started with a blond woman on the opposite side of the table from Lori. Her eyes changed, but her expression couldn't show surprise because the Botox wouldn't allow a display of emotion. Emily remembered her from the aerobics studio. The woman put a hand to her mouth and whispered to the redhead next to her. The redhead stiffened and clutched Lori's hand.

Lori turned and smiled at the two detectives, less than five feet away. She twisted her hips in her chair and tipped her face toward them. "Good morning, Detectives. Would you care to join us?"

In unison, the detectives raised their coffee cups.

"No thanks, Mrs. Townsend. We're only grabbing a quick cup," Emily said.

"And you came all the way out here . . ."

"The coffee's good here," Emily lied. It was bitter and stale from sitting on the heat too long.

Lori's eyes narrowed, and her voice iced over. She no longer played the role of the poor widow. "I'm surprised you have the time with a killer to catch. I'll bet my good friend Johnny doesn't know you're wasting the city's dime like this." She pulled out her cell, tapped out a number, and tucked it next to her ear.

"Johnny, it's Lori—yes, sweetie, I'm fine. But I would feel much better if your two officers would move on with finding the person responsible for Roger's murder." Then in a false tone projecting she felt hurt and scared: "They really should leave me alone on the morning of my husband's funeral . . ."

Emily watched the performance and wondered if Lori ever lived one genuine moment.

A smug look on Lori's face appeared as she handed the cell phone off to the detective. "The Mayor wants to talk to you."

Emily took the phone from Lori's outstretched hand and locked eyes with her. "Hunter here."

Emily listened briefly and calmly reported back, "Nope. Having coffee with Detective Medina."

She handed the phone back to Lori at the Mayor's suggestion, and Lori put the phone to her ear. "Johnny, will you—what? That's not acceptable, John. I will not tolerate these—these—incompetent people—" A slight paleness crept into her complexion as she listened to the voice on the other end.

She turned away from the detectives and replied in a harsh voice, "They don't need to have coffee in my backyard."

Lori stabbed a manicured finger, disconnecting the call, and threw the cell phone on the table, knocking over one of the women's non-fat-decaf-no-foam-something-or-another.

All four women stood, afraid the tan spill would stain their designer clothing. A young barista sensed the impending fashion disaster and swept in wiping up the mess with a large white towel.

Lori ignored the barista's attempt to clean the mess, left the table, abandoning her drink and her friends as she left for the parking lot.

"The coffee break is over," Emily said as she watched Lori Townsend huff over to her car.

The two detectives got up and gratefully tossed their cups into a garbage can on the way to their car. Lori was easy to follow because traffic on Douglas Boulevard slowed for repaving and the traffic merged into a single lane. The column of vehicles inched along toward Interstate 80 when Lori's Porsche jumped onto the shoulder and passed a small white truck on the right before veering into traffic on the interchange.

The Porsche settled in the traffic on Highway 65 heading northbound until it suddenly hit the brakes and exited on Galleria Boulevard toward the upscale mall.

"Shopping? She's going shopping," Javier stated, dumbfounded.

"Wouldn't surprise me. She needs to prepare for her performance this afternoon at Roger's funeral service."

Lori pulled her Porsche to the curb in a designated no parking zone in front of a delivery truck. She hopped out and trotted inside the entrance doors.

"Can you believe that? She thinks she gets to park wherever?" Javier uttered.

"So do we," she replied as she pulled the Crown Vic in front of Lori's Porsche, effectively blocking it in.

Emily popped out and tapped the front bumper of the Porsche with her hand and rushed to keep up with the woman.

Javier followed his partner inside and hurried to catch up with her. She wasn't running, but she moved fast enough to keep Lori in sight. Emily expected the woman to peel off for the Nordstrom store to the right side of the mall, but instead, Lori stopped at a counter near Pottery Barn. A Shopping Concierge Center.

Emily stood a few feet behind her and listened while Lori Townsend asked for a package from her personal shopper. The young woman behind the counter listened intently, nodded, and then lifted a garment bag from behind the counter. Lori slipped a ten-dollar bill to the young woman and hefted her black and gold garment bag, folding it across her arm. She turned and her face drew pale at the sight of the two detectives. Lori nearly stumbled over a runaway free-range toddler before she strode defiantly back in the direction of the glass doors.

She brushed past the two detectives and pushed her way through the light crowd to the exit. Lori noticed her car was blocked by the police vehicle, and she stopped dead in her tracks. Turning on her heels, she shook visibly.

"What do you want from me?" she shouted.

Emily leaned up against the fender of the Crown Vic and crossed her arms. She paused before she spoke. "I'm thinking who-ever killed your husband knew what they wanted. They may come for you next."

"The man who killed Roger and assaulted me got what he was after—money and his jewelry. I gave you the list. Johnny told me the man died in jail. Please, leave me alone. You've done your job. I need to prepare for Roger's service. Now please move your car."

Without another word, Emily circled around the police sedan, got in the driver's door, and started the Crown Vic.

Lori tossed the garment bag into the passenger seat of her car and circled around to the driver's side. She got in and caught Emily's eyes in the detective's rearview mirror, as they glared back at her. She started the Porsche, and the throaty rumble of the engine reverberated off the structure of the mall. She gunned the engine twice, and the detectives in the car ahead of her didn't budge.

Frustrated, Lori shoved the sports car in reverse and crept back-ward. A loud air horn from a boxy red truck stopped her before she backed into the delivery truck.

Emily noticed the widow's head drop into her hands after she nearly collided with the truck. Her shoulders shook, and she sobbed.

"I think she's where we want her. Do you have a copy of the divorce papers we got from Tooker?"

"Yeah—why?" Javier said.

"I got an idea. This should do the trick," she replied as she waved a copy of the formal document, titled PETITION FOR DISSOLUTION OF MARRIAGE from Javier's hand. She opened her door and left it ajar while she strode to Lori's vehicle.

She rattled the paper in Lori's window. The widow cried, and the tears appeared real. Emily rested her forearms on the window frame and got within a few inches of Lori's ear.

"We know Roger was divorcing you and you weren't gonna get a dime."

"What are you talking about?" she responded unconvincingly.

"I'm talking about this," Emily said while she held the document out in one hand.

Lori struck out with feline quickness and tried to grab the document. A guttural sound came from deep in her throat as she reached for the paper. She missed, and Emily felt the heat from her anger.

"Give me that. You have no right!"

"Now, now, now," Emily warned as she pulled the legal document away. "You sure are lucky your husband died before these were filed in court. Maybe too lucky." She folded the document, put it in her jacket pocket, and returned to the Crown Vic, without out a backward look.

Emily shut her car door and pulled away from the curb.

"She knew about the divorce action."

Javier caught a green blur of the Porsche flying past them, but clear enough to see Lori's extended middle finger.

"Aren't you going after her?"

"We know where she's heading. I slapped the GPS unit under her front bumper when we got here. We already know her next stop. She has a one o'clock appointment at East Lawn Memorial Park."

CHAPTER TWENTY-THREE

OUTSIDE THE IVY-CLOAKED walls of the East Lawn Memorial Park, Emily watched a parade of local celebrities and power brokers gather for Roger Townsend's funeral. Although the services were a half hour away, the mourners already numbered in the triple figures. One limo after another turned from Folsom Boulevard into the gated cemetery and deposited their passengers.

"I've already seen the Mayor, two State Senators, and a whole pack of suits who thought they were important," Javier said, looking through the telephoto camera lens.

"There goes Jonathon Anderson, Townsend's partner." Emily pointed up ahead on the elm tree–lined sidewalk.

"This is a 'who's who' in town," Javier said over the camera shutter noise.

"Whoa . . . whoa . . . whoa. What's this? Look who's hanging by the entrance gate," Emily said.

Javier turned the camera to the left and zoomed in on a face tucked away in a shadow inside the ivy wall. "I'll be damned. What's Josh Potter doing here?"

"Got me. He's not working security or crowd control, that would be uniformed guys. He's scanning the crowd coming in."

"Any guess who he's lookin' for?" Javier asked.

Emily shrugged and dialed a number on her cell. After a moment, she said, "Hey, Ortega, Hunter here. I'm looking for Detective Potter."

She listened and replied, "No—no message, I'll call back later."

"What'd you find?" Javier asked.

"The gang unit has him signed out to a surveillance gig in South Sacramento."

Javier snapped another picture of the out-of-place detective. "He's not here in any official capacity."

"Nope . . ." Emily pointed. "He's moving."

Potter stepped out to the sidewalk and stared in the direction of the Crown Vic.

"Shit. I think he's found us," Javier said and dropped the camera into his lap.

Potter ambled off of the curb, waited for a pause in the traffic, and dashed across the street.

Emily started the Crown Vic's engine and gauged the traffic flow to flip a quick U-turn. She checked the rearview mirror, and the endless flow of traffic prevented a quick getaway.

Hidden in the flow of traffic, behind a white Toyota minivan, a loud motorcycle roared past the detectives and pulled up next to Potter.

The biker wore the usual black t-shirt, leather chaps with metal studs, and a worn black leather vest. An elaborate motorcycle patch decorated the back.

"Can you get a shot of the guy and the 'colors' on his jacket?"

Javier pulled the camera into place and snapped several shots. "Got it—I can't see his face. His sunglasses and hair are in the way."

The biker's hair hung down to his shoulders and seemed greasy from a distance. He engaged in an animated discussion with Potter and the biker banged his fist on his handlebars. Suddenly, the long-haired biker pulled off the slick black helmet and held it in his right hand. They continued to talk, and Potter did more listening than talking.

Javier zoomed in with the lens and froze. "That's him. That's Artie Miller, the guy from Pelican Bay who Tooker said came with Potter when they hit the attorney's office."

"Let's see," Emily said, taking the camera from Javier. "Josh, what are you doing? And what the hell is an Aryan Brotherhood member doing here? He isn't here to attend the funeral."

At that moment, Potter reached out and delivered a quick punch to Miller's jaw. The biker didn't move from the blow and absorbed the jab full force.

Javier started to open his door to assist Detective Potter until Emily grabbed him by the arm and pulled him back.

"No—wait."

Miller swung the helmet in his hand and struck Potter on the side of his shaved head, knocking the detective off his feet to the sidewalk. Potter rolled on his side and rested on an elbow, looking up at the biker.

With a smooth, practiced motion, Miller put the helmet back on his head and drew a long-barreled pistol from under his vest.

"Gun—gun. He's got a gun," Javier yelled in the confines of the sedan.

Emily instantly regretted not allowing Javier to help the detective. She expected to hear a crack from the revolver and see Potter's head explode in a red mist at any moment. Miller used the gun to punctuate whatever he said to Potter. Anger, violence, and urgency poured from the biker's movements.

Potter put up his hand in a useless gesture of surrender. Satisfied with the response, Miller holstered his weapon, kicked his bike into gear, and roared away.

"What was that about?" Emily wondered aloud.

"Potter came out on the receiving end. Makes me think he didn't keep his part of a deal," Javier said.

Potter got to his feet, rubbing his head. When he pulled his hand away, he checked it for blood coming from a cut above his ear. It wasn't bleeding badly, but Emily bet he'd be left with one hell of a headache. Potter wiped the blood and held a handkerchief in place as a compress while he steadied himself.

The injured detective's attention switched from his head to the approaching hearse and two accompanying stretch limos. The limo's smoked windows blotted out the view of anyone within as they made the sharp turn into the memorial park.

Potter dropped the blood-soiled handkerchief and darted into traffic behind the black caravan as they entered the shadowy recesses behind the ivy walls.

Emily waited for a break in the traffic and opened the car door. "Let's go catch the show. I have a really bad feeling about Potter being here."

"He's gotta be here for Lori. You think he might take her out?" Javier said.

"In this crowd, that'd be pretty bold. Let's follow from a distance and find out how bold he is," she said.

The two detectives jogged across the street and blended in with the gathering inside the memorial park. A white tent, erected near a granite wall, faced rows of white folding chairs. With most of the front-row seats occupied, the mood mirrored the opening night of a Hollywood premiere.

The hearse arrived, and the remaining mourners gravitated toward the tent, filling in the seats quickly. The first limo opened, and Lori Townsend stepped out accompanied by an older woman. Lori wore black for her role as the distraught widow, but it was the only traditional thing in her appearance. The black dress was cut at mid-thigh; form-fitted across her hips and hugged the curves of her waist. A low-cut, plunging neckline revealed what God had provided, and a few surgeons enhanced.

Javier gawked at the skin display and whispered to his partner, "Is she advertising she's back on the market now, or what?"

A dozen couples whispered to one another and waited their turn to greet the widow. Lori basked in the attention, but the old woman on her arm shied away, put out and embarrassed.

A man in a conservative black suit opened the rear of the hearse, pulled out a highly polished metal urn, and held it gently with white cotton gloves.

"Apparently Lori upgraded the urn for her husband. It's bigger and more elaborate than the one she carried out of the mortuary yesterday," Emily said.

"I guess she's having second thoughts and felt Roger needed a classier send-off."

The glossy silver urn held the place of honor on a dark wood table in front of a marble wall and reflected the sunlight back onto the crowd. Lori guided the old woman to a seat in the front row. To ensure Lori remained the center of attention, she arranged to sit at a chair next to the table and the urn. The placement proved well choreographed—the radiance of the sun's reflection appeared to come from Lori.

Emily motioned for Javier to follow her to a nearby willow tree where they could watch the crowd from the darkness of the leafy canopy.

"Where's Potter?" Emily asked.

They both scoured the surroundings for the man, and as if on cue, Potter stood up on the pretext of allowing a woman to pass him along the row of chairs. He remained standing for far too long. He glared at Lori Townsend and wanted to make sure she noticed before he sat.

Her eyes cast in his direction and she dropped her head to a tissue in her hand. When she raised her head again, she held a practiced calm on her face.

A pastor of some undetermined religious denomination approached and stood at the podium.

The usual "dust-to-dust" pronouncements lasted about twenty minutes, and the assembled crowd started to fidget. Following a nod from the pastor, Lori Townsend stood and approached the podium. Rather than stand behind the wooden lectern, she removed the microphone from its cradle and stepped in front.

"I'm not going to offer any personal reflections on my life with Roger. Each of us has those memories, and we need to keep them in our own way. Roger would be very happy to see you here today. I'm very grateful for the support and friendship in this difficult time. Roger had a great many friends and you are invited to our home on 46th Street following this service. Thank you." Lori handed the microphone to the pastor and returned to her chair next to the metal urn.

"Please retire to the Townsend residence for a small reception. The interment will be a private family affair."

The crowd dispersed and ambled toward their limos, cars, and drivers. Lori, the old woman, and another older man stayed behind. Potter, however, waited by the limo that had carried Lori to the service.

Lori picked up the urn and hefted it to the man from the funeral home who then placed it inside a large niche in the granite wall. A dark maroon velvet drape pulled across the opening, and Lori stood silently for a second and then nodded to the memorial park employee standing nearby.

The man placed a brass plaque on the front of the niche and used a cordless drill to secure the plaque in place with security screws that prohibited tampering. The blank metal panel would bear Townsend's inscribed name—someday.

Lori hooked the old woman by the arm and guided her toward the limo and Potter.

Emily said, "Here we go."

The two detectives moved close but stayed in the shadows of the trees.

"Josh, what are you doing? You shouldn't be here," Lori said.

"You know why I'm here, and you have until four o'clock this afternoon."

The old woman's eyes clouded. "What's he talking about, dear?" she asked in a fragile voice.

"Nothing, Mother Townsend. Don't worry about it. He's one of Roger's associates."

The old woman's eyes glared at Potter. "Roger kept bad company—he always did. That was probably his undoing." Roger Townsend's mother had no idea how close she was to the truth.

"You hear me, Lori? Don't mess with these guys. I can't help you if you cross them," Potter warned.

"I'll give them what they deserve when I decide to give it to them." She pulled herself into the limo and closed the door.

Potter hammered his open palm on the dark window. "Lori, do what they ask, or we're going down!" As the limo pulled away, Potter stepped back to avoid being run over. He put his head down, slunk to the entrance gate, and passed within fifteen feet of Emily.

After he passed, Emily said, "Did you catch that?"

"Yeah, Potter and Lori are in a pinch and owe Miller and the boys. They must want to make sure the money doesn't dry up from the Townsend accounts."

"The RICO files," Emily added.

"The files the U.S. Attorney handed over?"

"Lori knows where they are. Roger played chicken with the wrong dudes when he didn't hand the files over. Miller and his thugs gave her a deadline."

"Think she destroyed them?" Javier said.

"They're too valuable to the right people, and she'll lead us right to them. And this ties together with Roger's murder. He made arrangements to force a U.S. Attorney to hand over the RICO files, and for whatever reason, Roger didn't follow through. That got him killed," Emily said.

"That means Lori knew why her husband was killed. She knew from the very beginning."

"Let's do a drive-by of the house on 46th Street. That's where she's headed next."

CHAPTER TWENTY-FOUR

FOLLOWING THE PROCESSION of limos and Ubers, Emily and Javier parked across from two blue and red catering trucks in the driveway of the 46th Street Townsend residence. Black-and-white-clad employees rushed from the trucks carrying trays of cheese, caviar, crusty French bread, and an assortment of hot dishes in covered serving crocks.

Through the front windows, the detectives watched men and women mingling inside the residence. Some held champagne flutes, while others carried plates piled with food as if they expected a looming hunger strike. Lori made her way from one gathering to another and collected supportive hugs and gestures from each of them.

"I'm getting hungry watching them," Javier said.

"Me too. Let's fix that." Emily got out of the car and set off toward the home.

Javier popped his head out her door. "What are you doing? You can't go in there!"

She found the back of one of the catering trucks. Javier noticed her talking to someone—the caterer caught his partner trying to rip off a few snacks from the truck.

Thirty seconds later, a young man followed Emily back to the Crown Vic carrying two heaping plates of prime rib sandwiches, a selection of cheeses, and a mixture of sliced mango, papaya, and pineapple. The catering employee handed a plate through the window to Javier and then one to Emily. She slipped the man a ten-dollar tip for his help.

"Sorry it took so long. He needed a couple of minutes to find paper plates."

"You're nuts, you know that?"

"You said you were hungry."

"Well . . . thanks."

They devoured the food in silence over the next few minutes while they watched the crowd begin to thin. The faces of the mourners were more relaxed and less concerned about Roger Townsend's passing. Funny how a few mimosas and crab puffs could make them forget.

Emily caught movement from a side door that opened up onto the driveway. Lori Townsend ditched her guests and headed for the garage. She changed into a pair of tight-fitting jeans, heeled boots, and a grey sweater. "The widow's done grieving," she noted.

The garage door opened, revealing the emerald green Porsche next to a black Mercedes.

"Uh-oh, I didn't count on another car. If she gets in the Mercedes, we could lose her."

Emily watched as Lori stopped and appeared to be considering which of Roger's vehicles to use. She started for the Mercedes, unlocked the door, and got into the driver's seat.

"Damn it. We don't have the GPS on the second car. We're gonna risk a close tail to wherever she's headed," Emily said.

"Wait. She shut off the engine. She's getting out—she's going to the Porsche. Why'd she change her mind?" Javier said.

"It was probably low on gas and the widow wasn't about to suffer the indignity of pumping her own gas."

Emily pulled the GPS monitor from a black nylon bag and tossed the bag on the back seat. She turned the monitor on and hoped in the rush at the mall she remembered to turn the little bugger on before she placed it on Lori's car.

A brightly lit colored map of midtown Sacramento filled the small screen, and in the center, a red dot confirmed the unit tracked Lori's car.

"We're up and running," she said.

Emily passed the monitor to Javier as she buckled her seatbelt.

"In the mood for a little drive, are we?"

Immediately, the dot jumped as the Porsche backed out onto 46th Street and made the turn on Folsom toward downtown.

Emily waited until the sports car sped out of sight before she pulled the Crown Vic from the curb. Lori would recognize the unmarked car in her rearview after the encounter at the mall.

"She's turning up ahead; getting on the Capitol City Freeway."

"Which direction?"

"North—she's heading northbound."

They followed the Porsche at a distance of over a mile, which wasn't difficult considering the speed Lori maintained, well above the posted limit.

"I'd say she's pushing eighty-five miles per hour," Javier said.

"Where's a cop when you need one?"

"She's approaching her four o'clock deadline. Maybe she's taking it seriously."

"She's slowing."

Emily backed off on the accelerator and pulled to the right-hand lane, anticipating an exit from the freeway. Before Javier could speak, she caught a quick glimpse of the Porsche at the red light at the end of the off-ramp for Antelope Road. She slowed and made sure other cars remained between the police sedan and the Porsche. After the light turned, Lori made a left and headed into a residential subdivision built in the late seventies, but without an ounce of preventative maintenance since.

"She's gonna end up carjacked in here," Emily said.

The monitor then showed Lori stopped at a house three blocks up to the left. Emily held the car a block away and watched as Lori pulled the car into the driveway of a beaten tract home, one with chipped paint and a completely brown lawn. The most notable features of the place were the three choppers parked near the open front door.

Lori exited the car, adjusted her hair, and strode up to the door. A burly man met her at the step and nodded. He turned away, spoke with someone behind him, and then seconds later, Artie Miller appeared. Lori strutted up to the gangbanger, gave him a peck on the cheek, patted his face with her hand, and walked on into the house.

CHAPTER TWENTY-FIVE

THE INTERIOR OF the home matched the weathered and dilapidated outside. It smelled of beer, sweat, and bedsheets unchanged since the Clinton Administration. A series of ragged unpatched holes decorated the hallway where fists, elbows, and bottles marked episodes of unchecked rage.

Lori passed through the kitchen, littered with beer bottles and pizza boxes and featuring half-broken cabinets, thick with grime. She paused at the living room and found the formerly tan shag carpet pockmarked with grease- and oil stains from motorcycles parked in the room—as evidenced by the two partially dismantled choppers now propped up on orange plastic milk crates.

A man with his back to Lori installed a new exhaust manifold on one of the bikes and tightened the bolts with a socket wrench. The muscles across his back flexed with each turn of the tool. The movement caused an odd fluttering on a large leprechaun tattoo between his shoulders. Even Lori recognized a prison tat. The color came from carbon paper, and the uneven lines were courtesy of an inmate artist with a heroin withdrawal tremor. This wasn't the quality work the kids bought at a street tattoo salon when they wanted to look hard. This was the real deal.

"Well, you took your damn time in getting here," the man said without turning his attention from his bike.

"I'm right on time," she replied, looking at her Cartier watch.

The man picked up a long chrome exhaust pipe and lined it up with the bolt pattern on the manifold. "You have it?"

"Yes—but not with me."

He lowered his head and put the exhaust pipe on the carpet. The biker slowly got up from the floor and faced Lori. Dean Sands stood under six feet tall, but his slate grey eyes, muscular build, and shaved head made an imposing presence, nonetheless.

"That wasn't our understanding. You were supposed to deliver it to me. That was the deal," Sands said.

Three of his men gathered behind her. Lori turned back to him. "There's been a change in plans. The files are safe, for now. As long as I stay safe, you have nothing to worry about."

Sands didn't often show his anger; one of the characteristics that struck fear into those who crossed him—right up until the moment he cut their throats. His eyes narrowed, and a furrow gathered on his brow. "You don't get to make that call."

Lori stepped closer to the White Supremacist and ran a manicured fingernail down his chest. "I hired you to kill my husband. I agreed to get the file from the federal prosecutor." She brought her hand back up and held her finger under his thickly bearded goatee. "I held up my part. But how can I trust you not to kill me after I hand over the files to you?"

A smirk formed on Sands' face, giving away the fact he considered it as an option. Without a twitch on his face, Sands quickly reached out, clenched Lori's wrist, bent it backward, and spun her around roughly. He wrenched her arm behind her back, pushed her face-first into the wall, and pinned her against it with his weight.

His breath smelled of stale beer and onion as he whispered in her ear, "Don't think I won't gut you like a pig." He pushed her harder into the wall, her face turned sideways against the stained drywall. "You bring me that file, or I'll make what I did to your husband look tame." With his free hand he plunged a sharpened blade into the wall, the Nazi insignia inscribed into the antique bayonet resting inches from her eyes.

"All right. I'll give it to you," she cried out.

Sands released her, and she turned her back to the wall, leaning against the surface. Lori pouted and rubbed her freed wrist. "I did everything you wanted."

"Hand over the file."

"I don't have it with me. I already told you. It's safe." She slowly turned around, a small welt showing over her right eye.

"Where is it?"

"I'll go and get it." Lori started to walk away, and Sands put an arm out to bar her escape.

"I don't think so. You'll stay here, and I'll have someone go pick it up. Now, where's my file?" She didn't see the sudden movement. Sands pulled the bayonet from the wall and pressed it to her throat.

She felt the blade trace a line on her skin, and reflexively she pushed back as far as she could, her back to the wall.

"You can't. I need to retrieve it. The file is in my safe deposit box." She sounded desperate.

He released the blade from her neck. A faint pink line remained behind as a reminder. "In that case, Artie here will go with you."

He turned to Artie. "Bring me the file. If she causes any problems—kill her."

Artie Miller yanked her arm. "Come on, Princess. Let's go make a withdrawal from your bank." He pulled her toward him.

Sands put the shortened bayonet in a sheath on his black leather boot and turned his attention back to the motorcycle. While he positioned the long metal exhaust pipe once more, Sands said, "Your only chance is to give Artie the file. I give you my word he will let you go after you hand it over."

Artie pulled Lori toward the front door, and she came with him; more or less willingly. Sands wiped his hands with an oily rag and made a gesture, dragging his hand across his throat. Artie nodded. He understood—as soon as he got his hands on the federal prosecutor's RICO files, he'd kill the woman.

CHAPTER TWENTY-SIX

EMILY CAUGHT THE movement in the doorway as Artie Miller pushed Lori outside. Miller shoved Lori away from her Porsche toward the street and a faded blue 1980s Buick Skylark. Lori got in the passenger seat while the biker circled around and got behind the wheel. Lori wasn't happy about the road trip with her new friend.

The Skylark pulled from the curb, and Emily put her car in gear, pulling from the house. Two skinhead thugs started the Porsche and backed it from the driveway. The sports car headed in the opposite direction and the skinheads stared at Emily and Javier as they passed each other.

"They made us," Emily said.

"This doesn't look good for Lori. She's being led off somewhere, and those goons are dumping her car," Javier said.

"Are you getting a soft spot for her?" Emily asked.

"No. But if she disappears, then our case disappears along with her."

He pointed ahead. "They're getting on the freeway heading back downtown."

There was no trouble following the Skylark because of heavy traffic downtown. Miller's car swerved and shot down the J Street exit, catching Emily by surprise. The detective cut off a semitruck and sped down the off-ramp, following the Skylark.

Miller crept with the flow of traffic in the left lane, and Emily ended up stopping right next to it at the red light. Emily kept her face hidden by looking down the street to the right. Javier kept watch on the Skylark and its two occupants.

He didn't look away quick enough, and Lori locked eyes with him. "Shit. Emily, she saw me."

Emily glanced over at the Skylark and the expression on Lori's face. Instead of the anger she expected, Lori moved her lips carefully and mouthed the words, "Help me."

Before she could say more, Miller cut her off, grabbing her by the hair, pulling her close. He clamped a thick hand around her throat and demanded her full attention, and she responded with a nod, pointing ahead. Miller's tunnel vision centered on his captive and where she directed them. He never noticed the two detectives in the next car.

The light changed from red to green, and Miller sped off, turning at 6th Street. He made an immediate right into an alley behind a Bank of the West branch. Emily couldn't follow the car into the alley—she knew Miller would see them if they came any closer. She pulled the Crown Vic past the alley and found a spot to park up the block.

*   *   *

Miller reached in the trunk and put on a worn green Army surplus jacket, under which a MAC-10 machine pistol hung on a strap slung over his shoulder. The .45 caliber weapon would make an obvious bulge in the jacket if he zipped it up. With the jacket open, Miller stormed around and pulled Lori out of the car by her arm.

"You bring me the files, and I'm done with you," he said.

"Wait here."

"No way, lady. I'm coming in with you, and if you try to screw me, I'll put a bullet in your head," he said menacingly and parted his jacket enough for her to see the stubby black barrel of the MAC-10.

She paused, and Miller shoved her in the direction of the door. She reluctantly complied, pushed open one of the glass doors, and entered the bank lobby. Artie Miller followed a few steps behind her, stopped at a long wooden counter, and fiddled with deposit slips. He nodded for her to get on with retrieving her safe deposit box.

Lori approached a small brunette woman at a central wooden desk, with a placard identifying her as Patricia Langston, Assistant Branch Manager.

"Hello, Patricia. I need to access my safe deposit box."

Langston recognized Lori from her frequent trips to the bank in recent months. "Good afternoon, Mrs. Townsend. Of course . . . please come with me."

The bank manager led Lori to a private area and said, "We're sorry about Mr. Townsend. Such a shock to all of us here. Please wait here while I get my keys."

*　*　*

Tucked away in a corner of the alley, Emily reached for her vibrating cell phone. "Hunter here."

"Detective Hunter? This is Patricia Langston at the Bank of the West. You told me to call if Mrs. Townsend accessed her accounts. She's here now and asking for her safe deposit box."

"Do you know what she keeps in it?"

"No, of course not," the bank manager responded. "What should I do, Detective?"

"Give her the box. Can you tell what she takes from it?"

"Only if she's carrying it openly." She paused. "Detective? She came in with a man. He's scary-looking and making some of our tellers nervous."

"We're right outside, Ms. Langston. Go ahead and give her the box and see if you can tell what she removes from it."

"Very well," and Langston hung up.

*   *   *

Langston returned to Lori and escorted her to the safe holding her deposit box. It required two keys to open. The bank manager inserted hers and turned it, and Lori followed suit and unlocked the second lock. Langston waited for a second, hoping for a glimpse of what caused the authorities to push her to snoop over Lori Townsend's shoulder. Probably drugs, or stolen jewelry perhaps.

Lori paused, sensing Langston hovering over her. "Thank you. I won't need any assistance for now."

Langston nodded and silently left Lori and the box behind.

Waiting for the bank employee's retreat, Lori opened her safe deposit box. She slid the lid back and quickly skimmed the contents—several bundles of cash, insurance documents, two velvet-covered cases holding expensive diamond and tanzanite necklaces, and assorted property deeds.

She knew what the box contained. She had lied to Sands when she told him the RICO prosecutor's files were here. Now it closed down on her. She couldn't give him the files. They were her only life insurance policy. Would Miller take a pile of cash instead?

"No, dammit. You earned this, and you can't let some dirtbag take it away from you." She felt each second tick by, and the pressure to flee ratcheted up with each passing heartbeat.

*   *   *

In the lobby, Miller grew impatient. He felt everyone staring at him, the tellers, the other bank customers, and the stuffy men and women behind the desks. "What's taking her so long," he mumbled.

"I'm sorry, what were you saying," a thin young man asked. He filled out a deposit slip on the table next to Miller.

"Mind your own fucking business," Miller replied.

Had the young man had a tail, it would've tucked between his legs as he slunk away from Miller.

His impatience reached its limit, and he started walking toward the station where Lori hid. A middle-aged, balding man with a potbelly over his narrow brown belt stood up and slowed Miller's progress.

"Excuse me, but you can't come back here," the bank man said, with the bravado of a former high school football player.

Miller didn't slow down, swung a quick right arm, and connected his elbow with the man's jaw, dropping him in his steps.

Nearby bank employees screamed as their colleague fell to the carpet. Before anyone else reacted, Miller opened the thin door, pulled the machine pistol up on the strap under his arm, and pointed it at Lori's head—or where Lori's head should've been. She'd disappeared along with the safe deposit box.

CHAPTER TWENTY-SEVEN

PROPELLED BY A scream from the bank lobby, Lori closed the box, tucked it under her arm, and ran to the back of the office. She noticed an employee's emergency exit door marked with a large red and white warning sign. THIS EXIT TO REMAIN LOCKED AT ALL TIMES. OPENING THIS DOOR WILL SET OFF ALARM. Lori shoved the push bar on the door and ran into the alley. The door alarm sounded a shrill electronic siren, which Lori hoped, added to the panic brewing inside the bank.

She found the stairs to the parking level, a secure garage tucked underneath the bank building. The slap of her boots echoed in the stairwell as she ran down the metal stair treads. She pushed a thin metal door at the bottom of the stairwell and ran into the locked garage. Trapped. A metallic clank came from one end of the parking structure. Someone outside activated the security gate into the garage. She ran to the gate and tore past the waiting bank patron with the box tucked tightly under her arm.

She ran blindly down the alleyway and gained speed until a hand tugged her from behind and spun her around. Lori expected Miller and the shadow of terror he brought with him. She didn't care that it was Detective Hunter who stopped her and Lori continued to struggle and try to pull away.

Seconds later, Artie Miller burst through the entrance of the bank and found Lori with the detective at the corner of the alley.

"You bitch!" Miller pulled the weapon up and began firing .45 caliber shells toward them. The MAC-10 was a powerful, intimidating weapon, but the recoil made it less accurate at a distance. The rounds stitched a path on the alleyway asphalt, each one landing closer to Lori.

Emily pulled Lori out of the path of the bullets, shoved her toward Javier, who caught the woman and put her down on the pavement. From concealment behind an electrical box, Emily got down on a knee and pointed her Glock down the alley.

Miller ducked behind the Skylark and leaned over the broad faded hood, firing toward the corner. The high rate of fire depleted the fifty-round magazine in seconds. He hit the magazine release button, and the empty long metal box fell to the ground. From a pocket inside the green jacket, Miller pulled another magazine and shoved it into the open magazine well.

Emily poked her head around the electrical service box and caught Miller reloading.

"Miller! Drop it!"

Miller's eyes were on fire after he finished reloading, and he aimed the machine pistol at Emily. The first shots landed ten feet in front of her, and Miller walked the path of the weapon forward toward his target.

Emily felt concrete from the alleyway fly up and hit her in the legs. She fired her Glock twice, shattering the Skylark's passenger window. Gunshots from the right cracked loudly, and Miller flew backward behind his vehicle.

From the rear bank steps, Detective Josh Potter held his weapon on Miller. Potter exited the bank and caught Miller while Emily distracted him. Potter waved to Emily while he kept his gun trained on the downed gang member.

Emily crept toward the Skylark. Miller lay sprawled on his back with a gunshot wound to the upper left chest. Blood oozed from Miller's mouth as he gagged for a ragged breath. Emily kicked the MAC-10 out of Miller's hand but found it tethered under the wounded man's arm.

Miller slowly turned his head, and his eyes focused sharply on Emily. He attempted to move his hand to grasp the weapon, but his muscles wouldn't react as directed. He fumbled around, and his fingers clawed at the pavement near the weapon.

The detective stepped heavily on Miller's groping arm, pinning it to the pavement. "It's over, Miller." Emily heard approaching sirens, pulled a folding knife from her pocket, cut the leather strap, and released the MAC-10 from the biker's shoulder.

The first uniformed unit arrived; the officer rolled Miller onto his stomach and secured him in handcuffs. The officer called for the paramedics to tend to the wounded gang member.

Emily felt the shoot was good, but immediately a cold lump in her stomach formed because the Sacramento Police Department's policy required the shooting to be investigated by the Homicide Unit, Internal Affairs Division, Professional Standards Unit, Crime Scene Investigations Unit, and the City of Sacramento's Office of Public Safety Accountability. An entire fleet of armchair slugs would take hours to dissect each and every aspect of the shooting where an officer on the streets had a fraction of a second to react. All this and she wasn't even the one who put him down.

A nagging, needling feeling crept into her mind. How did Potter manage to show up at the most opportune moment?

Javier joined Emily with Lori in handcuffs, leading her by the elbow. "Are you all right, Emily–Josh?"

Potter looked pale and shaken. He trembled and nodded as he tried to light a cigarette.

"Yeah . . . I don't think Miller's gonna make it," Emily responded.

"Good," Lori huffed. "Now turn me loose this instant!"

"Mrs. Townsend, I think we need to talk. What did Miller want in your safe deposit box?" Emily asked.

Emily caught a quick look between Potter and Lori, a glance passed between them, but she couldn't tell what it meant.

"Nothing," she complained. "Now turn me loose . . . I'm the victim here."

Javier held the deposit box under his arm and felt the weight of the contents. "This is too heavy to be nothing. And, honey, I doubt you've ever been a victim of a thing in your life."

Emily watched as Miller's gurney was rushed to a waiting ambulance. One of the paramedics slowly shook his head. The heavy white and red ambulance door slammed shut jarring Emily back to her partner and Lori Townsend.

Potter waved to the Internal Affairs investigator who responded at the location. "I'd better go get this over with. See you guys later."

Lori struggled against the cuffs, complaining they were too tight and then every breath or two she'd yell, "Let me go!"

The shooting gathered a crowd, and Lori's hysterical outbursts gained more attention. Before the crowd turned ugly, Emily called a uniformed officer over from the far side of the alley to give them a hand. As the officer approached, Javier recognized him, Officer Booty Bandit, Brian Conner.

Emily unconsciously tucked her hair behind her ear with the hand that wasn't occupied with her prisoner. She tried not to smile but found she couldn't help it.

"Detectives," Officer Conner responded, but his eyes were focused only on Emily.

Javier must have felt invisible—he cleared his throat loudly. He followed with, "Officer Conner, take this prisoner to holding. We're gonna have a nice long talk with Mrs. Townsend after we finish up here."

Conner gripped Lori by the arm and told Emily, "I'll bring your cuffs back to you." He smiled back over his shoulder.

"I bet he will," Javier whispered to his partner's hot, flushed face.

"I don't want to sound ungrateful, but don't you think it's a bit too convenient Potter happened to show up and shoot Miller when we were pinned down? How the hell did he know to be here?"

"Couple that with the argument he and Miller shared at the Memorial Park, and it makes it really troubling," Javier said.

Potter stood with the Internal Affairs people where he gestured to Miller's car as he described the shooting. "I don't understand how Potter got himself involved in this mess. First, Potter does the shakedown at Corona's law office, and now he puts Miller down."

"Makes you wonder if he's looking for the same thing." Javier pointed to the safe deposit box. "Potter didn't want Miller and the Brotherhood to get their hands on whatever's in this."

"Come on. Let's see if we can't put that mystery to rest. And I need my cuffs back," Emily said.

CHAPTER TWENTY-EIGHT

CHIEF CLARK WAITED in the detective bureau. Decked out in a crisply pressed dress blue uniform, the Chief perched on a corner of a desk. He held a television remote in his hand, and he pressed the mute button when Emily and Javier entered.

"You brought me another media circus, Detective Hunter."

"That wasn't my intent, Sir."

"Bright side is there won't be any protesters camped outside for a Nazi with an extra hole."

"There's that."

The television screen carried the images of the alleyway behind the bank in a montage of violence. The cameraman found his money shot with Artie Miller's bloodied body wheeling through the frame. The video image cut to a young male reporter; his dark black spiked hair held in place by industrial-strength hair gel. The reporter gestured to the back of the bank building and then to the electrical box where Emily had taken cover.

Emily got the sense the reporter headed in an odd direction with the story, and she asked the Chief to hit the sound.

"The former gang member was gunned down by police in what can only be described as an ambush. He was outgunned and outmanned and attacked in an alley, out of public view." The reporter moved to the Buick Skylark and panned the camera from one side of the alley to the other, littered with shell casings, clearly identified by the yellow numbered evidence tags sitting next to each one. There were fifty numbered markers littered in the shot.

"Sources close to the police department, who asked not to be identified for fear of retaliation, told this reporter the deceased is Michael Artie Miller, a reformed White Supremacist and ex-gang member. The once avowed racist was said to volunteer as a mentor at a local homeless shelter. Our source told us police officers followed Miller to this isolated location before killing him. This proves to be an interesting case of street justice. Back to you in the newsroom."

"Reformed, my ass. Who's this source, and where can I get my hands on him?" Emily said.

Chief Clark rubbed the back of his neck. "It's Detective Potter."

"Are you crazy? Why would he make up some pitiful story saying I ambushed Miller when he tried to kill us along with Lori Townsend? He's the one who shot the bastard."

"The source is Detective Potter. He told the IA investigators he's known Miller for a couple of years and Miller called him this afternoon. Said someone followed him. Apparently, Miller thought they were Aryan Brotherhood members who learned he was going to roll over and give up information on the gang."

Emily's mind replayed the earlier encounter between Potter and Miller once more. If anyone stalked Miller and threatened to kill him, Detective Potter fit the bill, she thought.

"Chief, you know that's a bunch of crap, right? Miller nabbed Lori Townsend and pressured her for what's in her safe deposit box. How did he arrange to leak this reformed racist narrative to the press?"

With a sigh, the Chief replied, "Yeah . . . I know. I talked with Lori Townsend while I waited for you." He rubbed his hands together, and continued, "Lori says Miller grabbed her as she left her home after the reception. He wanted her to give him the cash she kept in the box. She's not copping to any knowledge about the files."

Emily began to interrupt, but the Chief put up his hand and stopped her. "She claims he killed her husband. Miller came back because he didn't find the cash he expected in Roger's safe."

"We think he is good for the break-in at Corona's law offices," Emily responded. "Not enough to tie him to Corona's murder yet. But, Chief—there is a witness who puts Detective Potter in the law office at the time."

Javier nodded in confirmation and used it as a cue to jump in. "Chief, Potter and Miller tore apart Wayne Corona's home and offices. The attorney was killed after he couldn't deliver what they were looking for. We think they were after the federal prosecutor's files on the A.B. RICO investigation."

"The only explanation for Potter being there is Miller told him about the files," the chief said, putting the pieces together.

"I'm going to prepare the affidavit now for a warrant to open the box," Emily said over the tapping on her computer keyboard.

"Did you ask her to open it?" Clark asked.

"Well—honestly, no," Emily replied. "If the RICO files are in there, she's not gonna let us open it, Chief."

"If they aren't?"

Javier shrugged in a "Why not" gesture.

"Let's go ask—bet she won't, but I'll bring it anyway," Emily said as she shook the sturdy metal bank box.

*   *   *

Down the hall in another room, Lori Townsend waited in semi-darkness; her back straight, legs crossed, and her hands rested gracefully in her lap. She appeared bored, perhaps annoyed, but not noticeably affected by what she had experienced in the past few hours.

Her expression held neutral as Emily came in, holding the bank deposit box. She brightened somewhat when Chief Clark followed. Then Lori ignored Emily altogether.

"Chief, I see you've recovered my property. Thank you so much," she said warmly. "I'll be sure to let Mayor Stone know."

Emily slid the box on the desk. "Mrs. Townsend? What drove Miller to such extremes to get his hands on this?"

"Money. He threatened to kill me if I didn't hand over my cash," she said in a trembling voice.

"How did he know you kept money in this box?" Emily said, giving the box a nudge.

"I . . . he made me tell him." She paused, "When he carjacked me."

"*Carjacked?* When did that happen?" Emily asked, ready to confront her with photos of her walking into the biker's nest.

"Chief Clark, is this really necessary? I do appreciate the detectives saving me, killing that dreadful man, and for recovering my property. I wish to go home now to rest."

Emily ignored her plea to the Chief. "Will you open this for us, Mrs. Townsend?"

She waited for any sign of sympathy and found none, not even from Chief Clark.

"As soon as you open it up, we'll get you out of here, Lori," the Chief said.

Lori paused and appeared to consider her options. She shrugged her shoulders and pulled a key from her jeans pocket, inserting it in the lock, and gestured for the detectives to "have at it."

Emily slid the box lid open, exposing the contents. "We're gonna take an inventory of the contents, Mrs. Townsend. It shouldn't take long."

Javier pulled a property/evidence log form out of a drawer and scribed as Emily called out the items, one at a time.

"Ten bundles of U.S. currency." Emily paused while he counted each bundle and Javier recounted the same ones to verify the amount. "A total of fifty thousand dollars."

"One blue velvet jewelry box, containing a yellow metal necklace with five clear stones."

"A tan velvet jewelry box, containing a yellow metal bracelet with—ten purple stones."

"Property deeds to the Granite Bay home, the 46th Street residence, and a condo in Montego Bay, Jamaica."

Emily pulled the final document from the case, and stated for the record, "Insurance policy documents for personal property, liability, life, and vehicle." Emily turned the box over, showing it empty. There were no RICO files.

CHAPTER TWENTY-NINE

LORI TOWNSEND WASN'T happy she couldn't take her safe deposit box with her. Emily told her the District Attorney ordered the box retained as evidence until they completed their review of the shooting. The woman huffed out of the room and waited for someone to pick her up, while she chatted with the Mayor on her cell phone. God only knew what she filled the politician's head with.

Chief Clark motioned the detectives out in the hallway. "Look, you don't have a solid charge to hold her on. She has cash in her deposit box, so what? She says he abducted her and there's nothing to prove otherwise. There is no other choice—she walks," he said.

"Chief, she met Miller after the funeral services, and we know Potter had an argument with him at the cemetery. She knows more about the killings. We have video of her extorting a federal prosecutor." Frustrated, Emily slammed her palm on the wall.

"Emily, no need to preach to the choir. I agree she might be wrapped up in this mess more than she's letting on, but thinking it ain't enough. She'll claim her husband forced her. And he's not exactly able to refute her claims."

What the Chief said next surprised Emily and Javier.

"I'll give you cover from the Mayor's Office. I don't know how long I'll be able to hold him off, you need to work fast. Now, if there's evidence out there implicating Lori Townsend in a larger conspiracy, go find it." As he left the bureau, he said, "And get me Potter's ass while you're at it."

Emily followed Lori and watched her slip into a taxi, and as she slid into the back seat, she smiled at the detectives. Not one of those friendly smiles; it was one of those phony Mean Girl smiles with bared teeth that brought out her inner animalistic qualities. She'd beaten Emily, and she made sure she knew it.

A voice called out from behind Emily, "We need to talk to you, Detective."

Emily and Javier turned and found two investigators from Internal Affairs behind them. The taller of the two sported a no-nonsense military haircut, but his wire-rimmed glasses didn't fit with the harsh image he tried to project. His eyes gave away his reluctant disposition. The man's eyes shifted, couldn't lock onto either of the detectives.

The voice came from the shorter of the two, a soft, round man who shaved his head, which made him look older than the age on his ID card. "We interviewed Detective Potter after the officer-involved shooting. It appears he followed procedure at this point." He shuffled to a wall and leaned his bulk against the surface. "What I don't understand is how you happened to be there?"

"Is this an investigation? Aren't you supposed to read me an advisement of my police officer's bill of rights?" Emily asked— she'd been down this road before.

The shifty guy put his hand up. "No, no, Detective. But Detective Potter claims his informant, Miller, thought you two were A.B.'s going to hit him."

"Have you seen me?" Javier said. "I'm brown. I failed the Aryan Brotherhood skin pigment test by this much." He put his thumb and forefinger together.

"How would Potter know two gang members were after Miller?"

"Miller called him."

"Did you check his cell phone to verify the calls?"

"The phone apparently broke during the confrontation in the alley," Shifty responded formally.

"How convenient for Potter." She turned to Javier. "Can you print out the photos from this afternoon?"

"Already done." Javier dug in his notebook and handed them to Emily. Shifty snatched them from her hands.

"What's this," he demanded.

Emily pointed. "That's Miller and Potter getting into a discussion a few hours before the shooting."

The round man came off the wall to look over the images, and as the photos were shuffled to the one where Miller knocked Potter on the ground at gunpoint, he said, "These were taken today?"

"Yep," Javier confirmed. "I've got the camera and the memory card right here if you need them."

"Doesn't come off as your average informant and cop relationship, does it?" Emily said. "You gonna let Detective Medina and I talk to him?"

"You know we can't let you do that," he responded.

"Tell you what, I wanna watch as you hand him these photos. Oh yeah, don't forget to ask him what he wanted in Wayne Corona's law offices," Emily said with a smile.

The two IA investigators waited for the other to object. Emily took the photos and, together with Javier, strode off in the direction of the IA offices where Potter waited, sequestered since the shooting.

The Internal Affairs investigator caught up with them and took the photos from Emily. "You can come in, but don't say a word—you got that? Not one word."

"Sure—sure." Emily gave Javier a look, which told him she had no intention of keeping her mouth shut.

The round-shaped investigator moved with his feet splayed apart, which made him waddle penguin-style down the hall. He opened a door where Detective Potter and a union representative huddled behind an empty table.

Potter smiled at Emily and then said to Javier, "Lucky for her I showed up when I did, eh, Hunter?"

"Thanks for that. Convenient for you to show up and save the day," Emily said with her hands in her pockets.

"That's enough, Detective." The shifty-eyed investigator tried to make a stern face as the round bald investigator placed the photos in front of Potter.

"What's this?" Potter's coffee cup halted halfway to his mouth. "Where did you take these?"

Emily pointed to Potter's fresh cut on the side of his head. "Is that where Miller cold-cocked you?"

"Hunter!" the shifty-eyed investigator warned.

"What the fuck are you talking about, Emily? I saved your ass from this piece of shit!" Potter stood, and the union rep forcibly pulled him back down in his seat. The rep whispered in his ear, and Potter's face grew hot with visible rage.

"What were you looking for in Wayne Corona's office, Josh?" Emily asked.

"Are you sure you wanna do this?" Potter replied.

"Shut up," the union rep scolded him.

"We know you were there."

"What if I was?"

"Still can't find the RICO files, huh?" Emily said.

"Those files . . . what are you talking about?" Potter said.

The taller IA officer got up from the table and told both Emily and Javier to leave. They agreed without another word. They'd heard all they needed to from Potter.

Before they shut the door, Potter called out, "Fuck you, Hunter!" Then to his union rep, "Get me an attorney."

The rep got up and responded, "Yeah, good luck with that—you're gonna need one."

"Everyone wants those files," Javier said.

"Must be interesting reading," Emily said to Javier as they left the IA offices. She pulled out her car keys and said, "I think we need a little visit to Mrs. Townsend to pay our respects. Need to make sure she's okay after her traumatic adventure."

CHAPTER THIRTY

IN THE CROWN Vic, Javier called the Townsends' home, and the housekeeper answered after it rang for a full minute. Javier prodded the housekeeper until she admitted the lady of the house busied herself packing for her trip.

"What trip?" Javier asked and tapped Emily's elbow.

The housekeeper responded, "Señora Townsend is taking a vacation to relax after all that has gone on."

Javier didn't want to spook the housekeeper, but kept asking questions. "Is Mrs. Townsend leaving?"

"Where?" Emily asked, barely above a whisper.

"Do you know where she's planning to go?"

"No . . . Señor Medina. I think I tell you too much already." The housekeeper hung up on Javier.

"Lori's leaving on a flight tonight. The housekeeper didn't want to tell me where. She's at the 46th Street house now."

"Call Simon Winslow in Communications. See if he can pull flight information on Townsend before we drop by. Her passport wasn't in her bank box." Emily gunned the engine out of the police station parking lot and headed north toward Broadway.

The early, mercifully light evening traffic allowed them to pull up in the Townsend driveway in less than fifteen minutes. What greeted them did not bode well. The garage on the 46th Street home was open and empty. God only knew what happened to the Porsche Lori Townsend had left at the biker house. The GPS unit stopped sending a signal—meaning the battery died, or the bikers found it. Now the black Mercedes vanished.

"We're too late," Emily said.

A shape in the kitchen window moved and Emily turned in the direction of the glass pane. Javier trod through the planter between the home and the side patio and tapped on the glass with a knuckle. The rapping sound reverberated off the window and filled the backyard; no mistaking this for an aggressive woodpecker.

Sheepishly, the housekeeper poked her head up from the kitchen counter and wasn't sure what to do when Javier motioned for her to meet him at the back door. She'd likely heard stories from her friends and family about the police in America and getting deported back home. She pointed at the rear door to her left, and Javier nodded.

The detectives approached the back door and heard a series of locks being turned, unchained, or pulled before it actually opened. The housekeeper opened only wide enough for her eyes.

"Where's Mrs. Townsend?" Emily asked.

"No sè," the woman responded.

"Is she here?"

"No . . . no . . . Mrs. Townsend leave already. Five minutes ago."

"Excuse me . . . can I come inside so we can talk?" Javier asked.

Carmen, the housekeeper, stuck a bony finger through the partially open door and pointed at Emily. "The Señorita may come in. You—take off your shoes first."

Javier glanced at his shoes caked with black loamy potting soil from the planter box he waded through. He sighed, and Emily walked past him through the now open doorway into the kitchen.

"Thank you, ma'am. Men are such slobs," Emily told Carmen as she entered the tidy kitchen space.

A dull thud came from the porch where Javier knocked the caked mud from his shoes. He dropped them by the doorway and stepped inside before he noticed the pair of socks he wore had a hole in the toe. His big toe stuck through the gap. Quickly, he adjusted the hole under his foot so it wasn't too obvious.

The housekeeper turned her back while she selected two coffee cups from the shelf. However, Emily caught him with his secretive sock adjustment, and she bit her lip and rolled her eyes at him.

No sooner than Javier had seated himself at the table, Carmen placed an antique china cup of rich smelling black coffee in front of them both.

"Carmen, we need to find Mrs. Townsend. Can you tell us where she's gone?" Emily asked. Javier seemed reluctant to touch the fragile coffee cup.

"I tell the man, Mrs. Townsend gone. I do not know where she is going, but she left with three big suitcases. She could be gone a long time."

"Does she take off frequently?" Emily asked.

"Sí . . . Yes. Mrs. Townsend travels a great deal."

"What man?" Emily interrupted.

"What?" Carmen asked.

"You said you told the man. What man did you tell about Mrs. Townsend leaving?"

Carmen looked worried she'd face the wrath of her employer for talking with the police. She sheepishly put her head down and answered. "After I talk to you on the telephone, a man rang the doorbell and wanted to see Mrs. Townsend." She paused. "He was not a very nice man. He pushed me and came into the house looking for her." She furtively glanced at Javier. "His feet were dirty too. That's how I found out she already left . . . he got mad and left. Señorita, that man had evil in his eyes."

"Tell me about him, Carmen?" Emily asked.

She closed her eyes as if she were imagining him in the room. "A white man, no hair on his head, and a big mustache."

"What else can you remember about him?"

"Sí . . . he was not a big man. He was perhaps as tall as you." She pointed to Detective Medina. "But he had big muscles in his arms and shoulders. He looked very strong and *muy peligroso* . . . I mean, dangerous."

Emily remembered she had the lineup photos they used with Benjamin Tooker in her notebook. "Maybe you can help." She laid the photo six-packs out in front of Carmen.

Carmen put one hand to her heart, and the other tapped nervously on one of the photographs. "This one! This is the man who came looking for Mrs. Townsend."

Carmen identified Dean Sands, the leading Aryan Brotherhood member in the Sacramento area. Until now, he'd been hiding in the background. With Miller out of the picture, Sands had to do his own dirty work. That work included Lori Townsend.

Emily gathered up the photograph "six-packs," swept them toward her, and Carmen grabbed one of the cards.

"What is it, Carmen?"

She furrowed her brow and held the card up to her face. "This man! Mrs. Townsend was supposed to go to the airport with him today. She was mad because he didn't come on time and was afraid she was going to miss her flight, so she left without him."

Once more, Detective Josh Potter figured in the investigation. Fleeing with the grieving widow.

CHAPTER THIRTY-ONE

CARMEN RELOCKED THE rear door and gave Javier a glare through the window as he knocked another clump of loamy soil from his shoes. Emily waited while he tied them and he said, "Potter seems to turn up everywhere. You think he planned on running away with Lori and living happily ever after?"

"I think he was the means to an end for Lori. As soon as she had no further use for him, he'd be left behind. From what I've picked up about Lori, she's focused on her upward mobility and Josh can't add much to the equation." She peeked at the muddy trail behind her partner and shook her head at him as if he were a child.

"You think if Potter got his hands on Lori's cash, he'd be in the wind?" Javier said.

"They deserve each other," Emily replied as they reached the Crown Vic.

As soon as Emily got behind the wheel, her cell phone vibrated in her pocket. Freeing the phone, she answered, "Hunter here."

"I got your request for flight info on your subject, Townsend," Simon Winslow from the department's Communication section responded.

"Get a hit?"

"She has a JetBlue flight to New York leaving Sacramento International tonight, with a connecting American Airlines flight to London Heathrow. The system shows she's traveling with a companion, a J. Potter. That person hasn't checked in yet."

"You mean Townsend checked in for the flight?"

"Affirmative. Flight leaves in about two and a half hours."

"Winslow, do me a favor and ask the Sheriff's substation at the airport to find her and keep an eye on her. Don't let her board that plane."

Winslow agreed, and Emily backed out of the driveway. She dialed another number quickly and asked for Internal Affairs. While she waited, she asked Javier, "What's the guy's name . . . the one with the shifty eyes?"

He shrugged and shook his head.

"This is Detective Hunter; I need to speak with the investigator on the Potter shooting. I don't care—whoever you can grab," she said into the receiver.

A few seconds later a man's voice came on the line. "Detective Hunter? This is Hammstead." Emily placed the IA officer's voice—the one with the shifty eyes. "I'm surprised by your call, Detective. Have a confession for me?"

Emily ignored Hammstead's jab. "Potter in the room with you?"

"That's none of your concern."

"Knock off the games, Hammstead. Potter's booked on a flight out of the country tonight. And if you're not eyes on with him right now, then I'd say you got a big problem."

Hammstead stuttered and Emily pictured the man's eyes darting over the room as he spoke. "No . . . Potter went on administrative time off pending the outcome of our inquiry." He paused.

"How did you come by this information? If you're interfering in my—"

"It's called investigation . . . I wouldn't expect you or any of the rubber gun squad to understand."

"Detective Hunter . . . you are to have zero contact with Detective Potter. Are you clear on that point?"

Emily struggled to contain her anger. "Listen, pinhead, if Potter leaves the country, you can kiss your precious administrative inquiry goodbye."

Finally, a sigh from Hammstead. "Detective, we know Potter is dirty. There's a two-man team parked watching his home."

"Then what are you waiting for?"

"We wanted to see who contacts him," Hammstead responded.

"And you thought it was gonna be me?"

A forced cackle came through the line. "You really don't know, do you, Detective?"

A pause. "Know what?"

"Miller's alive, and he came out from under sedation about a half hour ago. He's talking. Potter's been working with the Aryan Brotherhood for the last couple of years. Potter didn't even know you were there at the bank. Miller called him for backup. Potter's focus was Lori Townsend and the United States Attorney's RICO files she said were in her bank deposit box."

"Miller's alive?"

"He's messed up and will be for a long time. Can't move his arms or legs and he's struggling to speak. But, what he's been able to say is all about Potter. He wants him bad."

Emily pointed the Crown Vic north on Interstate 5 at eighty-five miles per hour, and barely kept pace with the traffic. She hung up on the Internal Affairs investigator so she could change lanes to avoid hitting the back end of a yellow and white bread truck tooling along at fifty in the fast lane.

"Miller's alive?" Javier repeated what he'd heard his partner say.

"Apparently—and he's ratting out Potter. Miller puts Josh deep into the shit with the Brotherhood."

She couldn't believe Josh got involved in the gang's activities, but everything she experienced in the last few days said otherwise.

As Emily exited at the airport turnoff, she said, "I get it, you know? I mean, I can see how it can happen. You work with the scum of the earth, day in and day out, and the closer you get, the more you get manipulated, or get talked into, doing some little thing to buy you credibility with the gang. Drop off some dope, shake down some shopkeeper, and it's part of your cover. But then they have you—they own you."

Emily pulled the car to the curb at Terminal B, one of two terminals at the regional airport. She held her identification to a Sheriff's Deputy working security in front of the terminal.

The deputy started to complain about leaving the car in the white passenger-loading zone, but noticed the police ID and waved them on.

Hundreds of passengers snaked around and through the security funnel at the top of the escalators. Only two of the six metal detectors were staffed during the late evening shift, and the glacial pace of passenger screening took a toll on travelers' nerves.

At the far left of the security lines, the detectives approached a Sheriff's Sergeant standing next to a TSA employee watching passengers as they left the security area of the terminal. After showing their IDs, the Sergeant radioed a deputy in the terminal and advised them two armed Sacramento Police Officers were on their way to the JetBlue gates.

The departure lounge for the New York JetBlue flight teemed with waiting passengers. All of the seats were taken, and a group of twenty to twenty-five high school students sat on the carpet. A slim woman in a black Sheriff's Department jumpsuit stood near one wall of the gate area and watched the passenger traffic. The bulk of the ballistic vest under her uniform did little to conceal an athletic body. Her utility belt cinched impossibly small and was crowded with her gun, extra magazines, expandable baton, two sets of handcuffs, a radio, and a pouch for latex gloves.

Emily approached the Deputy, and before she introduced themselves, the deputy said, "You must be the two detectives the Sarge called about." Her yellow and black name tag identified her as Brown.

Looking at the crowd, she asked, "Who are you looking for?"

Emily described Lori Townsend and suggested Javier walk to the end of the gate area and see if he spotted Lori, or perhaps she would see him and that would flush her out.

Javier nodded, but from the expression on his face, Emily knew he would rather wait here with the young deputy. He paced to the far end and searched the faces of passengers on both sides of the walkway. Tourists in bright Hawaiian shirts seized one corner of the lounge while they waited for their flight to Honolulu. Directly across the walkway, the New York–bound passengers waited. Some calmly read, listened to music through headphones, or chatted with people around them. No sign of Lori Townsend hiding in the busy crowd. Javier made it three-quarters of the way back, turned to Emily raising his hands in failure.

On cue, between Emily and Javier, Lori Townsend popped out of the women's restroom. She held a slim cell phone to her ear, and her expression turned from a carefree smile to frozen fear in a split second as her eyes locked with Emily.

The detective approached Lori, and she bolted in the other direction. The sudden movement alerted Javier before he spotted Lori.

"Oh crap—there she goes," Emily told the deputy.

Javier ran to intercept Lori, but Townsend turned a quick right and tried to lose her pursuers in the food court. Emily followed on Javier's heels into the bustling cafés and bistros. The sight of three running people drew a few panicked screams and sent food trays clattering to the floor. Lori pushed her way through a thickly packed coffee line and gained separation from the two detectives.

She reached an opening on the far side of the food court, thirty feet from the detectives, before a blur with blond hair and a black jumpsuit tackled Lori and pinned her to the ground. Deputy Brown held Lori down with a knee in the middle of the struggling woman's back.

Javier arrived, slightly winded. " . . . pretty . . . impressive."

Deputy Brown smiled and replied, "Three older brothers."

Emily put her handcuffs on Lori, and both women pulled Lori up from the floor. Two additional black-clad Sheriff's Deputies arrived, took custody of Townsend, and escorted her to the security offices located by the rows of metal detectors. Passengers in the lines temporarily stopped inching forward and watched the petite blond woman struggle with the deputies.

Javier told a worried curious older woman near the security lines that Lori tried to take more than the allowed number of carry-on bags. Within a minute, a flurry of bags piled at the security checkpoint for baggage check-in.

Lori waited in a holding room where she tried to regain her composure until Emily entered. "Going somewhere?"

CHAPTER THIRTY-TWO

LORI TOWNSEND'S AGITATION prevented her from sitting down in the sparsely furnished interview room. The beige walls and grey and brown carpet tiles did nothing to disguise its intended purpose, a temporary holding area for unruly passengers. It smelled of bitter vomit, an odor a heavy industrial disinfectant couldn't mask.

Emily and a sheriff's deputy entered the room, and Lori's eyes burned with contempt. "How dare you! I'll have your job for this, Detective," she said, directing the outburst at Emily.

Emily took one of the metal chairs at the table and wearily responded, "You want my job? You can have it." Emily shifted the chair, put her elbows on the table, and rested her chin in her hands. "Why the hurry to jet out of town, Mrs. Townsend?"

"I have every right to travel wherever I goddamn please," Lori spat back. She noticed her expensive light blue cashmere sweater bore dark coffee stains from her sudden landing near the food court. Lori absently wiped the stain with her hand.

"But in your case, it's called 'Flight to Avoid Prosecution.'" Emily added, "We know you planned on leaving with Josh Potter."

She rubbed the coffee-stained sweater vigorously, ignoring Emily momentarily. "It's ruined. This is worth more than your salary for a month."

"Well, get used to it. A spoiled, pampered woman like you is gonna get all chafed and break out in hives from the cheap prison jumpsuit you'll be wearing."

She momentarily stopped rubbing the sweater and responded, "What are you talking about, Detective Hunter? Did you forget, I'm the victim here?"

"You killed your husband to prevent him from filing for divorce. If he managed to file, you'd be left with nothing," Emily said and tried to bait her into a response.

Lori laughed loudly at the notion and said, "Detective, you don't know what you're talking about. I didn't kill Roger."

"Why don't you tell me how he died?"

Lori didn't bite. She finally sat down across from Emily and glared at her. She said, "As I've told you before, I returned home, and these men accosted me. They obviously did this. I don't know what happened before I came home."

Emily drove the first small crack in her story. "You've always said you didn't know if more than one man was involved; now you're saying *men* . . . plural. And you told the Chief Artie Miller was the killer. Which is it?"

"That's what you want to focus on, Detective? How many people beat me?" she said as she smoothed her blond hair.

"Who killed Roger? You? Artie Miller? Johnny Parkes? Josh Potter? How much does a hit cost nowadays?"

Lori leaned over the table and said in a low, controlled voice, barely above a whisper, "I don't know what you're talking about. I told you, Miller attacked me. Josh didn't have anything to do with it."

Emily said, "Really? Josh wasn't involved? Why should I believe you?"

Without a break in eye contact, she said, "Because I was on my way to see him the night Roger died. I wasn't really going to my yoga class."

"Can you tell me if anyone can verify your story?"

"Since I didn't make it to my class—no. Josh can tell you we planned to meet. Anyone who could tell you different is dead, Detective."

A knock at the interview room door preceded Javier entering. He bent to his partner's ear.

"I need to talk. We have a problem," Javier said.

Lori's icy gaze followed Emily to the door. "Hum ... let me guess?" she said. "Josh isn't going to meet me on the plane? That's a shame."

Outside the interview room, Javier said, "Potter's gone."

"What?"

Javier continued, "Internal Affairs watched his house, they checked on him again, and no one answered the door. They broke in, thinking Potter put a bullet in his head, but he'd gone."

"Let me guess, IA parked out front and Potter simply strolled out his back door."

"That's what I'm hearing. He didn't take much with him, but he left his badge on the kitchen counter," Javier said.

Emily thought for a moment. She put her hands on her hips and watched the snaking airport security lines. "He's not going to be here. Potter would know we'd be waiting for him," she said.

"But I thought the creep planned to meet up with Lori Townsend and leave the country together?"

"That was *his* plan. I'm beginning to think Lori never intended for him to join her."

Javier leaned back on the wall, jacket off, and shirtsleeves rolled up. "Lori's luggage was pulled from the plane and searched. Nothing there—no RICO files, no cash, nothing out of the ordinary for a vacation."

"Now what do we have on her? If Potter's in the wind and Miller doesn't pull through, we've got nothing on her." The frustration was evident on her face.

"We've got the extortion of the federal prosecutor for the RICO files on the Aryan Brotherhood," Javier responded. "That's how this mess started. The RICO files, the extortion, Josh Potter working for the AB, Roger Townsend's murder, the ransacking of the law office and the death of the attorney, Wayne Corona. All interconnected, but not quite linked up. You know?" he said.

Emily's expression brightened. "Then let's link them. We're gonna recruit the Aryan Brotherhood to help us find Potter."

"You've gotta be joking," he said.

"Nope. The AB isn't gonna be too happy Potter shot one of their own."

"It's all over the news, but why would they help us?"

"Because we're gonna ask real nice."

CHAPTER THIRTY-THREE

WHILE JAVIER MADE arrangements with the airport Sheriff's detail to transport Lori Townsend to the Main Jail downtown for booking on the extortion charge, Emily called the Police Department's gang unit. They were reluctant to talk to her because they'd discovered the Aryan Brotherhood compromised Detective Josh Potter. Months of investigations would be pulled into the spotlight, and only then would they find out how deeply the corruption crept into the unit.

Several minutes of begging and assurances got Emily an address. A different address from the house they'd watched Lori Townsend leave with Artie Miller before the gunfight at the bank. The gang unit gave her the location of an apartment building on Marconi Avenue. Dean Sands owned the small twelve-unit complex and resided in Apartment 10.

From the outside, the building blended with the scores of others lining the busy four-lane thoroughfare; most were at least four decades old with attractive names with visions of Villas, Garden Apartments, or River views. The villas, gardens, and rivers had long dried up and evaporated behind the metal gates, if they ever existed. The horseshoe-shaped apartment building featured a tan stucco arched entry in the front, with parking for the tenants along the rear of the complex. A faded brown and green sign hanging from the cracked stucco façade proclaimed the structure as the Palm Garden Apartments.

Javier pointed to an alley to the left of the building, and Emily pulled the Crown Vic down the narrow passage.

"No sneaking up on this bunch," Emily said as she glanced at more apartment windows occupied by watchers who clocked their slow drive to the parking area.

A few cars dotted the small parking area behind the building. An old Camaro, a Trans Am, and a battered Barracuda were the only ones without flat tires, or crazed windshields, and evidence of recent use. A faded 1970s green and white pickup truck with landscaping equipment rested in the back row. Parking the police sedan amongst the once proud relics, Emily felt eyes burning into the back of her skull.

"I didn't know this place was fancy enough to warrant a doorman," Javier said.

At the rear entrance of the complex, a large man stood with his tattooed forearms crossed. He tried his best to look imposing, and he did a pretty good job.

Before they got within ten feet of the man, he said, "I think you got lost," revealing twisted yellow teeth.

"Why's that?" Emily asked.

The biker flexed his thick neck muscles, and popping sounds came from his neck. His eyes were dark brown dots surrounded by a yellow cloud, which narrowed as he said, "We didn't call no cops."

Emily caught some movement above him and to her left. Another man, long dirty blond hair, in a black sleeveless t-shirt, appeared on the balcony railing of the second floor. He drank a beer from a green bottle, but the thick black Pachmayr gun grip sticking out from the man's waist drew Emily's attention.

"We need to talk to Dean Sands," Emily advised.

"I don't know any Sands," the man at the gate responded.

"Why don't you let him decide if he'll talk to us?"

"I don't know who you're talking about."

"We have something to tell him," Emily said, tired of the game.

"I don't care."

"It's about Artie Miller. He's been shot."

"You don't say? What's that to me?"

Emily stepped closer to the man, close enough to smell the sour breath behind the yellowed teeth. "I'm here to give you the man who shot him."

The man said nothing in return, the silence broken by the shatter of a green glass beer bottle at Emily's feet. The biker at the balcony railing threw it down and nodded to the gatekeeper to let them in.

Inside the courtyard of the apartment complex, there were neither palms nor any garden in view. More than a dozen motorcycles, spare parts, and four large barbecue grills filled the cement surfaces. Where a pool once served as the central feature of the courtyard, the empty chipped blue tile pit now served as a garbage dump, motorcycle oil stains evident on the sides.

One of the apartment doors opened, and a man with an impossibly thick mustache running down both sides of his mouth and into a stump of a goatee motioned for them. He wore dark, thick-framed sunglasses, even though the sun had set.

"This isn't a good idea, Emily," Javier mumbled to his partner.

"Yeah—something tells me this isn't your typical college student apartment building."

"You really have a future as a detective."

The man at the door motioned them inside with a sideways nod. He didn't follow them inside and shut the door after the detectives entered.

The living room space of the apartment came furnished with a table and four cheap folding chairs. In the dim light, they found the walls covered with White Power posters and Nazi flags. Torn newspaper articles featuring hate crimes, cross burnings, and church arsons were mementos tacked to the walls.

Emily wiped her hand across the table and smelled the odor on her fingertips. "Gun oil. I guess this is a multipurpose room. I bet the armory is in there." She pointed to a heavy door with a commercial deadbolt, which had replaced the bedroom door in the apartment.

Behind them, the door to the courtyard opened, streaming in light from a halogen lamp into the dark space. The bright yard light reminded the men of home—in prison. Dean Sands entered first, the only one of the small group who didn't carry the build of a professional wrestler.

"Please take a seat," Sands said while the two muscled thugs stood behind him.

The two detectives sat in the folding chairs facing the gang's shot-caller.

Sands leaned back in his chair and said, "I understand you wanted to talk . . . so talk."

"I thought you'd want to know Artie Miller has been shot," Emily said.

No outward reaction came from Sands. "Why would a shooting be of any interest to me?"

"I know who shot him."

A throaty laugh came from Sands. "Let's cut the bullshit, Detective. You know who I am and I know who you are. That's why I didn't ask you to turn over your weapons. Call it professional courtesy." Sands leaned in. "I haven't heard of any shooting, but if one of my brothers got himself stabbed or shot, that's my business, and I don't need your help to make it right."

Javier jumped in, "Even if one of your own brothers shot Miller?"

Sands' eyes didn't acknowledge Javier; they stayed locked onto Emily. "That's not possible. No one makes a move against a brother without a green light from me—or so I've heard."

"Why don't we take you to see Miller in intensive care?" Emily said.

Another phlegm-coated laugh from the gang leader. "So I can walk into some sting you set up? Fat fucking chance."

"Then you go see him on your own. I'll make sure no one bothers you going in or out. Call it professional courtesy," Emily said.

Sands leaned back once more and silently pondered the detective's offer. "Why?" he asked. "What's in this for you?"

"I need your help," Emily replied.

"Last time the cops 'helped' me, I ended up in Pelican Bay. What do you need my help for?"

"I need to find the man who shot Miller."

"If this is true, then why would I turn over one of our own?"

"Let's say our interests are temporarily aligned," Emily answered.

"If I go along with your little plan, what's in it for me?"

"You get the man who pulled the trigger."

Javier's face tightened. He pulled his partner's arm and whispered, "What are you doing? You can't have him killed." His eyes betrayed the panic she felt.

Sands caught the slight shock registered in the detective's eyes and said, "Hum, someone doesn't agree with you. Must be good." He paused, then said, "Okay, let's take this one step at a time. First, you tell me who supposedly shot Miller. Second, I talk to Miller, and you walk away—no questions asked."

"Fine," Emily replied.

"Emily, you can't do that." Then to Sands, "Find him and turn him over to us."

Sands said, "If we find him, there won't be much left to turn over. Think of it as my contribution to reducing prison overcrowding." He leaned forward again, staring at Emily. "So . . . give me a name."

The two thugs behind Sands tensed waiting for the disclosure of one of their own who they were now obliged to kill in retribution.

"Detective Josh Potter," Emily said.

Javier slumped and dropped his head.

"Well, well," Sands responded. "But you got it wrong. Potter never rose up to become one of us—too weak minded. Why you telling me another cop shot Miller?"

"Potter's dirty. We know he worked for you."

"He was an errand boy—that's all."

"You gonna find him or what?"

"I'm thinkin'."

Emily waited for a second, then added, "He mentioned something about a file."

"What file?" Sands' interest was piqued.

"Some file he stole from a woman," Emily said.

She hooked him, as Emily knew she would.

The gang leader silently nodded and then asked, "Let me talk to Miller."

Slowly, Emily reached into her jacket and pulled out a cell phone. "We can do this either way. You go and talk to him at the U.C. Davis Medical Center, or by phone." Emily dialed the number for the nurses' station in the ICU.

"This is Detective Hunter—put me through to patient Miller."
A pause in the conversation, then, "Yes, I know he's not supposed
to get calls, but tell the officer watching him to pick up the phone."

After two full minutes, a voice came on the phone. "Who the
hell is this?"

"Detective Hunter. Who's this?"

"Officer Phillips . . ."

"Put Miller on the phone, would you?"

"Detective, we're not supposed to do that."

"It's on me. I need to talk to him."

Silence from the officer's end of the phone.

"Phillips . . . you there?

"Um . . . Yeah."

"Put Miller on the phone now. I'm taking full responsibility."

A rustling noise followed another voice, this one much weaker.
"Yeah?"

"Miller, I've got someone who wants to talk to you." Emily
pushed the speaker button and put the cell on the table.

"Artie, is that you?"

"Yeah, dude. I fucked up and—"

Sands cut Miller off and instructed him to listen. "Don't say
nothing, 'cept yes or no. You got that?"

"Yeah."

"Okay . . . I got a cop here who says Josh Potter shot you. That
right?"

"Yeah."

"Did Potter get our file?"

"Yeah, probably. That Townsend bitch supposed to get it from
her . . ."

"No names!"

"Sorry. But he might have it," Miller admitted.

"You need anything, dude?"

"Nah, they giving me all kinds of drugs . . . it's cool."

"We'll make this right by you, brother. I'll take care of this personally," Sands promised.

"I know. I ain't worried," Miller said in a drug-induced fog.

Sands ended the call and slid the cell phone across the table toward Emily. The phone now held a slight oily sheen from the gun lubricant.

"I think we're done here. We'll take care of your little problem."

"You gonna tell us when you find him?" Emily asked.

Sands shrugged. "Maybe." He got up from the table, and the two thugs led him to the door of the apartment. At the door, Sands turned around and said, "Don't ever come back here again."

"And miss the hospitality?" Emily said.

The mustachioed doorman appeared, and once more silently crooked his head for them to leave. He escorted the two detectives to the rear of the courtyard, where the iron gate stood open for their departure.

Javier brushed Emily aside and quickly returned to the sedan. Emily followed and got in behind the wheel. Sullen, Javier couldn't look at his partner. His face and neck flushed.

"What the hell have you done? You put a contract out on another cop?"

"Do you trust me, Javi?" she said.

"I used to, I want to . . . but I . . . I don't know if I can do this," he replied. He cast his eyes down and watched his shoe pick at a hole in the floor mat.

"Trust me. We're gonna follow Sands, and he'll lead us right to Potter. We'll take him down before he has a chance to get him."

"You're playing a game with Potter's life. Sands and the rest of the AB don't mess around."

"Remember, Javi—Potter put himself in this position. He's the one who aligned himself with the Nazi assholes. He's the one who shot Miller. And I want him to pay for it. Having the AB hit him is the easy way out. Sands already knew Potter shot Miller. News like that travels at the speed of sound. We needed Sands to think we'd let him get rid of Potter. That's the last thing I want. I want him to spend the rest of his life in prison."

As they backed out of the parking slip, Emily's cell phone vibrated in the center console. She hit the speaker button. "Detective Hunter," she said.

"Emily . . . it's Lisa." Lisa Gonzales was a friend who worked the booking area of the Sacramento County Jail.

"Hi, Lisa, what's up?"

"I processed a case and you were listed as one of the arresting officers . . . Lori Townsend."

"Yeah, she's a piece of work. She won't give your accommodations a great review."

"I'll bet, but that won't be a problem, that's why I called. She made bail within ten minutes. Quickest damned thing I ever saw. She—"

"What did you say?" Emily stiffened behind the wheel.

"She cash bailed with a hundred and fifty thousand dollars. I've never seen so much money in my life."

"How . . . who . . ." Emily stuttered.

"Some guy walks in and says he's here to bail her out and pops open a briefcase full of cash. Oh and get this . . . he's a cop."

"Josh Potter?"

"How'd you know?"

CHAPTER THIRTY-FOUR

"POTTER BAILED OUT Townsend?" Javier asked after he overheard the phone conversation with the deputy at the jail.

"In cash," she replied.

"Should we head back to the airport?"

Emily pulled a blue rectangular object from her jacket pocket. "Nope, I kept her passport. She's not leaving the country this time."

"Where's he taking her? Where can they hide?"

Emily pulled the Crown Vic into a corner gas station and mini-market combination. The small establishment posted signs in at least four different languages other than English, one of which exhibited the sharp lines and angles of Sanskrit. Emily nudged the sedan behind the building, came up slowly along the side, and watched the traffic on Marconi.

"If we got a call, I'd bet Sands did too," Emily said.

"Right. Someone at the jail tipped them off the moment Johnny Parkes got booked—it makes sense they would know if Lori Townsend made bail."

"And we'll follow Sands. That's the best bet we have. Potter wouldn't risk going to either of the Townsend homes or his own. He knows we'd be watching those places."

They scanned the cars, almost empty public transit buses, and delivery trucks roll by their hiding spot. The red light at the intersection backed up the flow enough to allow the detectives to search the vehicles for Sands and his crew. All of the cars and trucks started to look the same. The people in them didn't match Sands, with his bald head and muscular frame.

The traffic light turned red once more, and the traffic piled up. They both spied the aged green and white pickup truck pull behind the line of cars.

"Kinda late for gardening, don't you think," she asked her partner.

"It's Sands behind the wheel. He's all by himself. That's odd. Maybe it's not him."

Emily started the sedan's engine. "It's him. It just hit me. It's the truck we saw drive in at Lori's Granite Bay house after we met with her out there. Damn. Sands drove right by, and we were that close."

"We didn't know Sands then."

Emily waited for the light and let the traffic clear before she pulled in the street. She followed the green and white landscaping truck at a distance. It pulled on Interstate 80, headed downtown, and Emily held back. The old truck trudged along in the slow lane, and the detectives continued the surveillance at a distance.

"This could take a while," she sighed. She pulled out her cell and hit a speed dial button. "I'm gonna check on Mom and let her know I'll be late."

No answer on the home phone. "The phone must be turned off, straight to voice mail."

"Don't worry, Emily. She's safe at your place with my mom."

"It's not her safety in the house that worries me now. She could walk out the front door the second your mom turns her back, and that worries me."

"You got her that GPS pendant, right?"

"I still worry, Javi."

"Yeah—you make that an Olympic sport."

"I don't want to trust Mom's well-being to a fricken app."

Anxious to change the conversation, Javier asked, "You wanna tell me about you and Officer Booty Bandit?"

"There's nothing to tell."

"Nothing?" Javier said.

"Nothing I'm going to tell you."

"Too bad. You want me to drop you off at the convent?"

"Ass."

"The nuns at the convent won't appreciate your language."

Javier switched into a serious mode. "He's getting off at the exit up ahead."

"I got him."

"He's slowing. Shit, he's pulling off to the shoulder. Shit . . . shit . . . shit," Javier said.

"He made us. I don't know how, but he did." Her eyes flicked to the rearview mirror. "How could I have been so stupid?"

Behind them, the battered Trans Am tailed the Crown Vic, and she never noticed.

"This could get ugly—call it in," Emily ordered as he slowed the car behind the green and white pickup truck.

She didn't hear what Javier said into the radio. Her attention locked on Sands and the evil smile on his face. The man leaned casually against the tailgate of the truck with his arms folded.

The old Pontiac Trans Am pulled to a stop about three car lengths behind the police sedan. The two occupants made no move to get out of the muscle car.

Emily and Javier exited the vehicle at the same time. Javier pulled the stubby Winchester 12 gauge shotgun from the rack under the front seat, pulled the slide back chambering a round, and pointed it at the front window of the Trans Am. Emily held her Glock trained on Sands.

"Well, Detective, I didn't know you came out for roadside assistance calls," Sands said.

"We heard there was garbage on the road."

"Now, Detective, we can do this the easy way," Sands said as he took a step forward toward Emily.

"Don't fuckin' move, Sands."

Sands put up his hands and continued. "Or we can do this the hard way. I'm gonna pull my cell from my pocket."

Emily tensed and followed the gang leader's hand to his shirt pocket. "Something you need to see. Here," he said as he tossed the phone to Emily.

She didn't attempt to catch it and kept her pistol aimed at the AB's chest. Emily called out to her partner, "Javi? How we doing?"

"Two in the car, not moving."

Emily freed one hand from the grip on her pistol and knelt for the cell phone.

"There you go, Detective. I decided to pick up a little insurance policy. Look at the picture on the screen."

Emily glanced down, and her knees nearly buckled. An ice ball formed in her chest and threatened to explode over the image of her mother and Lucinda Medina.

"What—what have you done?" Emily said.

She kept her Glock on Sands, but it suddenly felt heavy.

Sands took another step closer, close enough to take the phone from Emily while the detective's pistol pressed against his chest. Sands pressed buttons on the phone and a short, blurry video played on the small screen. It showed her mother and Lucinda talking as they entered a movie theatre.

"Where is she?"

"What's going on, Emily?" Javier asked while he kept the shot-gun on the other vehicle.

"As you can see, Mom and her little friend are at the movies. If you do exactly as I tell you, she'll go home after and live to see another day." Sands' face transformed as he continued, "If you don't, I'll cut her fucking head off and toss it in the river."

"How do I know—you—haven't already—hurt her?" Emily asked.

"You don't. But that's the chance you have to take, isn't it?"

Emily re-gripped the pistol tightly and yelled, "Where is she?"

"You're coming with me. Deliver me Potter and the RICO file, she'll be allowed to leave the movie and go home. If not, well—"

"Emily—no!" Javier yelled.

Emily slowly lowered her pistol to her side.

"Don't do it. You can't believe a thing that asshole says."

"I have to . . . for them."

Emily staggered forward toward the green and white pickup truck. The last thing Javier heard before the truck sped away was the metallic clink of the magazine from his partner's Glock hit-ting the pavement along with her cell phone. The Trans Am spit gravel as it passed Javier; he ducked behind the Crown Vic. A shiver raced up his spine. He realized he might never see his part-ner again.

CHAPTER THIRTY-FIVE

THE VIEW OUT the truck window came as a blue-green blur dotted with amber. Emily couldn't focus on the buildings or street lamps as the landscaping truck drove through a residential neighborhood. The cruelty to prey on an old woman with dementia struck an all-time low. Emily knew Sands would kill her, but if her sacrifice let her mother live out the rest of her life in peace, then so be it. She resolved she would do anything to save her.

The detective felt the truck slow before she noticed Sands had turned off the truck's headlights and crept the old truck to a stop.

Thick tree limbs blocked most of the light from ancient street lamps, and the few rays managing to pierce the canopy left dark, complex patterns in the shadows. Set back from the street, a murky outline of a Victorian-style two-story house was hidden in the overgrowth and shadow. A dim light shone from behind a yellowed curtain on the second floor.

"That's where you're goin', Detective," Sands said as he seized Emily by the elbow.

"What is this place? What makes you think Potter is here?"

"We have eyes everywhere. He's here. You screw this up and your mom's dead. It's as simple as that. You got it?"

Emily pulled her elbow away from the gang leader's grip. She stared back at the lifeless eyes and responded, "Yeah, I get it. You expect me to go in there and grab Potter with an empty gun?"

"He doesn't know that. Besides, I'll be right behind you. Now go."

The dull interior light flicked on when the truck's doors opened. Sands gestured with a machete he withdrew from the assorted landscaping tools piled in the back of the truck and told Emily, "Move."

The detective did as he ordered and left the truck door slightly ajar. The lamp in the cab glowed, but Sands anticipated the confrontation in the house and didn't notice. Emily hoped someone would see the light in the truck and come check it out. That someone, she hoped, would find her detective's badge on the front seat. She recognized it was a desperate act, and if this was a neighborhood where everyone kept to themselves, no one would see the light in the truck, nor the badge glimmering on the seat, signaling for help.

Sands pushed Emily in front of him, poked her back with the tip of the machete, and urged her forward, up the wide wooden stairs to a covered patio spanning the entire width of the front of the home. In the darkness, Emily couldn't pin down the house color; blue, green, or grey; it didn't matter, it was dark and foreboding.

A stair tread gave slightly under her weight and creaked. In the enveloping silence, the noise felt amplified; it provided a certain warning to those who hid inside. Emily expected Potter to burst through the front door at any second. Yet, another step, and then another, with no sign of Potter.

At the landing, Sands prodded Emily again with the machete, a small arc slicing across her shoulder blade. The detective winced at the searing pain as she moved to the door.

The tarnished and broken brass doorknob limply spun in a helpless circle. A new-looking deadbolt was installed in the door above the old knob. The gleam of the new metal reflected back in the darkness.

"Now what?" Emily asked.

Sands dug a ball of keys from his pocket and sorted through them until he found one. He handed the ball to Emily, the correct key held between his fingertips.

In the dark, she considered using the bundle of sharp jagged keys as a weapon, gouging out the gang leader's eyes. What would happen to her mom and Lucinda if she failed? She decided against action, for now, and slowly slid the key into the deadbolt. Through the thin metal, she felt the pins traveling up against the pressure of the key. The deadbolt turned smoothly and slid from the door frame, opening the home to Sands and his captive.

The gang leader hurried into the shadows beyond the door so his silhouette wouldn't be an easy target.

Emily reached for her weapon before she entered the home, only to remember the Glock was unloaded. A musty smell of urine and vomit overtook her senses. She removed the ball of keys dangling from the lock and stuffed them in her pants pocket before she followed Sands inside.

The entry hall remained still, and the thick black spread out into the distance. Rooms, walls, and doors stood nearby, concealed in the pitch dark in front of them. Emily felt her way along the wall to her right and hit a heavy table with her leg. A vase fell to the floor, where it shattered into pieces. Her feet crunched through the debris, and the sound crackled in the thick air.

A sliver of light appeared at the top of the staircase. The shadow of a man reflected off of a wall at the top of the stairs, and if Emily stayed in place, she would be in the open. The shattered fragments of the vase crunched under her quick footfall to the side of the staircase.

The stair treads at the top creaked as the shadowed man's weight tested them, one by one. Emily recognized the profile in the dark—Potter. Emily ducked to the side of the staircase and curled up, making herself as small and invisible in the dark as possible. The sound of steps on the stairs came closer. She held her breath when a warm and hairy creature brushed against her hand.

A pair of small green eyes reflected back, and a mouth full of sharp white teeth exposed themselves as a feral cat hissed loudly. A deep guttural yowl rose from the depths of the feline as she announced the stranger's presence. Potter came halfway down, judged by the groan of the stairs.

Emily caught the cat under its matted fur underbelly and tossed her out at the base of the stairs. The animal slid through the pieces of the vase, batting a few of them in anger. The cat slunk down low on its haunches, gazing up the staircase, and issued another deep yowl before the stray bounded into the darker recesses of the first floor.

The stairs were silent for at least a minute before Potter's voice broke. "Fucking cats."

The creak on the wooden stairs reversed as Potter retreated, satisfied one of the strays who claimed the first floor as their litter box was responsible for the noise.

Emily let out her breath, unaware that she'd held it in. Sands watched her with amusement, tucked back in a shadowed corner.

"Move," Sands whispered harshly.

Emily pulled herself up from the floor and kept to the far edge of the stairs where her weight made it less likely to squeak. Behind her, Sands didn't care to hide his approach. The wood bent at the fourth step, and the sound shot straight up Emily's spine. Potter had to hear that, she thought.

Rather than being caught in the open stairwell, Emily ran up the remaining eight steps, making as little noise as possible. She'd been right—Potter heard the sound and opened the door to the right of the stairs. Potter didn't expect to be face-to-face with Emily when he opened the door, and the man froze for a second.

That gave Emily her opening. She sent a knee up into Potter's groin and came across with an elbow to his nose, which resulted in a satisfying crack. She whipped the ball of metal keys to the back of his head sending Potter to his knees, clutching his testicles. Blood wept from a laceration on the bridge of his nose while Potter glared back at Emily.

"What are you doing here, Hunter?" Potter groaned. "This has nothing to do with you."

"No, it has to do with you and me and some unfinished business," said Sands from behind Emily.

Sands moved quickly and kicked Potter in the jaw with his steel-toed black boot. Potter fell backward into the room, unconscious. Sands kicked the former cop several more times in a frenzied attack and rolled the unresponsive Potter on his stomach. Kneeling on Potter's back, Sands pulled the man's head up by his hair with one hand and pulled the bayonet from the sheath on his boot with the other.

"No!" Emily yelled.

Lori Townsend emerged from the shadows, holding a blue steel .38 caliber revolver. She cried out, "Stop," and trained the short-barreled revolver at Sands.

"Now you get brave, bitch?" Sands growled as he put the knife to Potter's limp throat.

Sands dropped his machete in favor of the smaller blade. With her back pressed to the wall, Emily slowly sidestepped away from the door and squatted for the machete.

Lori pulled the trigger on the .38, and a bullet slammed into the floor, sending wood splinters from the old oak boards. "Nobody move," she ordered.

"Let him go," Lori directed at Sands.

"Give me the file," Sands countered.

"I told you it's in a safe place."

Sands stiffened and drew the knife lightly across Potter's throat, a thin line of blood oozing from the wound. "I'm not falling for that again. Give me the file now, or I'll kill him."

A strange look came over Lori's face, one of resolve. She turned to Emily and said, "Detective Hunter—Sands killed my husband."

"Shut up, bitch," Sands snarled. "Where is the file?"

"He and Johnny Parkes forced their way into my home and killed Roger." Without any trace of emotion, Lori pulled the trigger repeatedly until the hammer fell on an empty cylinder with a click.

Dean Sands lay on the floor next to Potter, both men bleding profusely. Lori Townsend had shot them both—Potter twice in the back and Sands hit three times in the chest.

Then Lori Townsend pulled the trigger again, and the click of the hammer finally registered with her. "Are you working with them, Detective?" she asked.

"No," Emily responded.

Lori dropped the gun and rushed to Emily and said, "Thank you for finding me, Detective."

Emily wasn't sure what happened, exactly. One minute Sands threatened Lori to hand over the files—or he'd kill Potter. Then she gunned them both down and implicated Sands in Roger

Townsend's murder—not Miller; and Sands hadn't denied her accusation.

The sound of heavy footsteps and light from a score of flash-lights came from the front of the house. Emily was caught in the spotlight with a trembling Lori Townsend.

CHAPTER THIRTY-SIX

JAVIER CAME FROM behind one of the lights. "Let's get the paramedics in here!" He stepped aside while two blue-clad men with heavy equipment bags reached the two men on the floor.

"Javi . . . how did you?" Emily asked.

"I think you'll need this," he said as he handed over her detective's badge she'd left in the pickup truck. "Miller. He told us about this house. One of their safe houses apparently."

Lori stiffened at the mention of Miller's name and backed away from Emily. "Miller's dead . . ." she said, a measure of uncertainty in her voice.

"This one's a goner," one of the paramedics announced. "Call in for the ME, would you."

"Miller's alive and talking, sweetheart," Javier responded to Lori.

Lori stood rod straight, her superior, standoffish manner returning.

"Sands killed my husband and threatened to kill me if I told you."

Javier closed in on Lori. "Miller said you hired them to kill your husband."

"That's a lie—I didn't. You can't prove it. I had nothing to do with it," Lori spit back. "They did it. They killed Roger."

One of the paramedics yelled, "I've got a pulse on this one! Let's load him up!" In spite of the three bullet wounds to his chest, Sands had survived.

Emily turned from the wounded gang leader to Lori; the widow's expression changed, from a mask of confidence to one of uncertainty.

"Miller says you hired them, and I'm gonna take a statement from Sands while he's in the emergency room."

Lori cut Emily off, "They're both criminals . . . who'd believe them? That animal isn't giving a statement to anyone."

"Oh, I'll get a statement from him," Emily said. "If he dies on the operating table, all the better. Then it's called a dying declaration, and it's worth its weight in gold in front of a jury."

"He's a thug, no jury would believe him," Lori said, not sure of herself.

"Don't forget Miller," Javier piled on.

Lori backed away from the two detectives and pressed herself against the wall.

"Javi, what do you think a jury would say? Lori here finds out her husband is about to file for divorce and she hires the dirtbag to kill Roger. Then, to cover their tracks, they ransack the Corona law office, but they can't find the divorce papers, because they were sitting on the fax machine."

A look of surprise in Lori's eyes betrayed the fact she believed the police had found the divorce papers in some hidden safe, or file, not simply tossed on a fax machine. A crack formed in her foundation.

Emily continued, "I wonder how much she paid Sands for his—um—services?"

Lori remained silent.

Javier responded, "Miller can fill in the blanks on that."

"I think it's time I speak to my attorney," Lori said as another crack showed.

"Too bad, Wayne Corona's dead," Emily said with mock sincerity.

Lori's eyes cast to the ground; she pulled inward, unresponsive to any further prodding from the detectives. A far cry from the gregarious socialite they had encountered a few days earlier.

Javier gestured for a uniform to book her downtown. Emily called him off. "This one's mine," she said.

Emily gripped Lori's hand, forced her around, and held Lori's wrist behind her back. While the handcuffs ratcheted on each of Lori's slim wrists, she remained sullen and mute.

A uniformed officer escorted her out to a police car parked at the curb outside. For a split second, Emily swore a wry smile grew on Lori's lips as she left the scene.

"Son of a bitch," Emily muttered.

"What?"

"She played us."

"What are you talking about? We've got her on murder. She killed Potter and attempted to kill Sands. Add that to the extortion and her attempt to jump bail . . . she's toast."

"She'll claim she ran in fear of her life from the Aryan Brotherhood. The shooting will play out in court as a distraught woman trying to save her most recent lover, Potter, and in her panic, shot them both."

"But the divorce?"

"There's no proof she knew what Roger planned," Emily responded. "She'll lay off the whole RICO file thing as Roger's doing. The last desperate greedy act of a dying man."

"She could pull that off?" Javier asked. "Oh, here. I found this. Might need to get the screen fixed." He handed Emily the cell phone she was forced to toss when Sands took her away. A diagonal crack in the screen ran from corner to corner.

"You've seen her act. Yeah, she can pull that off."

CHAPTER THIRTY-SEVEN

Lucinda Medina helped Connie Hunter out of the movie theatre and put a sweater around the old woman's shoulders to ward off the evening chill. The twelve-screen theatre complex ended four films on the hour and the lobby filled with popcorn-scented moviegoers. The exiting pack flowed out to the parking lot from the exit doors.

Unseen by the old woman and her attendant, a man in the back of the parking lot watched their progress. He blended into the background with a black leather motorcycle jacket, dark jeans, and boots. Through the lens of a small pair of binoculars, the biker followed the old women as they came out of the multiplex.

The biker's instructions were clear. If he didn't hear from Sands by the time the movie got out, the old woman dies.

"Oh well, the old bird had a good run," he thought aloud. The biker put the binoculars down and picked up an M-4 military-issue rifle. The compact scope drew his target in close.

"What did you do to piss off the Sandman, you old broad?" he mumbled.

The old woman's face filled the scope and looked back at him. Her eyes grew wide, and her face showed shock and surprise. She couldn't possibly see him among the trees behind the parking lot.

A dark blur covered the scope, obscuring his view of the woman. The biker jerked his head up at the sight of another woman between him and his target. A younger woman rushed toward the shuffling old crone with her back to the rifleman.

"What the hell?" The biker lowered his eye to the scope, and the picture cleared once more. The old woman's face was exposed. Centering the crosshairs on her forehead, the rifleman let half of his breath out and caressed the trigger.

In the millisecond before he put enough pressure on the trigger to fire the weapon, he stopped. The younger woman's face turned under a streetlight. He recognized the bitch detective Sands had met with earlier today. What brought her out here?

The biker slung the rifle over his shoulder and pulled out a cell phone. He hurriedly pecked out a number with his gloved hands. He put it to his ear and heard it start to ring. Then he heard a phone ring out in the parking lot.

He watched as Emily fumbled with a plastic bag and pulled a black object from the wrapping. "Yeah?" Emily said into the confiscated gang leader's phone.

"Detective? I take it since you're holding Sandman's phone, he's off the board?"

"Yeah, what's it to you?"

"Is she your mother?"

Emily turned in a quick circle and scanned the area around the parking lot. The lack of lighting beyond the edge of the lot turned the distance into an inky fog. She hugged her mother and pulled her and Lucinda down behind a car. Emily didn't know from which direction the threat came.

"What do you want?" Emily said.

"Ah . . . the old woman is yours," the voice said. "Sands told me to take her out, and I have to ask why?"

"She's not part of this . . ."

"I agree. Sands crossed a line if he targeted family."

Emily expected a gunshot to ring out from the darkness beyond the parking lot at any moment. She pushed her mom down on the pavement to make the smallest target possible.

"What did she do to get a green light from Sands?" the biker asked the detective.

"She's not involved in any of his business."

"Somebody thought she was and Sands gave the order."

"Do you have family?" Emily asked in return. The threat implied if the man killed her family, his family would face retribution.

"Tell them to get the hell out of here."

Emily knelt down and put an arm around her mother. She felt her tremble under her touch. Softly, she told Lucinda, "I need you to take her and leave now."

Frozen in place, Lucinda made no effort to move. Her eyes filled with tears.

"I'm scared," she said in a slight whisper.

"You need to leave . . . now. Come on." She pulled her mother to her feet.

Lucinda put an arm around Emily's mother, trying to calm her. She pointed somewhere in the parking lot and asked, "The car?"

Emily nodded, and Lucinda prodded the older woman along, and within seconds they sped from the parking lot, leaving Emily alone. Her mother's placid face peered out the rear window. She'd already forgotten the trauma in the parking lot. The only benefit of the frail mind and memory of dementia.

"Now what do we do?" Emily said into the cell phone.

"I'd be within my rights to take you out—you're a cop," the biker said as he sighted in on Emily through the scope of the military rifle.

Emily caught the glint off of the lens of the scope, fifty feet from the edge of the parking lot. She raised her chin and stared back.

"In a sense, you did us a favor. Sands went renegade. If you took him down, that's good for me. With him and Artie out of the way, I'm next in line."

"I'm so happy for you," Emily said.

"Dude got sideways with the Boys up North and wasn't pulling his end on paying tribute. His name was in the hat anyway."

Emily knew he meant Sands hadn't sent enough money and drugs to the Aryan Brotherhood members at Pelican Bay State Prison and Sands was marked for a hit from within the gang.

"I hear Miller is talking—that's unhealthy," the gang member said. "That's too bad, 'cause Artie used to be a solid Wood, but he's weak minded."

"At least he's alive—I'm not sure how Sands will end up—he didn't look good."

"Did you shoot him?"

"Wish I did . . . but no."

"Who?"

"Why is that important?"

The biker paused and in a laugh that scraped like sandpaper in her ear, said, "It was the bitch, wasn't it? I knew she'd fuck him up. I knew it the minute we got the contract to hit Roger Townsend."

"Why are you telling me Lori Townsend put out a hit on her husband? We know she did." Emily wasn't sure why this guy decided to get chatty all of a sudden.

The man laughed the sandpaper chuckle again. "Roger Townsend came to us and wanted us to kill him. He was dyin' of cancer or somthin'."

"What? You're telling me Roger put out a contract on himself?"

"Yep. But that's where Sands got sloppy. He got to the wife, and it turns out she wanted him dead too." The sandpaper laugh sounded once more. "Dude was gonna divorce his ol' lady before Sands did the job."

"Sands got greedy and wanted to be paid twice for the same hit," Emily replied.

"Uh-huh. 'Cept for things got real squirrelly when the lady didn't come up with her end."

"The RICO files?"

"I'm not saying any more. You know the gun you found taped to the desk in that dirtbag attorney's place? Check it out—check it out."

The cell call disconnected, and Emily thought briefly about running into the darkness ahead and going after the man on the other end of the call. Her mind felt scattered with concern for her mother and the revelation that Roger Townsend had contracted with the Aryan Brotherhood for what amounted to assisted suicide.

She leaned against the trunk of a car and tried to make sense of everything. She called Javier on his cell and recounted the story provided by the biker.

"You believe him?"

"I don't know. Part of it sounded like bullshit to me. He wasn't too upset about Miller and Sands going down."

Javier paused. "Do you need me to take the gun for processing again?"

"Might as well. Nothing to lose. I'll meet you back at the office, say twenty minutes?"

Emily disconnected from the call and punched in another number. She wasn't going to allow her mother to be threatened again. She needed to call in a favor.

CHAPTER THIRTY-EIGHT

JAVIER PUSHED INTO the detective bureau and found Emily at her desk. She acted surprised to see him, even though he'd told her he was on his way in. "Whatcha up to?" he mumbled.

Emily got up from the desk and met Javier by the door, blocking his path. She kept stepping in his way as he approached, a sheepdog herding Javier away from her desk.

"I asked the techs to pull the report on the gun again, and they're gonna bring it up for us. They already finished the ballistics on the gun yesterday and confirmed the gun was used to shoot Roger Townsend in the back," she said.

"What's going on?"

"I told you," she said a bit defensively.

He sniffed the air and said, "What do we have here?"

"What's this?" he said as he pulled a tall glass vase with a dozen red roses from the floor space under Emily's desk.

Her face flushed as Javier placed the bouquet of red flowers on the surface of her desk. She reached out to grab the card from the vase, but Javier beat her to it and held it out of her reach. As Javier opened the card to look at it, Emily ripped the card back.

"Ass."

"Let me guess . . . Officer Booty Bandit?"

"His name is Brian . . . and yes," she admitted.

"Must've been some date last night?"

"Shut up. No, we needed to cancel. Weren't you listening?"

Nina Sommers, a young woman recently assigned as a crime scene technician, entered the room. She sniffed the vase and said, "Wow—nice flowers. Who are they from?"

Nina handed a document to Emily and brushed her long dark hair off her shoulder while she put her nose close to a rosebud.

"A friend," Emily responded, while she glared at Javier. The look meant not to open his mouth.

"Honey—this is more than a friend." She gave Emily a knowing look.

Javier started to speak, but Emily cut him off and made sure to change the direction of the conversation. "What do you have for us? This is your report on the gun?"

"Nothing unusual. The serial number checks back to a 1998 burglary in Oakland. The owner reported it missing the next day. We pulled prints from the frame, barrel, and cylinder."

Emily examined the report and said, "This ties Sands to the Townsend killing; his prints were on the barrel. Did you get any hit on the other prints?"

"Nothing was in the system when we originally processed the weapon—" A smile appeared on Nina's face.

"And?" Emily asked.

I ran another search, including the exclusion prints we pulled at the crime scenes, and the prints on the weapon belonged to Townsend."

Javier replied, "He could have done that in a struggle over the gun."

Nina wrinkled her forehead and then said, "No . . . no . . . no. Not Roger Townsend. I found the wife's prints on the gun. And that speck you thought was blood. . . was a flake of red fingernail polish."

CHAPTER THIRTY-NINE

A HEFTY DOUR-FACED male deputy in a black jumpsuit led Lori Townsend into the interrogation room at the Main Jail. She glowered at Emily and Javier, but she brightened when she noticed Michael Bartson, the pale, rumpled-looking attorney Emily had encountered at Roger's office in the meeting with Jonathon Anderson.

The attorney stood as Lori entered, and he whispered urgently into his client's ear for a solid minute.

Emily interrupted, "Can we get started here?"

The attorney sighed with an agitated glance at the detective. "This is a waste of time."

Lori perched uncomfortably on a metal chair bolted to the grey cement floor.

Emily read from a card advising Lori of her Miranda rights and then began, "Mrs. Townsend, we have some questions to ask—"

It was the attorney's turn to interrupt. "Michael Bartson, representing Mrs. Townsend. She has nothing to say."

Lori glared across the table at Emily and Javier; a smug attitude crept back into her persona, in spite of the baggy orange jumpsuit.

"She'll answer—or face Obstruction of Justice charges," Emily said.

Bartson laughed. "Are you threatening to violate my client's Fifth Amendment Rights with some trumped-up obstruction beef? This is nonsense. You can't force her to divulge anything."

"Then tell your client we have her cold on the murders of Detective Josh Potter, her husband, and attempted murder of Dean Sands. That's in addition to the extortion nonsense."

Lori's eyes widened as Emily recited the list of crimes. She started to respond and Bartson calmly placed his hand on hers. He answered, "I'm only recently retained on this case by Mrs. Townsend, but I already know you're full of shit, Detective. Mrs. Townsend saved your ass earlier tonight when she shot Sands and that dirty cop Potter. You know that. I'll have fun with the facts in front of a jury. The widowed lady struggles for her life and saves a cop in the process. You should be awarding her a medal, not jailing her."

Javier changed the line of questioning. "Why did you shoot your husband?"

Lori jerked at the statement. "What are you talking about?"

"That's enough, Lori," Bartson warned.

Bartson's cell phone, which he failed to disclose at the front desk, interrupted the interview. He pulled it from his jacket and listened.

"Yeah? When did this happen?"

"Hey, can we get back to this case, if you don't mind," Emily said.

Bartson smiled and shoved the phone back into his jacket. His face morphed into a Cheshire cat grin, the "I got you" look, the smug face corporate attorneys must practice in the mirror.

"Let's move on with a discussion about letting my client go."

"Are you serious?" Javier asked.

"You bet. You got nothing but a nice story; you have nothing to back it up," Bartson said.

"We have Miller and Sands. Both implicate her in the murder-for-hire conspiracy. And—"

Bartson cut her off in the same soft tone. "Sands died on the operating table, and it seems Miller has taken a turn for the worse. Apparently, one of the other inmates in the jail ward at the Med Center beat him with an IV pole."

Javier popped out his cell phone and spoke in the hallway while Emily responded to the attorney. "That doesn't change a thing except add another count of murder," she said

"Oh, please." The attorney bounced in the chair. "You would do this to the woman who saved your life?"

"My ass—she ran out of bullets, or I'd be on a slab next to Potter and Sands," Emily came back.

"Really? Can you prove that?" Bartson paused. "I didn't think so."

"We know you shot your husband. Your prints are on the gun."

Lori bit once more. "I didn't kill Roger."

"Lori—Stop," Bartson said.

"I didn't say you killed him with your shot, but you did shoot him. I missed it at the time. Your right index fingernail polish was chipped that night. I know it was because the trigger recoil snagged your nail." Emily leaned forward and placed a photograph of the flake of red polish on the trigger guard of the murder weapon.

"You shot your husband first and now Detective Potter and Sands. Seems you got more confident; I gotta ask, was your husband practice?"

"You bitch," she blurted out.

"Lori, shut up," Bartson warned.

"Fuck you, Michael," she shot back.

"She's baiting you—calm down," the attorney warned.

"I bet Roger told you to shut up. Didn't he?"

"He won't anymore," she said behind a clenched jaw.

"Lori, stop. I'm your attorney. Listen to me."

"You are the company's attorney—Roger's attorney—not mine. You were probably involved in Roger's plan to leave me high and dry."

Bartson shook his head and took Lori's hand once more. "Please don't say anything more."

She pulled her hand away from the attorney. "That bastard planned to leave me penniless. After everything I put up with!"

Bartson yelled back at his client. "Everything you put up with? What about Roger? He put up with your whoring around. He thought you'd tire of it and stop. I showed him our web page and only then did he agree to set you adrift."

Emily perked up. "You put up the web page?"

"We were forced to act before she brought down Roger and the company. It wasn't hard to do, follow her around for a few days. She never really tried to hide it."

Lori turned and slapped her attorney hard across his face, and the deputy stepped in, restraining her in handcuffs. He said, "You done with her?"

Javier came back in response to the commotion from within the room. He noticed the red mark on Bartson's face immediately. "You know you're not supposed to beat the confession out of the attorney, right?"

Emily smiled, said, "Turns out Bartson here is the website porn king we hadn't tracked down."

"Oh—I feel overdressed."

"It seems Roger's company feared Lori's exploits were going to affect their bottom line. They convinced Roger to start the divorce proceedings."

Bartson laughed. "We paid a couple of guys to sleep with her, and she took the bait."

Emily thought that was doubtful, but the statement got Lori riled up again.

"Roger hadn't paid any attention to me in months. I deserve—" Lori said.

"That's because he had terminal cancer," Emily reminded her.

"How was I supposed to know that?"

"Maybe if you weren't constantly in heat?" Javier said.

Lori huffed and turned a deeper shade of red, not from embarrassment, but from seething anger. "Roger deserved to die."

"That's what Roger thought too. Did you know that?" Emily asked.

Lori glared back at the detective.

"Yeah, it appears Roger hired Sands to kill him before the cancer became too much for him, but after the divorce was filed."

"What?" The revelation hit Lori hard. She slumped back in her chair.

"Miller got a bang out of you paying for Roger's death too."

"That son of a bitch! He's screwing me from the grave."

Bartson rubbed the bridge of his nose and said, "Lori, stop."

"You mean to tell me if Roger handed over the federal prosecutor's files, Sands was going to kill him anyway?" Lori asked.

"Looks that way. Roger was ready to die, you wanted him dead, and I'm not sure his company wanted him around anymore either," Emily said.

Bartson picked up on the last bit. "What the hell are you talking about?"

"Remember the unexplained account withdrawals? One of them, the Community Growth fund, was an account you managed and traced back to a local landscaping company. Sands did landscaping. You sent a hundred grand to the account."

"This is preposterous," Bartson said.

"Sands killed Roger—not me," Lori yelled.

Javier stood behind her for a moment and put his hand on Lori's shoulder. "You told us Roger was already dead when you got there."

"The autopsy indicated Roger was shot before he died from getting his throat cut," Emily added.

"Lori—" Bartson warned once more.

Javier continued, "Why did you shoot him?"

"I didn't want to."

"Jesus, Lori. Shut the hell up."

A knock at the door and Emily motioned for the deputy to open it. The detective watched Lori's face turn chalk white as Dean Sands entered, chained to a wheelchair.

"What the . . ." Bartson gasped.

"Did you see a ghost, Counselor?" Emily asked.

CHAPTER FORTY

"WE KNEW WE had a leak in the jail. Thanks for helping us track it down," Javier said.

Bartson licked his lips and asked, "And Miller?"

"That's true. Another white boy trying to make his bones beat the snot out of Miller, but nobody could reach Sands, so we kept him safe and leaked the story that he died on the operating table."

Sands wasn't in great shape, listing to one side and pale. A weeping bandage visible under the hospital smock.

"A miracle of modern medicine. Other than a collapsed lung, no major tissue damage from the slugs. Sorry, Lori.

"I'm gonna ask Mr. Sands here a couple of questions," Emily told Lori and her now apoplectic attorney.

"Did Roger Townsend hire you to kill him?"

Sands nodded.

"Did Lori Townsend hire you to kill her husband?"

Another nod.

"This is bullshit," Lori exploded. "He killed Roger!"

"Did you?" Emily asked the gang member.

"Yes," Sands said with a hissing sound deep from his throat.

"See!" Lori said.

Javier responded, "But you hired him to do it, Mrs. Townsend."

"But Roger hired him too—so it doesn't count," Lori cried.

"Oh, but it does count, Mrs. Townsend, as if you killed him with your own hands. Speaking of which, why did you shoot him?" Emily asked.

"Stop," Bartson said without much effort.

"He—he made me," Lori said, pointing at Sands.

"What about it, Sands? Did you force her to shoot her husband?"

Sands laughed and then coughed painfully. "She needed some blood on her hands. I told her I wouldn't do it unless she shot him, so she did. Didn't really do much to talk her into it. She shot him in the back," Sands wheezed.

"I should've shot you too."

"You did, remember?" Sands laughed again.

Sands turned to Emily. "We still got our deal?"

"I ain't the District Attorney, but as far as I'm concerned, yeah, we got a deal."

Officers wheeled Sands out of the room, and after he disappeared, Bartson asked, "What deal is he talking about?"

"In exchange for a recommendation for Protective Housing Unit placement in prison, Sands will testify against your client and your company."

Bartson got up from the chair. "We're done here. We'll see you in court, Detective. This whole house of cards will come down on you."

"Yeah, we'll see you in court, Counselor. You're under arrest for conspiracy in the murder of Roger Townsend. You set up the Community Growth account for Lori to pay for the murder. You knew what she had planned." Another deputy put the attorney in handcuffs, and Bartson nearly fell as his knees gave out on him.

"Mrs. Townsend, I think you need a new attorney," Javier observed.

Emily nodded for the deputy to take Lori Townsend back to her cell. Defiant to the last moment, Lori glared at the detective. She pulled away from her escort and faced Emily. "You can't do this to me! I know people, and I'll bring the world down on you."

Emily thought the display pitiful. This woman had it all, and it wasn't enough for her. Now she'd lost everything she held dear, and it ripped at her very core. "You do that, but you'll do it from a cell at the Central California Women's Facility in Chowchilla," Emily said.

Lori struggled against her escort as she left the room.

"I think she handled that well," Javier snickered.

"She's bought or sexed her way out of everything in the past, and that's not gonna work this time."

"How did you roll Sands? You didn't see him at the hospital?" Javier asked.

"I figured the same leak that gave up the information on Miller would run with the news about Sands being in trouble with the AB leaders at Pelican Bay."

"Where did the 'deal' come from?" Javier asked curiously.

"Sands knew he was already in the hat with the AB, and he knew a long prison term loomed ahead for him. He couldn't go to general population, so I had someone suggest lockup placement to him."

"Is that protective custody?"

"Yeah—something along those lines, where they put gang dropouts, inmates hiding from drug debts, and priests doing time for child molestation."

Javier thought for a second and asked, "Who did you convince to ask Sands to snitch on Lori?"

"Someone he would believe, and I needed to send a message at the same time."

"What are you talking about?" Javier said, clearly confused from her response.

"Sands threatened our families. He sent one of his men to kill my mom," she said. "While she went to the movies with your mom."

Emily's voice quivered. "I had to make sure he knew there were consequences for going after them. I sent a car to go by and pick up his mother."

"You what?"

"His mother has custody of his two kids. I figured if she told her son the police took his kids and put them in the foster care system, he might be a bit more cooperative."

"Why would she tell him that?" Javier asked.

Emily pressed up from the table and started for the door. "Because I told her if she didn't I'd get Children's Protective Services to do a knock and talk on a neglect allegation."

"Those kids don't deserve to get lumped in with Sands and everything he's done."

Emily's face grew tight. "Exactly. He crossed a line when he put our families in the line of fire."

"Emily—"

She cut him off. "Now he knows what it feels like when your family's threatened." The exhaustion showed on her face, and her shoulder muscles knotted up in her spine. She rubbed the back of her neck until it turned red.

He caught up with her and slid inside the elevator as the door slid shut. They rode to the main level of the jail in tense silence.

No sooner than the doors parted, Javier continued past the security desk and flung the glass door open. Javier stopped when he realized Emily held the keys to the car. He faced the lobby while his partner slowly made her way to the security counter.

Inside, Emily studied the faces of the family members here to visit one of their loved ones detained in the jail. They held a mixture of sadness, shame, and anger. A grey-haired old woman with slumped shoulders waited in a corner, her eyes filmed with cataracts, as they tried to focus on Emily.

Emily knelt next to her, and the old woman struggled to stand from the hard waiting-room chair. Next to her, two small children sat with their legs dangling and swinging back and forth.

Javier watched Emily take the old woman's hand. She nodded as she spoke to her, the gang leader's mother's filmy eyes glistening with tears. The old woman checked over her shoulder at the two young children and turned back to Emily. The old woman suddenly grasped onto her arms, and the tears fell from her eyes. Emily handed an envelope to the woman and left her in the waiting room.

Javier watched the woman open the envelope, pull out a few twenty-dollar bills, and quickly tuck the small package into her worn floral-patterned purse.

Emily pushed open the door and joined Javier on the sidewalk.

As they neared the car, he asked, "What was that about?"

"Nothing," Emily replied.

"That was Sands' mother, wasn't it?"

"Yeah," she answered.

"She had his two kids with her? I don't understand. I thought you said . . ."

"I needed Sands to believe if I could reach his family, so could the Aryan Brotherhood. I think he got the message."

Javier fell silent for a second, trying to put the pieces together. "But what did his mother tell him to get him to flip?"

"She told him only what a mother could. She feared her son was doing nothing but having his children follow in his path."

"A guilt trip?"

"A mother's guilt trip."

"You gave his mother money for the kids."

"I don't know what you're talking about," she replied.

CHAPTER FORTY-ONE

SILENCE FILLED THE car on the remainder of the ride back to the Detective Bureau. Javier was tense, and Emily could feel the waves of sadness coming from his side of the car. He didn't even notice they'd pulled into the department parking lot.

"Javi?"

Lost in his own thoughts, he replied, "Yeah . . . yeah," and pushed open the Crown Vic's door.

Emily paused at the double glass door and turned around.

"Javi, what's up with you?"

She followed but gave him some distance while Javier booted up his computer.

She tossed her jacket on the back of her chair and collapsed heavily in the worn wooden rocking desk chair. An ancient creak came from the springs under the thirty-year-old hand-me-down chair from detectives long retired.

Emily closed her eyes and put her head back; the events of the past few days ran through her mind. Lori Townsend was a real piece of work. How much could you hate your spouse to make you hire some thug to kill him? She had a ton of money, she had her looks, but was never satisfied with what she acquired, and always manipulated for the next score.

She reached for the pile of phone messages, which had multiplied since she last checked. Emily glanced at an evidence bag on the desk and picked up the clear envelope: Josh Potter's wallet, driver's license, Omega watch, a mechanical pencil, thirty-five cents in change, and a small tube of lip balm. That's all that's left, she thought as she tossed the bag back on her desk.

A strange metallic clanking sound came from the bag. Emily picked it up again and shook it. She pinpointed the sound from the lip balm tube and opened the bag. Emily held the tube in her hand, and it felt heavier than it should. Carefully removing the top, she poured the contents onto her desk blotter. A metal tube slid out and rolled off the desk into her hand.

"What the hell is this?"

Javier didn't turn around. "What?"

"I found this hidden in Potter's personal effects. It's a metal stamp or tool of some sort."

Emily rolled the tube between her fingers and found four stubby little prongs protruding from one end. A small dark cloud entered her mind. She figured Potter's secrets would go with him to the grave. She stiffened, and an idea smoldered as she held the metal object.

"Javi—let's go."

"What now?" he responded wearily.

"Come on, would you?"

Javier didn't respond.

Emily approached him, and he jerked away, startled from her touch.

"I'm sorry, I was thinking," he said.

"About what?"

Silence.

"Javi, what's going on?"

"Those kids. Man, seeing them hit a little close to the bone for me."

"Javi—what is it? Tell me."

He leaned back against a railing overlooking the building atrium and let out a breath. "That whole business with CPS and foster homes—it—it brought back some memories I thought were long buried away."

"What are you saying?"

"You know I was caught up in the foster system as a child."

"I knew you were adopted when you were a kid after your birth parents were deported."

He nodded.

"I was given up as a baby. My biological mother was undocumented. I don't know what happened to her—or where she went after I was born."

"I didn't know." Her eyes welled.

"Why would you?"

"But, you turned out okay. You got adopted, and your mom is incredible."

Javier fell silent again.

"You wanna talk about it?"

"It wasn't good—I was a possession, not a kid. You know?"

"No, I can't imagine what you felt," she replied.

"No—no you can't. Passed from one home to the next. When I was ten, I ran away from the home because my foster parent, the man who promised to look after me, abused me." Javier lowered his head. "You must think I'm a wimp," he said.

"No, Javi, I don't. It takes a strong person to survive that. Those experiences made you who you are—the good and the bad—and I think you turned out pretty good."

"We're okay? You willing to work with a wimp?"

"I wouldn't have it any other way."

Javier exhaled and relaxed.

Emily held up the metal object she'd pulled from Potter's property. "I've got a hunch Potter told us where we need to go next."

"Potter? He's dead."

"Exactly."

CHAPTER FORTY-TWO

THE DRIVE INTO East Lawn Memorial Cemetery took longer than expected due to the procession of cars creeping behind a hearse as it turned through the park's thick old stone walls. Emily pulled the Crown Vic behind the last car and followed the mourners.

People assembled and gathered in the chairs arranged near a newly prepared grave, covered by a swath of improbably green artificial turf tossed over a mound of loose soil waiting to cover the silver casket after it was lowered into the yawning hole.

Emily broke away from the group and angled to the left and the wall where dozens of bronze plaques hid the cremated remains of Roger Townsend and others. Then she strode to a workman's van parked behind the mourners and reached inside the open back doors. The workman was busy tending to the pulleys and straps preparing to lower the coffin into the hole at the end of the ceremony. He didn't notice Emily lift a cordless battery-operated drill from his tool bin.

Javier watched her insert the metal tube found in Potter's property into the drill and tighten the collar to hold the bit in place.

She headed to Townsend's memorial plaque. When she placed the drill on one of the security screws, the four points slid tightly in place. She flipped the switch to throw the drill in reverse and began to back out the retaining screw with a loud whirring.

"Em, you can't exhume a body without a court order," he pleaded.

She started on the second screw and responded, "If I'm right, there's no body to exhume."

"But we watched the funeral. Lori put Roger's urn in the niche," he said.

The second screw dropped to the ground, and Emily started on the third. "We saw what she wanted us to see. Remember, the urn was different, bigger, and better, right?"

She started on the last screw and backed it out of its threads. The plaque was sealed around the edges with putty, but it hadn't hardened. Emily pulled the plaque with her fingers and after initial resistance, the brass plaque popped off in her hands, revealing the urn within.

Emily carefully reached in, pulled the heavy urn toward her and out of the niche. When she turned around, a cemetery workman stood behind them. He held a thick metal pipe in one hand.

"Put that back." The man raised the pipe and took a menacing step toward her.

Javier pulled out his badge, said with authority, "We're on police business."

The workman hesitated and rubbed his patchy beard. "You can't be takin' no remains from here," he said. "There's laws against that—ain't there?"

Emily pulled the cover off the urn, tipped it upside down, and shook it.

Both Javier and the workman gasped in unison.

A thickly wrapped round bundle fell out of the urn, but no sign of Roger Townsend's cremated remains. Emily put the urn in the niche and picked up the bundle.

"Is that what I think it is?" Javier asked.

She tore open the plastic wrapping and exposed a Department of Justice seal on the front of the thick document. "The federal prosecutor's RICO files."

The workman stared at the official document, then at the urn. "What's goin' on here?"

Emily tossed the drill to the man and said, "Just picking up some mail."

CHAPTER FORTY-THREE

SIX MONTHS AFTER the RICO files resurfaced, federal organized crime indictments named Miller, Sands, two other Aryan Brotherhood members, and a Sheriff's Deputy who, following Potter's example, involved themselves in the gang's street activity. Sands testified at Lori Townsend's Preliminary Hearing and provided damning evidence that she hired him to kill her husband. The court found sufficient evidence to hold the matter over for trial, and Lori returned to custody, without bail.

Lori Townsend's legal team fought and obtained continuance after continuance. They hoped Sands or one of the other prosecution witnesses would recant their testimony, or simply change their minds. The court prevented Lori from drawing from her dearly departed husband's financial reserves, which made her high-priced attorneys sever their ties to the destitute woman.

In exchange for guilty pleas in the murders of Roger Townsend and Josh Potter, the District Attorney agreed to drop the death penalty. A sentence of fifty years-to-life guaranteed the rest of Lori's life within a small concrete box.

Emily stood at the rear of the courtroom with Javier as the judge passed down the sentence. The only reaction from Lori came as the judge hammered down the gavel, signaling the end of the proceedings. Lori jerked in her seat at the defense table and glanced over her shoulder at the sea of media and interested people who had come to witness the hearing.

Lori's eyes tunneled through the crowd until they locked with Emily. A smile parted her unglossed lips.

Two bailiffs pulled Lori from her chair and escorted her through a side door, with Lori never breaking eye contact with Emily.

"She didn't give a shit about going to prison," Javier whispered.

"That's because she's not," Emily countered.

Mike Riner, the Deputy District Attorney, gathered up his files and stuffed them into a worn leather satchel. He avoided the two detectives and left through the same side door Lori used.

"Come on," Emily said.

They hurried through the empty courtroom and used a side door into a hallway where Riner and a tall, thin man in a dark blue suit stood talking. The Deputy D.A. wasn't happy to see Emily and Javier.

With a look of exasperation, Riner threw his hands up. "Detective, there is nothing you can do about this. It's out of our hands."

"Where's Lori Townsend?" Emily said.

"Leave it alone," Riner said.

Emily attempted to step around the Deputy D.A. but a tall blue-suited man stepped in her path.

"Scott Paulson, U.S. Marshal's Service," he said while holding his badge.

"What interest does the Marshal's Service have in Lori Townsend?" Emily asked.

"We don't make the deals, but it turns out Mrs. Townsend is a key witness in the RICO case against the Aryan Brotherhood."

"She's a murderer. What kind of witness is that?"

"I said, I don't make the deals. I move 'em where they tell me to."

"What are you saying?"

"Mrs. Townsend is going into witness protection. My job is to relocate her."

Emily pushed past Riner, said, "Relocate, my ass. She got sentenced to life in prison."

"That was part of the deal. She fails to live up to her part, she goes to prison for a long time," Paulson said.

"She walks on two murders?" Emily asked.

"I don't see it that way," Riner said. "We got our guilty pleas. If she tries anything stupid, we've got her."

"You'll never see it coming," Emily said.

At that moment, an ear-splitting explosion tossed the rear courthouse door from its hinges, sending it into the hallway. Thick acrid smoke filled the space, and the pressure from the explosion knocked Emily and the others to the floor.

Paulson got to his feet and ran through the smoke to the exit door. He stopped outside the charred opening where the transport van burned. The windows shattered and flames licked the dripping headliner, melting it into the passenger compartment. White-hot flames sizzled around the outline of a figure in the van.

Emily and Javier joined Paulson, where he knelt over one of the U.S. Marshals who had escorted Lori Townsend out of the courtroom minutes earlier. The unconscious man bled from a gash to the back of his head; his clothing and exposed skin were heavily charred.

Emily crept close to the heat of the van, shards of molten metal melted into the pavement, which made a direct approach difficult. She shielded her eyes from the intense heat and found charred bits of a jail jumpsuit on the asphalt. The sizzling lump of human flesh inside the van wore a burnt U.S. Marshal's windbreaker evidenced by the jagged abstract emblem melted across the man's back.

"She's gone. Lori's gone," Emily said.

CHAPTER FORTY-FOUR

PAIN. SEARING PAIN throbbed with each heartbeat. Lori prayed for it to stop. The words turned to ash in her mouth. *Run away from the flames*, her mind ordered. Her body didn't respond. The blast threw her away from the open van door only seconds after the U.S. Marshal uncuffed her for the ride to her new life away from Sacramento. The van door lay over her and shielded her from the force of the explosion. But, she felt wrong, very wrong.

She tried pushing the door off, and her hand didn't move, the flesh stuck on the metal. With her free hand, Lori pulled her skin from the steel. Chunks of charred flesh stayed behind. Her scream was lost in the rumble of the fire and hissing engine parts. She rolled out from under the warped, bomb-damaged door and slumped over. Her head ached, and her face screamed with every speck of dust in the air. Lori noticed the darkened, blurred vision in her right eye and a wave of nausea swept over her. She touched her face and felt instant pain on the slick burnt surface.

The smoke, fire, and chaos following the explosion provided the distraction Lori needed to make a hasty escape from the transport van. She knew the Aryan Brotherhood wanted to prevent her testimony, but not to the extent of blowing up the transport van. Their overzealous attempt on her life might give her a chance. The gang might think she died in the explosion. She limped out of the smoke in her tattered, soot-covered orange jail jumpsuit and made her way up the courthouse parking ramp into the street.

Lori fell in with the path of a homeless woman and her two young children. The two boys hid behind their mother when Lori collapsed on the sidewalk. The homeless woman bent down and touched Lori's shoulder. "Hey. Hey, lady, you need me to call for help?"

"No, don't touch me," Lori said. She pulled herself to her knees, and the two boys recoiled when she faced them.

"Mommy, what's wrong with her?" one said.

"She's ugly," the second boy said.

"Stop it. Remember what I said about people less fortunate than you?"

Through the veil of pain, Lori could not understand what these—these lowlifes were saying. Less fortunate, my ass. I can buy you a hundred times over. Must be the black soot-covered jail jumpsuit, she figured.

Down the block, emergency vehicles swarmed the courthouse and closed in on the burning van. There wasn't much time before they figured out she wasn't in the wreckage.

The burnt-out transport van smoldered; wisps of hot steam from the water from a half dozen fire hoses spraying overhead. The charred remains of the U.S. Marshal waited for the Medical Examiner, trapped in his metal mausoleum. The only evidence that Lori Townsend had perished in the explosion consisted of burnt fabric remnants from her clothing and chunks of flesh from her right hand on the underside of the door. That might be enough.

Lori stood and staggered away. Passersby gave her a wide berth on the sidewalk. She needed to disappear and start over. First, she wanted to dump these disgusting jail clothes. Then, clean up, take care of the pain, and blend in.

CHAPTER FORTY-FIVE

ONCE THEY REALIZED Lori wasn't in the rubble of the charred van, the search began for the escaped fugitive.

"She can't go far; we have her passport, remember?" Javier said.

"I've underestimated her before. I'm not going to do it again," Emily said.

Marshal Paulson sat on the curb while paramedics tended to his unconscious, injured man. His eyes were puffy, and his hand left a black smudge where he tried to wipe away tears.

"Is he gonna be okay?" Emily asked.

Paulson nodded. "They said he hit his head on the wall after the force of the explosion threw him backward. Something shielded him from the incendiary charge."

"Or someone."

"You think the Townsend woman took the brunt of the blast?"

"Makes sense from the burnt jumpsuit and if that is her skin melted into the door."

"Danny had a wife and a two-year-old kid." Paulson paused as he pointed at the charred body in the van. "What am I gonna tell them?"

"Who knew you were moving Townsend today?"

"The Public Defender, the D.A., the Clerk of the Court, the usual folks," Paulson said.

"Who pressed for Witness Protection in exchange for her testimony?"

Paulson shrugged. "The Marshal's office doesn't get involved in the deal; we pick 'em up and move 'em, that's all."

From behind, the Deputy D.A surveyed the destruction. "It wasn't her Public Defender who arranged witness protection," Riner said.

"What are you saying?" Emily asked.

"Lori Townsend wanted witness protection for her testimony; her first attorney was a corporate law guy and didn't know how to arrange a protection deal. Lori told him to reach out to Stephen Lawson."

"Wait a godamned minute! Stephen Lawson, the ex-Assistant U.S. Attorney?" Emily said.

"The one we busted for giving the RICO files to Lori?" Javier said.

"That's the one," Riner said.

"He's in jail, what could he do?" Emily said.

"All I know is her attorney met with Lawson and within a couple of days, the Townsend and Associates legal team dropped out of the case, and I got a call from the Public Defender talking about a witness protection plan," Riner said.

Paulson excused himself and met the Medical Examiner's team at the van. He needed to be there when they moved his man, but he didn't expect the dead man's charred face frozen in a silent scream, and the muscle tissue contracting the man's hands into tight fists. Paulson's knees weakened, and one of the Medical Examiner's staff guided him to a location away from the van.

A uniformed patrol Sergeant motioned for Emily.

"We covered a ten-block radius—no sign of the woman," the Sergeant said.

"Keep looking. She's wearing a bright orange jumpsuit for Christ sake," Emily said.

"Javi, let's pay a visit to the ex-U.S. Attorney and find out what he said to Lori's lawyer."

CHAPTER FORTY-SIX

STEPHEN LAWSON WAITED in the jail interview room. He smiled as the detectives entered.

"I knew you'd be coming."

Lawson smelled the soot wafting from the detectives' clothing. "They got her, huh?"

Emily chose a spot opposite the prisoner while Javier leaned against the wall. Emily held a copy of the jail's visiting records. "Haven't you been popular, Lawson? Visits from Lori Townsend's attorney and Tommy Shannon. Now the attorney, I get. But what did you and 'Irish' Shannon, a known A.B. enforcer, talk about?"

"Lori destroyed my life. I lost my career, my family; I lost everything because of that bitch."

"Your gambling debts didn't speed things along," Emily goaded.

Lawson ignored the jab. "I figured with Lori out of the way, everyone wins, so I gave her attorney the plan for a witness protection deal."

"Knowing it would force Lori out in the open," Javier said.

"The trick was finding out the time it was going down. The Marshal's Service is nothing but predictable. The move would happen after her sentencing."

"And you told Irish Shannon," Emily said.

"That's the best part. I didn't need to tell them. They already knew. Roger Townsend's old attorney—Bartson—funneled the information from the firm's lawyers to the gang shot-callers on the outside."

"Why did Shannon come to see you, if they knew about the transfer?"

"He told me my slate with them was clean. I did my part, got the RICO files to Lori. She screwed them, not me. I'm going away for a long time, and they want me to act as their in-house writ writer for the gang."

"You're going to help these criminals by filing appeals and writs of habeas corpus?" Emily said.

"You do what you gotta do."

"Even if it means innocent people are killed," Emily said.

"Lori was far from innocent."

"What about the Marshal who got fried in the explosion?"

"Regrettable." Lawson showed no outward signs of emotion.

"That's all you got to say? *Regrettable?*"

"Lori had a way of infecting everyone around her. The Marshal's unfortunate passing is another example of her collateral damage."

A jail deputy knocked on the interview room door. He stepped inside and said, "Excuse me, which of you is Detective Hunter?"

"That's me," Emily responded.

"An Officer Conner is here for you. He says it's urgent."

"I'll bet," Javier said.

Emily pointed at her partner. "Don't start."

She ducked out of the interview room and followed the deputy down the hallway where Officer Brian Conner waited.

"Brian, I'm kind of in the middle of something right now."

"I bet, but I thought you'd want to know."

"Know what?"

"We got her."

"*Got her?* You mean Lori Townsend?" Emily said as her excitement ratcheted up a notch. "How? Where?" She grasped Conner by the arms.

"I responded to a call at Loaves and Fishes. A volunteer found a burnt jail jumpsuit in a trash bin."

"The high and mighty Lori Townsend stepped through the door of a homeless shelter?" Emily said.

"A couple of men who were getting food spotted her stealing some clothes out of a donation box, and they started to chase her off. When they caught her, they said she dropped and howled in pain. Burns. Her face, neck, and arms were covered in burns. The shelter staff called an ambulance."

"Where is she?"

"I found her at U. C. Davis Medical Center, the burn unit, listed as a Jane Doe. She's under direct observation by two of our guys."

"Great work," Emily said and rose up on her toes to give Conner a peck on the cheek.

She didn't notice her partner duck out of the interview room, and he caught the last snippet of their conversation. "Get a room, Hunter."

Conner's face flushed red, and Emily turned in surprise and nearly tripped. "Brian—I mean Officer Conner—has Lori in custody," Emily said as she regained her composure.

"I heard."

"Let's go see her," Emily said, in a hurry to get away from Javier and Brian.

Javier stepped closer to Conner, paused, and said, "Good work, Officer. I'm confused—am I supposed to kiss you, too, or what?"

Brian squirmed. "No, sir. I think you've said enough." Brian slowly edged past Javier and made his way out.

Javier joined Emily at her car and paused before he opened the door. "How come you never rewarded me like that for good work?"

"Do some good work, and we'll talk. Now open the door, ass."

The Regional Burn Center served as the central hub for treating thermal and chemical trauma and was the first stop for local fire-fighters who found themselves victims of an out of control blaze. Its twelve Intensive Care Beds were in constant demand, but Emily had no trouble narrowing down which room held Lori Townsend. Her screams reverberated down the hallway, but the staff didn't react to the cries; they were used to the sound of pain.

From the doorway, Emily found the source of Lori's torment. A team of doctors and staff were carefully pulling debris and bits of charred clothing from the open burn wounds. Javier gagged and covered his nose.

"That smell," he said.

Lori rocked her head to the side and locked her gaze on Emily. The woman's face was charred from the crown of her head down to her neckline. One eye disappeared, hidden in a blackened clump of flesh on the side of her face. The remaining eye was shocked wide in a cocktail of anger, pain, and frustration, as she pulled against the restraints.

"You. You did this," Lori hissed at Emily.

"No, Lori, this is on you, and you can't buy your way out of this one."

Lori bared her teeth and screamed.

Emily recognized this wasn't all about pain. It was the recognition that Lori's life would never be the same. At best, she'd be a shell of her former self.

Lori's breath grew uneven; she started to panic, unable to take a breath.

"Laryngeal swelling. We need to intubate now," an attending doctor said.

Emily whispered to a nearby nurse, "What's happening? Why can't she breathe?"

"It's pretty common for face and neck burns. The heat causes the tissue to swell, and along with any toxic vapor, or debris, it blisters and restricts the airway."

A young woman doctor deftly inserted a tube down Lori's throat; the muscles on her chest relaxed as she started breathing.

The doctor turned to Emily and Javier and shook her head. "Tough luck if you're planning on interrogating my patient. My priority is keeping her alive."

"Will she make it?" Javier asked.

The doctor glanced over her shoulder. "It won't be easy. She'll require months of surgeries, therapy, and some reconstruction work—not cosmetic, but a few procedures so she can swallow, breathe, and speak semi-normally. But, yeah, she'll make it."

A nurse inserted an IV in a patch of unburnt skin and began pumping a bag of IV fluids and morphine. As much as Emily despised the woman, she didn't wish her physical pain. There would be internal psychological anguish for years to come, and Emily believed that was justice enough.

*   *   *

After leaving the hospital and fighting traffic, Emily made it home and changed out of her work clothes. She swore she could smell Lori Townsend's rendered flesh in the fabric. She bound up the clothes in a plastic bag and carried them out to the trash can. Part of her felt it was a fitting end for everything associated with the case.

At the back door, Emily found a trespasser.

"Don't you have a home?" Emily said to the cat that wasn't her cat. She reached down and scratched the black cat under the chin. "Oh, all right. You can come in, for a while."

The cat sashayed in behind Emily and waited in the kitchen. As Emily poured cat food in a bowl, she heard her mom's voice.

"Honey, are you home?"

"In here, Mom."

Connie and Lucinda came in from the living room and joined Emily in the kitchen.

"When did you get a cat?" Connie asked.

"I didn't."

Connie's face scrunched up. "I know I'm not as quick as I used to be, but that is a cat."

"But it's not *my* cat. It's a long story. What are you two doing out and about today?"

Lucinda prodded Connie. "Go ahead, tell her."

Emily tried to decipher the expression on her mom's face, serious, tense, and excited at the same time. She gestured to the kitchen table. "Come and tell me."

Connie clutched her hands together, the vision of a nervous child confessing some imagined failing.

"Mom, come sit and talk."

"I'll let you two catch up," Lucinda said.

Emily caught the slightest nod from Lucinda as she headed for the living room, the kind of gesture meaning, it's okay.

Connie perched on the edge of the kitchen chair and furrowed her brow in search of the words, so Emily started.

"What's on your mind, Mom?"

The older woman thought for a moment. "I don't want you to worry about me. I can't be that kind of burden to you."

"You're not a burden, it's—"

"I've decided to move into a facility with people who have my— people who need a little extra help sometimes."

It was Emily's turn for a loss of words.

"I'm sorry, dear, but I think moving in with you has been too imposing. You need your space, and quite frankly, you're not getting any younger, and having an old woman around isn't going to help you find a man."

"I can get a man, on my own, thank you very much."

"From what Lucinda tells me, you've already done that." A sly smile from Connie told Emily that Javier was telling secrets out of school again.

"You can stay here with me, Mom. There's no reason we can't make it work."

"I've made up my mind. Lucinda showed me a couple of places, and I think I've found one where I will feel comfortable."

Emily had feared the time she was going to rush to find a place for her mom. Connie erased her concern and made the decision for herself while she was able to think things through. That was a slight relief, although Emily felt a twinge of guilt she was "putting Mom in a home."

"This is what I want to do," Connie said.

Emily got up and hugged her mom. "Okay then. But I want you to know you can live here if you change your mind."

They shared a moment, and both knew this placement was final, even if it went unspoken. Connie's dementia would only get worse, and she would require ever-increasing levels of care. Some things were best left unsaid. Tears began to stream down Emily's cheeks.

CHAPTER FORTY-SEVEN

THE CITY EXHALED in the year after the courthouse bombing, and the flow of new homicides washed Lori Townsend from the media, a fitting exile for the former socialite, fading away as another Sacramento crime statistic.

Emily and Javier visited the Central California Women's Facility, where they interviewed another inmate who had witnessed a murder in Sacramento. The woman provided very little for them to pursue in their investigation. The years of drug use had riddled her memory of the months on the street before her incarceration. The trip from Sacramento to Madera turned out to be a waste.

Before they left the housing unit, Emily noticed a photo board at the officer's station. The board held a booking photo for each of the one hundred and twenty prisoners in the building. One photo stood out among the vacant faces on the board with hard, jagged scars, a sagging right eye, and sparse tufts of greyish hair.

"I'll be damned. Lori Townsend," Emily said.

"You know her? She's a real piece of work," the Correctional Officer at the desk said.

"Yeah, we've made her acquaintance. What's the red outline on her picture for?" Javier pointed to the thick red square around her photo. Six other photos showed the same red marking.

"Staff assaultive. Mostly gassing," the Officer said.

"*Gassing?*" Emily said.

"She throws urine and feces on staff every time we open the tray slot to feed her."

"How the mighty have fallen," Emily said. "What happens to a prisoner who does that? What consequences are there? I mean, she's already in prison."

"We write her up, and they take time from her. It don't matter to her. She's doing life anyway." The officer stood and picked up a clipboard. "I've got to give her a copy of some legal mail. Wanna say hello?"

"I'd like to, if you don't mind," Javier said. "After what we went through with her, it seems like closure, you know?"

Emily and Javier waited for the Correctional Officer in the control booth above them to secure the dayroom before the electric lock on a chain-link fence popped open. The officer led the two detectives to the last cell on the far end on the bottom tier.

The housing unit vibrated with the catcalls, threats, and crying of a hundred women. The sound echoed in the concrete and steel housing unit. Half of the windows set in heavy steel doors filled with the faces of inmates checking out the visitors to their world—a world of predator and prey. Emily and Javier followed the officer to the cell.

"Townsend. Legal mail," the officer said through the solid cell door.

The cell was cloaked in darkness, the interior light off, and paper covered the back window of the cell, rendering the inside stark black.

"Townsend, take down the paper. You know better."

A shaft of light penetrated the back cell window as Lori pulled down her makeshift curtain.

Melted chin and cheek implants, congealed collagen from repeated injections, formed a thick, hard layer of scar tissue over Lori Townsend's face. The formerly blond hair burnt off the right side of her head, the right eye malformed and twisted into a hideous mask of permanent horror. She'd grown to tolerate the constant physical pain, but the mental anguish screamed and tormented her in her waking moments and it took a heavy toll.

Lori covered the mirror in her prison cell and avoided contact with other prisoners. In addition to the self-imposed isolation to avoid the constant gawking and abuse, prison officials placed Lori in a segregated housing unit due to the threats from other inmates. The officer explained inmate Townsend spent all day–every day in her cell and refused to come out for designated exercise periods. The only time she left her cell was to shower, and she endured catcalls and reminders of her disfigurement as she passed down the tier to the shared shower stall.

"You gonna sign for your legal mail, or you gonna refuse as usual?" the officer asked as he unlocked the tray slot to pass the mail.

No sound came from within the concrete cell. Lori teetered on the edge of her bunk, the less damaged side of her face toward the front of the cell.

"Got some friends of yours here to see you," the officer said.

Emily stood in front of the cell window, and the person in the cell was a shell of the former Lori Townsend. Gone were the trappings of a pampered existence. Her most precious assets, her beauty and sexuality, had abandoned her.

Lori never turned or outwardly acknowledged the detectives' presence.

"Why aren't there any sheets or blankets in her cell?" Emily asked.

"Oh, that. We've had to cut her down twice now. She's torn up her sheets and tried to hang herself. Came back from suicide watch in the treatment center last night. Promised to be good, didn't you, Townsend?"

"I can't imagine what this must be like for her. Destitute and alone, facing the rest of her miserable life in a concrete box, and she can't manipulate her way out."

The hard metallic click of the tray slot closing made Emily jerk. Emily took one last look at the emaciated, frail woman in the cell. She had had it all, and her greed robbed it away. This was the *face of greed*.

"Goodbye, Lori."

ACKNOWLEDGMENTS

The spark for *Face of Greed* lies within a case I investigated many years ago. A trio of gang members forced their way into a home, killing the homeowner after forcing him to open a safe. During hours of interviews, gang members told me the victim was a drug dealer and was rumored to keep large quantities of product and cash in his safe. There was never any evidence the victim was involved in criminal activity. The jury saw through the false claims, and the shooter was convicted and sentenced to death. The other two home invaders received long prison terms.

That event always stuck with me. *Face of Greed* twists the facts a bit and asks *what if there was more going on in that home invasion?* Of course, the names, places, and events of that original crime have been changed.

While a novel like *Face of Greed* might be written in isolation, it only comes to life with a team pulling together. I'm forever grateful to Bob and Pat Gussin and the team at Oceanview who gave Emily's story a chance. Thanks to Lee Randall, Faith

Matson, and Tracy Sheehan for their help whipping the book into shape.

Thanks to Elizabeth K. Kracht of Kimberley Cameron and Associates for not giving up and finding the perfect home for this book. Thanks, Liz, we did it again!

A special thanks to my advance readers, Jessica Windham, Janis Herbert, and Megan Cuff, who aren't shy about telling me what works and what doesn't. Thanks to Tricia LaRochelle for a last look before submission.

The book community is incredible, and I appreciate the support of independent bookstores like Face in a Book (Tina Ferguson and Janis Herbert) and Book Passage (Kathy Petrocelli and Luisa Smith). They make a bookstore feel like home.

For *Face of Greed,* words of encouragement came when they were most needed. J.T. Ellison, Wendall Thomas, Karen Dionne, Hank Phillippi Ryan, and Shawn Reilly Simmons, I thank you endlessly. A special shout-out to my fellow Capitol Crimes Chapter of Sisters-in-Crime members for the love and support.

Thanks to my kids, Jessica, whose snarkiness may have influenced Emily's character, and to Michael—I love you guys.

I wasn't always alone at the keyboard, and I owe Emma and Bryn, the Corgis, extra treats for all the plot points they helped me work through during countless walks. Then there's #NotMyCat who finally got her debut in this book. The book would have been done a month earlier if not for her walking on my keyboard.

A special thank-you to Ann-Marie L'Etoile for tolerating my nonsense over the years. You let me disappear behind my keyboard and still love me when I come up for air. Love you.

And finally, thanks to you, dear reader. It's only possible because of you.

BOOK CLUB
DISCUSSION QUESTIONS

1. Emily Hunter is a smart cop with a strong moral compass. What do you think she's had to sacrifice and compromise to succeed in a male-dominated profession like law enforcement?

2. Emily's mother, Connie, and fifty million people worldwide, suffer from dementia. How do you think Emily will be able to cope with Connie's worsening condition?

3. Police officers like Emily witness a tremendous amount of violence and trauma on the job. What are some of the survival and coping mechanisms she uses?

4. Popular culture—movies and television—often portray the detective as a lone wolf. Emily's relationship with her partner, Javier, is much more the norm. Why do you think detectives are often partnered up in this way?

5. *Face of Greed* exposes political influence used to control a criminal investigation. Do you think there is widespread

political interference in police departments? Do you think the corruption evidenced in *Face of Greed* is a common or a rare example of police department reality?

6. It's often said, "Money is the root of all evil." While greed does play a huge role in the story, what other motivation do you believe was behind the murder we discover in the opening pages?

7. Javier Medina is a competent detective, one who cares about the people caught up in the system. What in his background makes him so effective?

8. Emily Hunter and Lori Townsend are both strong female characters. They're both pursuing very different goals. But, in what ways are they similar?

9. Did you learn anything new about the city of Sacramento? Did any preconceptions change?

10. What do you see in the future for Emily's romantic relationships? Her career status?